ABÉCÉDAIRE evolved o⌐
throughout which the auth⌐
for the length of the analytic hour. She followed
Freud's model of train travel for his theory of free
association, assuming a line of thought that connects
seemingly disconnected ideas, and continually echoes
other women…

'Not only skilled fancy work but profoundly moving,
Kivland unpicks the stories of the women whose repeated
patterns are entangled, interwoven. If you follow her
thread, you will reach the heart of a labyrinth.'

Joanna Walsh

'Sharon Kivland's *ABÉCÉDAIRE* is a dark, shimmering
archive of the remainder. The book's figures, its Annes,
Annies, and Annas, come into view as *tableaux vivants* from
which they look out, beyond us, eluding us, eluding
definition. They disappear into Kivland's beautiful and
mysterious network of passages.'

Sarah Bernstein

'How to describe *ABÉCÉDAIRE*? A garden of fathers, a
labyrinth of sisters, a ballet of daughters, a primer of
desire, a treasure trove, a tapestry, a reader's dream.'

Isabel Wohl

'Sharon Kivland, emerges as if a nymph reborn from a
Viennese fountain, her beautifully written daily quota of
words configured as a learned novel of two-hundred-and-
fifty-seven scenes, sometimes floral, sometimes
hardcore in their eroticism.'

Michael Hampton

Sharon Kivland

ABÉCÉDAIRE

MOIST

First published in 2022 by Moist
https://www.moistbooks.com

A catalogue record for this book is available from the British
Library

This book is a work of fiction. Names, characters, businesses,
organisations, places, and events are either the product of the
author's imagination or are used fictitiously. Any resemblance
to actual persons living or dead, events or locales is entirely
coincidental.

Cover: Sharon Kivland, *Cou au genou*, 2011. Silverprint
photograph, 136 mm x 273 mm. Courtesy of Galerie Bugdahn
und Kaimer, Düsseldorf.

All images are the author's own or from her archive, save for the
photograph of Sigmund and Anna Freud on page 14, reproduced
with the kind permission of the Sigmund Freud Archives, Library
of Congress, Washington, D.C., USA

An alphabet primer (based on the first four letters of the Latin alphabet: A, B, C, D) is a visual support (book, poster, embroidery) presenting all the symbols of an alphabet, almost always listed in alphabetical order, then followed by one or more words with the first letter starting with the initial.

The many errors in this book are solely those of its author; they are due to her misreading, misinterpretation, mistranslation, and misremembering, and occasionally, misconstruction, unconsciously or wilfully.

The unconscious is the chapter of my history that is marked by a blank or occupied by a lie. But the truth can be refound: most often it has already been written elsewhere.

Jacques Lacan

As everyone knows, when you recognise yourself in the mirror, it's already too late.

Mladen Dolar

I have hardly anything in common with myself, and should stand very quietly in a corner, content that I can breathe.

Franz Kafka

This ABC is the way I wrote it.

M. F. K. Fisher

I

[Often I would show the first image in this book when I was invited to speak about my series *Freud on Holiday*. I would say it is a photograph of my father and me on holiday. Then I would admit that it was not, of course, and would show the second image, a photograph of my father and me (and others) on holiday.] On 13 September 1913 Sigmund Freud sent a postcard from Rome to his daughter Anna. He wrote simply 'Papa to his future companion'. On 22 September he sent her another postcard, a view of the waterfalls in Tivoli, writing 'In order to convince you'. In September 1923 Freud travelled to Rome with Anna. It was Freud's last journey to Rome, his seventh visit. He wrote to Lou Andreas-Salomé: 'Here I am again in Rome, and I feel this will do me good. It is here that I realise just what excellent company my little girl is'. On 16 September Freud sent a postcard home, remarking that Anna is as gay as a chaffinch. There is little correspondence from this holiday, though a detailed list of what they did on the three last days exists, noted by Freud and Anna. One evening they went to the cinema.

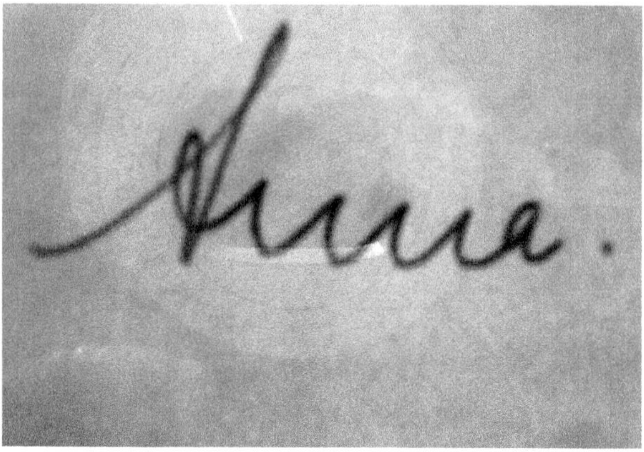
Anna.

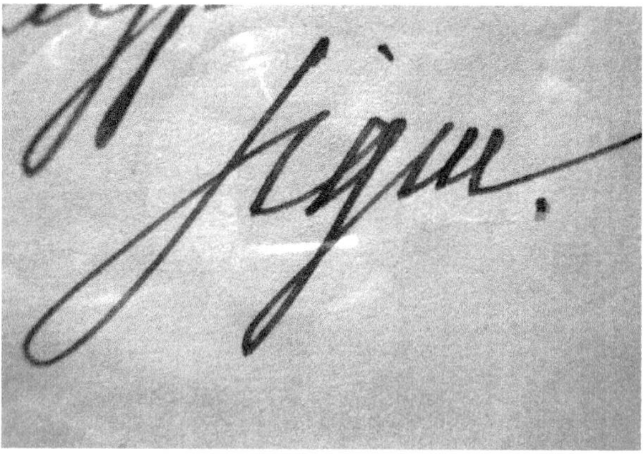

II

[Anna, my sister.]

III

[The second photograph was taken in Athens in 1967. There are others in the photograph, my mother, my sister, and another woman who may be a family friend. I am seized with the sentiment of sibling rivalry and a more complex feeling of competition for possession with other women, all women, sisters, mothers, and friends of the family. Opposite there is another photograph of my father and me on holiday; the others have been eliminated: there are no siblings, no mother, no unnamed woman friend. On the steps of a hotel, in Nice or Cannes, on the French Riviera certainly, I have my father to myself at last, for once, and that is certainly one way of resolving conflict.]

CARTOLINA POSTALE ITALIANA

(CARTE POSTALE D'ITALIE)

17

ROMA 13 · IX · 1913 FERROVIA

DEN HOTEL ROMA

Sig.l Anna Freud

Klobenstein a/Ritten

Austria, Tirol — Posthotel

IV

When Anna F. received the first postcard of 13 September from her father, he was staying (again) at the Hotel Eden. The postcard had the hotel's stamp. Anna was staying at the Posthotel at Klobenstein (Collalbo) am Ritten, near Bolzano in the Tyrol. The postcard was a colour image of a painting by Ernesto Richter, 'No. 9. Castello S. Angelo e Cupola di S. Pietro'. In the picture, a picturesque scene, there is also Ponte Sant'Angelo and a section of the Tiber with the boats of fishermen. Freud was travelling with his sister-in-law, Minna Bernays, but there should be no vulgar speculation on the nature of their relationship. The weather was splendid. In 1913 Anna was bursting with jealousy of her sister Sophie, who had just married Max Halberstadt. It was then that Freud's incomprehension towards the sexual orientation of his youngest daughter began, and he made allusion to her 'bad habits'. She wrote that she herself did not want these to overcome her. Freud called her his 'only' daughter. He was convinced that she had transferred her rivalry of Sophie to a jealousy with regard to her sister's husband, and he exhorted Anna not to be frightened of men; no, what he said is rather that she should not be afraid of being *desired* by men. The following year, when she was welcomed by Ernest Jones in London, Freud wrote to Jones that Anna did not ask to be treated as a woman, being 'still distanced from her sexual desires and quite refusing men'. He did not see that his daughter was not attracted by Jones (a dreadful womaniser), but rather, by his mistress, Loe Kann, of whom she dreamed, of her beautiful white body. Frau K. also had a beautiful white body, 'Dora' said.

V

Anna, Anne, Ann, all those women who are not my sisters, who are my sisters. Once they pledged sorority, against fraternity. Once they called it sisterhood, which is also a clothing label with an emphasis on sustainability and a range of timeless dresses, and a creative design programme for helping young girls reach their creative potential. Oh, that Greek life, with instruction on etiquette, on dress and comportment, on networking and social opportunities. *Soror*, 'sister', 'cousin, daughter of a father's brother', or 'female friend'. Oh, my friends, there is no friend. Oh, my friend, there are no friends. Or look, my friend, you can read Aristotle's (Montaigne says it is Aristotle's aphorism) opening vocative omega as aspirated, and thus pronouncing it with the exhalation of breath, it is a dative, and so he who has friends has no true friends. Matter is drawn from the body, aspirated. A-A-A-Ah. The A is drawn out, then a *hah*. Ah, ah, ah. Montaigne might enter, with another woman, stage left. He leaves, well, he dies, in fact, and she stays: Madame de Gournay, who taught herself Latin and became Montaigne's 'adopted' daughter. I permit myself to mention her, for the heroine of her *'histoire-tragique'*, *Le Proumenoir de M. Montaigne*, which she dedicated to him in memory of a walk they took together, is called Alinda. Alinda, and to add her to my list of sisters who are not my sisters, Alinda who, seduced and betrayed, pours out a rhetorical declamation in a monologue addressed not only to herself but to generations of women yet to come, bittersweet.

The persuasive philosopher Giorgo Agamben argues that by constitutively excluding *zoē,* the *polis* includes natural life in its logic. He calls this the inclusive exclusion: something is included solely by virtue of being excluded. His understanding follows Carl Schmitt's concept of the state of exception, where the rule of law is transcended in the name of public good. It is the sovereign decision, the moment of drawing the line between what is inside and what is outside, what is in the *polis* and what is in the *oikos.* It is always a matter of what is inside and what is outside, what is introjected and what is extrojected. And logically, in order to be spat out, something must first be taken in. Achille Mbembe extends this in his theory of a walking dead: some may live while others die and some exist only between life and death. No place. ZERO.

VII

[Anne B. sent me two photographs from her notebook, surprised that she did not make more notes. Usually, she wrote, she made many notes. She had written on one page that a lecture is something that wants to die. She might be quoting Roland Barthes, because that day we were all quoting him. We could not stop. Then later we were all quoting Anne, I think, whom we did not see again until the next morning. The photographs I received were of the same two pages; one photograph was taken with the notebook laid on a leafy path, the other on a blue-grey quilt with a motif of small red flowers. She had just given away a green satin Givenchy trouser suit. Once she wrote: 'There is a lot of meaning-space inside a "no" spoken in the tremendous logic of a refused order of the world'. So, no, and no, and again no.]

VIII

In 1912 Freud was treating Loe Kann for morphine addiction, after treatment for renal stones. Freud said about her that if she were not his patient, he would have been pleased to expend his fantasies, that she aroused his feelings with full symptoms. Can it be believed, that this reserved and proper man remarked this, and to whom? To Sándor Ferenczi? Yes, to his friend, he wrote that Loe was a jewel. In his calendar of patients, Freud referred to her as 'Frau A.'. She wrote to Freud expressing her desire to retain him as a friend, that she loved him in friendship-love, that she found in him the father she had never recognised. In 1923 she sent him a letter in which she enclosed some pressed snowdrops, with a little bill for this free gift, planted and cultivated by nature, manured by birds, irrigated by God and her old dog, gathered by her in the middle of the night, in thin slippers in wet grass, in her nightie, in the drizzle, at the expense of her health. The total cost came to nothing. NIX. Nothing to pay.

IX

Fräulein Anna O., the patient of Joseph Breuer, had frightening hallucinations of black snakes. She saw her hair, ribbons, and similar things turn into snakes. She told herself not to be silly, that she was only really seeing her hair but she could not think, complained of the profound darkness in her head. She had, she said, a 'bad self', and a host of hysterical symptoms; she could not think. She nursed her father at Ischl, and woke up one night in great anxiety about him while waiting for the arrival of his doctor. Her mother was away and Anna was seated at the patient's bedside, her arm over the back of her chair, where she fell into a waking dream. She saw a black snake come out of the wall to bite her father in his bed. Breuer thought it likely there were snakes in the fields behind the house, which had frightened her. Though she tried to fend off the snake, she was paralysed, and the fingers on her right arm, which had gone to sleep, turned into little snakes and her nails turned into death's heads. The snake vanished and she tried to pray, but language failed her until she thought of some children's verses in English. A train whistle, that of the train bringing her father's doctor, broke the spell. The next day she threw a quoit into some bushes and when she went to get it out, there was a bent branch that revived her hallucination of the snake and her right arm became rigidly extended. From then on the same thing happened in the encounter with any object with a snake-like appearance.

X

When Anna F. visited England, Ernest Jones met her with
a bouquet of flowers. The flowers are not described. What
kind of flowers would an older man buy for a young girl?
Perhaps he might buy white daisies, pink roses, red and
orange tulips. Or asters, lilies, ranunculus, even sunflowers.
Before she left Vienna, her father warned her that Jones had
serious intentions of seeking her hand. He had this from the
best sources. He told Anna that she should discourage any
courting while avoiding all personal offence. It is a delicate
balance to ask of a young woman. No and yes, no and maybe.
It is to *effeuiller la marguerite*, pluck the daisy, to pick off
the petals, one by one, loves me, loves me not, a little, a lot,
passionately, to madness, or not at all. There are many flowers
and their pluckings in the ballet *Giselle*, a haunted ballet that
appears in 1841. Giselle tests Albrecht's fidelity with a flower
growing by her house. When she returns to the grave she
lets fall a little white flower for Albrecht. Jones had already
overstepped the limits of sexual comportment. He believed
he could have any woman. Freud wrote to Jones, telling
him he should not make any sexual advances towards his
daughter, who was the most gifted and accomplished of his
children, interested in learning, in understanding the world.
At home, she was called 'the Black Devil'. She was moody
and petulant. Her father told Jones that she did not claim
to be treated as a woman. He told Jones there was a tacit
understanding between them that she would not consider
marriage or the preliminaries for another two or three years.
Anna was eighteen. To Sándor Ferenczi, Freud wrote that he
had made the matter clear to Anna, and that he thought Loe
would keep watch like a dragon.

There is always a problem with fathers, even with adopted fathers, even if they are good and kind, like Montaigne, even with loving fathers who analyse their daughters, who, like Freud, buy them dogs, lovely Alsatian dogs who will be called Wolf, a kind dog who is fed from the table in the apartment in Berggasse, against the mother's wishes. Ann Q.'s dark farce, *histoire tragi-comique*, opens with the line: 'A man called Berg, who changed his name to Greb, came to a seaside town intending to kill his father'. The man, Alistair, Aly, lived in a lodging house, like Ann. In the adjacent room there lived his father and his father's lover, Judith. The plot is complicated; it is not even certain that it is a plot. There was an intention to kill a father. The book has erratic directions. It lurches and mutters. It was a joke, this patricide, one that makes its way violently, hysterically, without much of a punchline, though a budgerigar fell down the stairs, but it was already dead, starved or strangled, and the cat was killed in the street. And in the end, the father disposed of, Alistair tried to fuck Judith, but potatoes needed peeling, and new curtains should be bought, and a new cat, a Siamese one, had been ordered from the pet shop, so no, not now. There was a man, motionless, bound by a velvet-covered couch and a woman whose hands fluttered around a brooch in the shape of a butterfly, and they stared at a piece of wood, shaking every now and then. There was an ellipsis ... an animal thumping its tail ... and it ended on an ellipsis. Ann, this Ann, drowned herself off Brighton Pier. A man, Albert Fox, saw a woman walking into the sea.

XII

In one apartment, there was a velvet-covered sofa, a very dark
red, with a pattern of fleur-de-lis, a damask, woven into the
fabric on a jacquard-loom, one warp-face linen and one weft-
face sateen. On it there was a blue blanket, with beaded tassels,
a folded quilt, and another blanket, woollen, woven in blues
and greys. There was a pile of cushions: dark-red velvet, with
a scattering of tiny curled white feathers, orange with a trim
of cotton bobbles, fuschia-pink velvet, and one made from a
kilim flat-weave rug. Anna F. composed her psychoanalytic
papers while working on her loom. Anna's couch had a
brown knitted cover. Anna was not good at knitting when she
was a child and Sophie laughed at her efforts. The nursemaid,
the *Kinderfrau* (who is not a child-wife, no), Josefine taught
Anna to knit. Anna was her favourite among the children
and Anna felt she was Josefine's only child, and it was not
true, not at all, that her father had a sexual relation with the
nanny (Josefine was not the pretty little Paula) and certainly
not with her Tante Minna. All the women in the house
knitted together, though Tante Minna, who did not have a
sexual relation with Anna's father, no, she did not, was the
most spectacular producer. The cushions on the sofa were
woven in natural colours, modest in technique and muted
in tone. On Freud's couch, there was a Persian q'ashqai rug,
woven with assymetric knots and a deeply depressed warp
and red-dyed weft. Anna often used weaving metaphors to
describe the development of the mind. Her father thought
weaving covered a 'genital deficiency'.

XIII

[Jacques M. told me she was like an object made of glass, his Anna X., *née sous X*, father unnamed, mother unnamed, an anonymous birth. A woman who gives birth under X may choose three names, the last of which may serve as the surname, the *nom de famille* where there is no family to name; or another, one in a position of authority, the mayor, for instance, may choose. She was a resident in the home in Versailles where he was director for eight years. People who had lived on the streets for many years, blind and mad, were made welcome there, to live out the days that remained to them. Often their time was short. Each year there was a party, and once he danced with Anna. He held her very carefully in his arms. He told me he knew she was a subject and not an object, but at the same time, he held her like a fragile thing. She was a hundred years-old, blind and mad, but she liked to dance.]

XIV

Of Anna O., said another Jacques, let us drop this story of O and call her by her real name. In her case, transference was discovered, and Breuer was delighted by the smooth operation. The more Anna produced signifiers, the more she chattered, another little *pinson*, *see* and *weet* and *pink* and *twink* and *chink* and *chaffey* and *pinkery* (but the male finches, the bachelor birds, always sing more than the females, out-voicing them), the better everything went. If finches were blinded with hot needles, they were thought to sing better. It was a case of the chimney-sweeping treatment, but without anything embarrassing, even though *ramoner*, with its back and forth movements, has a more vulgar meaning at least since the seventeenth century [once my friend R., before finally he left his long-suffering wife, who continued to suffer while he did not, remarked that he had not ceased to *ramoner* for months and I did not know what to say but murmured oh-o to myself. And then he told me how hard it was to love two women at the same time. He is no longer my friend]. There is another story of O, and that was Jacques L.'s joke, one of submission by a woman, a beautiful Parisian fashion photographer, taught to be constantly available, offering herself to any man. She was stripped, blindfolded, chained, whipped, pierced, and branded. We could drop this other story of O and call her by her real name too. Look again, Jacques said. No sexuality either under the microscope or in the distance or under a name. Oh-o. Again, noughts.

XV

When Anna F. was eighty-five years old, she told her friend Manna Friedman that it was time she took up a new profession. She was joyful. She said she was too old for patients. She and Manna would weave together and sell their handwoven works under the name 'Mandanna'. At that time, she dreamt that she wanted to go to work but could not find the Clinic. In her psychoanalytic work, she used the metaphor of weaving to understand the mind and therapy, not her father's metaphor of archaeology. Her layers could be woven and unwoven. While she was being analysed by her father, he was too ill for several weeks to continue, and she wrote to a friend that during those weeks she had lived as she did in the time before she became an analyst, with the poetry of Rilke and daydreams and weaving. Warp and weft, leave and left, a pick and an end. A frame is filled. The weaver pushes the shuttle through the shed. The shed is an opening made by lifting and separating, so the shuttle may enter. There are harnesses and heddles. They go up and down, in and out, incessantly pricking and pumping. Athene, goddess of weaving, punished Arachne for the incest with her brother by condemning her to a life of eternal weaving. She also made Arachne hideous, undesirable. When Anna and her parents arrived in England, they found refuge, 'proud and rich under the protection of Athene'.

Anna O. was the first to call it the *talking cure*. Jacques called it the patient's little story—if the patient can tell it or not. He called her the queen of social workers. He said that one must understand what one is doing when one starts to classify. He said that one begins by counting the petals of a flower, its coloured organs. This is a rudimentary botany. Sometimes the petals are not petals at all, but sepals. The uninformed do not always know the difference. Floral reproduction is bisexual. Petals are the corolla, an attractive showy part, the inner perianth. Sepals surround the petals, leafy calyxes, the outer perianth. The perianth is an envelope, the defensive organ enclosing and protecting the reproductive organs. Sometimes the calyx or the corolla or both are much reduced or even lacking. Marguerites may reproduce through insect pollination, through rubbing and transfer of the flower's pollen from anther to stigma, or by asexual vegetative reproduction devoid of the manufacturing of seeds, without requiring ploidy, reduction, meiosis, or fertilisation. Breuer wrote that hysterias must be thought of as a secondary production of hypnoid states. He said they depend on a certain fertile moment. Jacques asked how one is to look for what is natural. In 1919, on holiday in Bad Gastein, Freud did not allow the rain to dissuade him from going out to search for the magnificent white orchid, *platanthera bifolia*, the lesser-butterfly orchid, with its incomparable perfume, night-scented, pollinated by the *sphingidae* moth, such as the hawk moth, which hovers in front of the flower, resting its forelegs on its lip, while plunging [yes, plunging] its proboscis into the spur, pushing between the pollinia.

XVII

Norbert Hanold, the protagonist of Wilhelm Jensen's novella
Gradiva, cannot say if the way a woman walks is different
from that of a man. He takes to following women on the
street (those that are less frequented), in all weathers, but
rain is better because it makes the ladies lift up their sweeping
skirts. It is easier to see the feet of servant girls, but they wear
clodhopping shoes, and what thick, working-class ankles
they have. He casts his searching glance at the feet of ladies
and notes that there are many different ways of walking,
from sliding to stomping, but none match that particular
raised step he seeks. He calls these observations his 'pedestrian
investigations'. Anna F. felt jealous of her sister Sophie's trim
waist and slender ankles. She felt jealous of her mother's love
for Sophie. She felt left out by her brothers and sisters. She felt
boring and bored and left alone. She felt herself to be '*dumm*'
and leaden. She felt her name to be common and plain. Plain
Anna, with such thick ankles. She made her dirndl skirts long
enough to hide them and to disguise her waist. She sewed her
clothes by hand, for it would not have been practical to use a
sewing machine while she saw patients. She embroidered or
crocheted or knitted (the accounts differ, and at least once it
is a mistranslation) silently, and most of her patients hardly
noticed it. One of her patients spent many sessions talking
about his worries about his wife's pregnancy, what having a
baby meant to him. He was irritated that she did not speak
about it with him but kept sewing, rather intensely, in silence.
He complained that she was not paying enough attention to
the serious matters he brought to his analytic sessions. When
he came to his session, announcing that his baby, a son, had
been born, Anna gave him the blanket she had been making
for the infant [knitting then, or crochet, I tend to think, but in
other accounts, it was a dear little jacket she made].

XVIII

In the poem 'A Partial History', Ariana R. writes 'We were lost in a language of images. / It was growing difficult to speak', 'Yet talk / Was everywhere'.

XIX

H. D. wrote that her facial muscles were stiff with the effort of concentrating on the dots of light forming a line on the space above her washstand. She felt she might become frozen like one of the enemies of the goddess Athene, when the enemy was shown the Gorgon's head by Perseus. She wrote that Perseus could wield the head, that ugly severed weapon, because Athene had told him what to do, that he would be protected from mortification by looking at it only in the polished metal of his shield. She kept her gaze steady at the wall before her. She felt she was like Alice with her looking-glass or Perseus with his shield. She knew she must drown in order to survive, that she must drown completely and come out the other side or rise to the surface, that she must be born again and break utterly. She called Freud the midwife to the soul. She wrote that he was the soul, and that thought of him bashed against her forehead like the sphinx-moth, the death-head moth. He showed her the objects on his table, the ivory Vishnu with serpents and snake heads. He held up a tiny figure of Athene and told her it was his favourite. Freud liked to look at the small figures arranged on his desk; from time to time he would reach out to stroke his favourites. They were kept only in his consulting-rooms and study. The bronze figure of Athene stood in the very centre of his desk. She is the only piece he smuggled out of Vienna in 1938. She is ten centimetres high, a Roman figure of the first or second century CE, after a Greek figure of the fifth century BCE. She holds a frontal pose. Her left hand is raised, to hold a missing spear. In her lowered right hand, she holds a libation bowl, decorated with a petal design. Her head is lowered and turns a little to the right. Her left leg is straight; her right leg is bent at the knee in a *contrapposto* stance.

XX

Anna P. danced *Giselle* with her own company in 1913. It was her favourite ballet. As a pupil in the Imperial Ballet School she was taunted, given cruel names by her classmates: 'the broom' and '*la petite sauvage*', because of her unusual physique. She was often sickly. One of her first roles was Zulma, the attendant of Myrtha, the Queen of the Wilis. In 1903 she danced as Giselle in Russia, and a year later, in Warsaw. The Wilis are spirits who attack the men foolish enough to stray into their forest; they drown them or better yet, force the foolish men to dance themselves to death. The Wilis are nasty vengeful creatures, young women who die before their wedding night and cannot rest, for they must satisfy their passion for dancing. Giselle arises from her grave to join the Wilis in their ecstatic dancing; touched with a branch of rosemary by Myrtha, she becomes one. Théophile Gautier's libretto drew from a passage by Heinrich Heine and a poem by Victor Hugo. In the latter, a young Spanish girl died after a night of frenzied dancing. To dance *en pointe* is to support the weight of the body on the tips of the toes, feet fully extended. It is assumed largely by women, who may start *en pointe* around ten years-old, or when they are judged by their teachers to be ready, physically and emotionally. The line of the body passes through the centre of the hips to the toes. There is a risk of injury. It is hard. It is damaging. Dancers suffer from sprained ankles, inflammations, stress fractures, blisters, calluses, ingrowning toenails, and bruises. They develop deformities: bunions, bunionettes, and dancer's heel: compressed tissue, a bony formation at the back of the ankle. Injuries are caused through, for example, the lack of cushion, ill-fitting *pointe* shoes (supplied without proper consideration of the strength of the ankle or the flexibility of the arch of the foot), and improper use of the technique.

XXI

Anna F. had a dream in which she was wandering barefoot. It was an image of wandering along and through all the walks, tracks, gardens, streets, a dream image that became a poem with eight stanzas. It was a poem about love, of course. As her analysis by her father progressed, the images and motifs in her dreams changed, as did those in her poems. In one poem, two men met at a crossroads: one had a sword, the other, a rose. There is often a great deal of walking in dreams, and when one is awake, of course there is also walking, there is much walking, there is endless walking up and down, pacing, sometimes throughout the night. There may also be dancing, when one is as light as a swan's feather or a snowflake.

XXII

Anna von L. was named Cäcilie M. by Freud—one might say, A under C—he called her his *Lehrmeisterin*, his master teacher or teaching master, though not his mistress. In a letter to Wilhem Fliess in 1897, he wrote that only this woman could have been his teacher. Yes, she taught him something about what would become psychoanalysis; she was his most severe and instructive case. She had consulted his master Charcot in Paris, who suggested to Freud that he try treating her diarrhœa with a few centigrams of silver nitrate, while also insisting it was upon her psyche that they must act. Extravagant, wealthy, demanding, she lived on caviar and champagne; she had a professional chess player waiting on call outside her bedroom all night. She played chess so excellently she could play two games at the same time, another *double jeu*. It is called a simultaneous exhibition or a simultaneous display, the exhibitor plays white, the one who moves first. She spent most of her life lying on a couch, even after her treatment. Freud said she wrote poems of 'great perfection'. She entitled one, 'Case History'. Anna von L. had a violent pain in her right heel, which appeared to stem from a time when she had been in a sanatorium abroad. However, closer analysis revealed that she had been confined to bed in the sanatorium precisely because of the pains in her feet. She had a shooting pain with every step, walking became impossible. In the sanatorium after a week in bed, she was to be taken into the dining-room by the house physician but the pain started then. It came on when he took her arm to leave the room with him, she said, and the new pains disappeared when she remembered this, when she realised her fear that she would be placed on the 'wrong footing', that she would put a foot wrong among the strangers in the dining-room. In any case, hysteria had a punning logic, turning foot into footing, figuring speech, as M. has written. A physical pain became a psychic trauma, and was talked away.

XXIII

Anna F. wrote to her father, addressing him thus:

Dear Papa!
My dear Papa!

Almost always she sent him a kiss, ended her missive with a kiss. Or she offered him all her heart, with all her heart, wholeheartedly, from the heart, *herzlichst*.

His Anna.

Oh, the maids, *mes bonnes* who are not good girls. [I did not intend to write about them but they arose nonetheless, those sisters who gouged out the eyes and mutilated, smashed up, the faces of their mistress and her daughter while the master, monsieur, was out.] They bared the genitals, then slashed the buttocks and thighs of one in order to smear the blood on the other. They used a pewter pitcher, a hammer, a kitchen knife, whatever came to hand. They washed up carefully afterwards, pleased with the clean job they had made of it, *voilà, c'est propre,* but they left the hammer unwashed, hair clinging to it, on a chair or a bedside table, or on the floor (the accounts differ). Their motive was mysterious, but it was true that Madame used to slam their heads against the wall and they had to work fourteen hours a day with only a half day off each week and that was to go to church in gloves and hats. They were silent; one did not speak to the other; they were haughty, they were rebellious. Monsieur had not spoken to them once in the seven years they worked there, and Madame only communicated with Christine, the older sister, through written instructions. Between themselves they called Madame, *maman*. Madame used to put on white gloves to check their dusting. Imagine her gloved fingers rubbing across surfaces. At her arrest, Léa said that from then on, she would be deaf and dumb. At their trial Christine tore open her blouse, baring her breasts, and cried out to Léa, say yes, please say yes. Later, in prison, Christine tried to tear out her own eyes.

XXV

Léa and Christine became Solange and Claire, and in that transformation into actresses by one man, they played at murdering Madame while she was out. There was no Madame to tell them how to behave. Claire accused Solange of being pregant, the fault of the gardener, but they called the imagined child theirs for there was no separation between them, though Solange cried out to Claire to keep her distance. One said that filth does not love filth. One said that the other was her own image thrown back at her by a mirror, like a bad smell. Everything that came out of the kitchen was spit, they said. They mixed their muck together, mingling their hairpins. They were Claire-Madame and Solange-Madame and Claire-Solange. They became Michèle and Marie-Louise in one film, and Sophie and Jeanne in another. [The subject of Léa and Christine arose because I was talking with E. about Aimée, or rather E. was telling me that she hoped she did not have to write about her. I hoped she would not, that she would leave her to me, that I could keep her for myself. I wanted to keep the maids for myself, too, but they had been taken already.]

XXVI

Oh, sister mine, *meine Schwester.*
Sorella mia.
Ma sœur.
Soror, dolorem.

Lovely Sophie, graceful Sophie, Martha's favourite daughter, fifth child, her father's Sunday child, Max's wife, Ernst's mother, Heinerle's mother. Anna F. was happy when Sophie moved out from the apartment in Berggasse. She would be able to spend more time with her dear father. She wrote to him that she was glad that Sophie was getting married, because the unending quarrel between them was horrible for her. Her parents made sure Anna was out of the country when Sophie married Max. She did not go to the wedding, of course, and that should not be thought of as strange under the circumstances. Later Sophie had complications following the Spanish flu, a pneumonia; there was no train to take her parents to Hamburg, not even for such an emergency. She was pregnant with her third child, a child who died with her, a child who was not to be but one who would haunt Ernst. Anna analysed Ernst but would not adopt him, her legal heir, her nephew, her first child patient. Tante Anna. Jealous Tante Anna, but she tended to Ernst, who spent long periods of time swinging on a home-made wooden swing, *fort–da, fort–da*. There was another child, Heinz Rudolf, Heinerle, who died three years after his mother. Freud wrote to Ferenzci: 'Wafted away! Nothing to say'. He wrote to Oskar Pfister that in the four or five days of her illness, it was as if Sophie had never existed. He wrote to Ludwig Binswanger that his wife and Anna were profoundly shaken, in the most human sense. Ernst took the name of Freud during his psychoanalytic training; it was not given to him. Ernst sat by Anna's side when she saw her patients. Sometimes he saw his own patients on the couch of his dead grandfather. Ernst did not go to Tante Anna's funeral. He did not visit her in her dying days. He could not bear to witness her fragility; he could not tolerate it.

The editor's note to Vladimir Nabokov's novel *Ada or Ardour: A Family Chronicle* [a fairy tale or an erotic masterpiece or a love story] is this: with the exception of [...], a few incidental figures, and some non-American citizens, all the persons mentioned in this book are dead. [I wondered how I might use this in thinking and writing about sisters, about families? Of course, they (we) are not all dead; many are living and breathing and writing and some are walking off into the distance without me.]

XXIX

In *The Nutcracker Suite* [it is so obvious really] the magician Drosselmeyer swept up Clara through a blizzard of dancing snowflakes—he was taking her to the Kingdom of Sweets, [of course he was]. The magician was her uncle, he was taking her to a sweet domain [of course he was, the uncles, the magicians always say this]. The dancers must transform; they must appear to defy the law of gravity. The snow must fall as they waltz in a forest glade, taking brisk *petit allegro* jumps. A tree, a Christmas tree, has grown to its full height, rising from the forest floor, the stage floor. Their movements are symmetrical: they stand with their heels together, their toes apart; breathing deeply, they raise their arms to the height of their bellies, their fingers do not touch and they pause. First position. They raise their arms higher, keeping their hands below their elbows; they breathe out, they glide their arms out to the side. Second position. They glide their arms down to their sides. Third position. They lift one arm above their heads. Fourth position. They lift both arms above their heads, as though their faces are enclosed in an oval frame. Their feet are close together, one in front of the other, turned out away from their bodies, maintaining straight legs. Fifth position. The taller dancers perform some arabesques, but largely there is running, jumping, *échappés* and *enchaînement*, and they must kick the snow, brushing their feet out as they run, turning them out. It makes their calves ache. The snow covers their eyes. It is sometimes hard to breathe as it falls into their faces and mouths. They are a blizzard. There is a wordless chorus that accompanies their symmetrical waltz—Tchaikovsky said there should be twelve sopranos and twelve altos, and it was all the more desirable that they should be youths from a choir. He thought it was a boring work, preferring *The Sleeping Beauty*. It is vastly preferable that beauties should sleep.

XXX

This is how snow is made to fall on stage. Large bags pierced with holes are filled with punch-outs of flame retardant paper, in the shape of stars or a plus sign. Sometimes shredded plastic is used. Each bag is held on two bars, and the bars move, sliding against each other to release the snow. It starts slowly, then gathers speed, until the snow falls like a blizzard. Of course, it does not melt like real snow. It must be swept up to be used again, and may continue to drift gently down for weeks. For a snow globe, a captured scene, the container must be filled with bottled water to which glycerine or baby oil is added, which will allow the glitter or artificial snow to fall slowly. It must not be lumpy but smoothly mixed; it must float as long as possible in the water before it sinks, and then the globe may be turned upside down and shaken gently and the snow will fall. Inside there is a miniature scene, perhaps a model town or a landscape. The *Schneekugel* was invented by an Austrian, Erwin Perzy, at the end of the nineteenth century. A maker of surgical instruments, he was attempting to make a brilliant light source for a surgical lamp. He poured semolina or something like it, a white powder in any case, into a glass globe, and the effect of it floating slowly to the bottom of the globe as it absorbed the water reminded him of snow falling. His first snow globe contained the Mariazell Basilica in Vienna, devoted to the veneration of the Virgin. There was a scene in Freud's analysis of 'Dora'—she told him about looking intently at a painting of the Sistine Madonna by Raphael for two hours in the art gallery in Dresden. Freud asked her a question which she could not answer clearly. He asked her what had pleased her so greatly about the painting. At last she said; 'The Madonna', and perhaps that was an answer after all.

XXXI

Anna K.'s narrator looked for a woman whom once he loved, a fragile and elusive creature, in a frozen wasteland. Snow smothered the towns and cities. Waterways were frozen. The landscape gave the impression of having stepped out of everyday life, into a field of strangeness where no known laws operated. The woman, whom he called only 'the girl', was an ice-maiden, as brittle as Venetian glass. She had long white hair; sometimes it appeared to be silver. She was held captive by her husband, a high-ranking officer, 'the Warden', who policed the country. The narrator had headaches, insomnia; he had hallucinations, horrible dreams, caused by his medication, His account could not be believed. She was a glass girl, albino pale, with glittering hair. The girl was dazed, she hardly knew what was happening, her normal state of consciousness interrupted, lost, the nature of her surrender not understood. The ice advanced. He saw her surrounded and consumed by ice. Everything was misty, indistinct. Everywhere there was white snow, which shut out the world. The girl saw only white weaving meshes of snow. The known world was excluded and the girl was alone with phantoms, tall as firs growing in snow.

XXXII

[Today I broke my own rules. I initiated an extra séance this
week. It was because of my dream last night. I dreamt of
snow. I dreamt of snow on the moon. There was so much
snow, so much silver light, that I could not see. I dreamt that
I had no shadow. I was on the moon and I cast no shadow.
It was as if I did not exist. I could see nothing but still I knew
that I had no shadow. It was inexplicable to me, although
I suppose it continued as residue from yesterday's session.]
In *Die Frau ohne Schatten* by Richard Strauss, an opera with
a libretto by Hugo von Hofmannstahl, there is another
woman without a shadow. She is the title. She is the Empress,
only half-human, captured as a gazelle by the Emperor and
assuming human form. She cannot have a child while she is
without a shadow, and without one, without a shadow or a
child, the Emperor will turn to stone and she must return to
the kingdom of her father. Once she could transform into
any creature, she remembers and mourns. She must find a
woman who will sell her shadow. She dreams... She dreams
and behind the doors where she dreams, she knows her father
is waiting for her. Often Anna F. dreamt after his death that
her father was alive again, and that he longed for her, that
he showed her the tenderness he had rarely demonstrated in
reality. In one dream, he said quite clearly that he had always
longed for her so. She dreamt about losing and being lost.
[Snow blind, I thought to myself, thinking about reflection,
inflammation, blurred vision. Then I thought about haloes,
the glowing light of the moon and the arc around the Virgin's
head that sometimes she shares with her beloved son.]

XXXIII

Anna F. had bad posture. Her father worried about her curved back, her hunched shoulders. She was sent to Merano in the South Tyrol, noted for its temperate climate, even in the winter months, even when there was snow on the mountains. She hoped her father would visit her at Christmas; they could walk together on the most splendid paths. Some days she felt well, but on others she still had severe back pain, and was generally very tired. Her father wrote to her to wish her a happy new year. He hoped she would continue to gain weight. He advised her to abandon her embroidery, for certainly it could do no good for her back. She gained a kilo and a half in December but her father felt it was nothing. If she had been able to travel in Italy with her aunt for eight months, she would have returned as fat as butter. In her letters, she referred to her illness only as 'it'. What is it? It has no name. It never has a name. Or it has different names at different times. Anna would place an antimacassar on the couch of her consulting room. She had a different antimacassar for each of her analysands. Sometimes she worked on her knitting or crochet during the session. There was the clacking of her needles, as several patients reported. It was a work of the hand, always industrious, patient and persistent, useful, and even lovely. Ernest Lefébure wrote in *Embroidery and Lace* that 'few men would care to dispute [...] the right of using those delicate instruments so intimately associated with the dexterity of [...] nimble and slender fingers'. Needlework and similar preoccupations leave women especially prone to daydreams, as Freud and Breuer noted, aligning handiwork with hypnoid states, as the material forms of psychic disturbance: an embroidered symptom. Anna O. was fond of embroidery; she collected lace and, oddly, small objects made of cast iron.

XXXIV

[A nutcracker brings good luck to a family, well, that's what they say. It is a watchdog, baring its teeth.] On Christmas Eve, the magician Drosselmeyer gave an enchanted nutcracker doll to Clara. As the clock struck midnight, Clara and Drosselmeyer shrank down to the size of mice. On stage the Christmas tree grew to enormous proportions and the Nutcracker doll turned into a grown man. In E. T. A. Hoffman's story, Clara was not Clara but Marie—Clara was the name of her doll. Clara who was Marie fell in love with a nutcracker, which came alive when she fell asleep. Her brother Fritz told the story; her sister Luise barely appeared in the account but it was her fault that the mice ran riot, for she could not bear cats. The parents ridiculed her, poor dreamy Marie; she could not separate her dreams from the real world. She fell onto a glass cabinet and cut her arm badly. It was her uncle's fault, she said. Her nutcracker was more handsome than her uncle, despite his marvellous toy palace; for Marie, it was love at first sight. Oh, his lovely shiny boots. But he was disfigured.

XXXV

Aimée, beloved, was in reality, in her real life, in her own life, Marguerite Pantaine, a thirty-eight-year-old railway clerk. In 1931 she attacked the actress Huguette Duflos, wounding her with a knife as she entered the theatre. That year Duflos starred in *Le Parfum de la dame en noir*, a mystery film directed by Marcel L'Herbier, adapted from the novel by Gaston Leroux, and featuring an amateur sleuth, the reporter, Joseph Rouletabille. It was his nickname: *roule ta bille*, roll your marble—it can mean one who has been around the world, a globe-trotter, and so has seen it all, or one who is cool-headed. He was a little man with a head as round as a marble and a face as red as a tomato. He found a left foot in the rue Oberkampf, the remains of a dismembered woman, cut in pieces, *un corps morcelé*. Aimée was imprisoned, then hospitalised. Aimée thought the actress was the associate of a famous writer who had revealed details of her private life in a book. Aimée thought the actress, and another actress, Sarah Bernhardt, and the woman writer had been slandering her, all meant to harm her son, that they were in it together to persecute her. She tried to write; she wrote, and her poems and novels were rejected by all the publishers to whom she submitted them. She wanted to go to America where she would write and make her fortune for the sake of her child. Her sister cared for her child, the sister cared for her husband, and Aimée lived alone. She felt a need for direct action, she said; it increased with the rejection of her novel. She wanted to look her enemy in the eye. No longer could she guarantee the order of the world. She would approach strangers, entertaining them with her vague enthusiasm. She believed she had a mission, one she had to carry out among men, often going with them to hotels, whether she liked it or not. She confessed to having a great curiosity for the thoughts of men.

XXXVI

Amor nel cor

Rodolphe put the wrong seal on his letter breaking the end of their liaison to Emma. He wondered what excuses to tell her, how to sign his letter. He wrote that he would be far away when she read his lines, that he was fleeing from the temptation to see her again. He thought then that his addition of a second *Adieu*, this time written *À Dieu*, was in the most excellent taste. He signed it 'Your friend', and he thought that the whole letter was very good indeed. He felt that he should allow a few tears to fall on the page, lest she thought him insensitive, the poor little thing, but was unable to summon them, though that was not his fault. He poured water into a glass, dipped in his finger, and allowed a fat drop to fall on the page, making a pale stain on the ink. He reached for a seal, choosing one that did not fit the circumstances. Oh, well, he thought, *pshaw*, he said, never mind, he thought, and then he smoked three pipes, after which he went to sleep. In the morning, he had a basket of apricots sent to Emma, hiding his letter under some vine leaves. Louise Colet gave Gustave Flaubert a silver cigarette case engraved with *amor nel cor*. Louise Colet wrote a poem with the same title: the writer was poor, with little to give, but he whom she loved like a god mocked her gift in a flat-footed phrase, yet kept the fine agate seal. Flaubert said her effusion had sealed their relationship with a funereal bouquet.

XXXVII

[I was diverted again; I missed a session. I lost a day and I knew it would not be the last. I felt ashamed. I was thinking about endings and the deferral of beginning. I had been reading an essay on photography by Ariella A. She wrote that the idea of an ending is overthrown because of the spectator's agency and the groundlessness of the ending is revealed. The potential of the act of photography is never fully extinguished nor fully realised. Already I could see the problems that faced me, though ending was at this point nine months in the future (and yes, I understood the significance of the timing, as I am not an idiot) and I would have to read myself backwards, in the partly repressed knowledge that none of what I had written was mine, apart from some sentences that might be considered as insertions or asides or even a voice-off. Though I have no specialist voice talent, at times I might allow myself to provide ironic counterpoint. Hannah A. wrote of Walter Benjamin as 'producing a work consisting entirely of quotations, one that [...] could dispense with any accompanying text'. I was reading his *Convolute* on the Commune; I was speaking it for the project of my friend S., who was intent on an impossible speaking assembly of phantasmagoria. I told myself that I should dispense with interjections of this kind. And that I must keep to my rule of not speaking about myself. Ever.]

XXXVIII

Anna F. had a dream about her father, a curious double dream (one might say half-hearted, she said). It was actually in two parts, running alongside each other. In the first part, she was to marry a man, rather indistinct, youngish, a doctor. She was very unwilling. In the second part, her father and mother were lost in a dark place. It was in the city, Paris? Vienna? And she was looking for them with search parties. Her mother was found after a while but not her father and she was quite desperate. She urged the people to search more and more, but it seemed completely hopeless. Half awake, she interpreted her dream thus: that she had lost her father through marriage with another man. However, that seemed too glib to her to be true. Anyway, she was very glad to be awake again. She dreamt this in 1947, in London. Once she was asked if her father would return to Vienna. She answered: never. She noted: wanderer, immigrant, eternal Jew. She was herself a dream work before she was born, an explanation for a troubling symptom in her father's 'specimen' dream of Irma's injection. During the Blitz, she started a folder which she labelled 'About Losing and Being Lost'. Therein she collected dreams and their associations with the deaths of those loved, all the lost beloveds.

XXXIX

In Offenbach's operetta, *Le Voyage dans la Lune,* the moon princess, Fantasia, does not know what love is when Prince Caprice, the earth-dweller who arrives on the moon in a shell fired from a cannon, seeking air, light, space, courts her. On the moon, love is a disease. A child is conceived only in relation to the area of commerce in which it may prosper. Caprice eats an apple, the only food he has brought with him, and Fantasia tastes it, and oh, she is astonished by this unknown fruit, and oh, the taste makes her fall madly in love with him. She is mad, quite mad with the sickness of love, she is shut up in her chamber, the palace women, ladies-in-waiting, hear her calls, her cries of love for Caprice, they try to release her. She escapes, of course, and finds Caprice, who wants to save her. He will give her father an apple elixir, a love potion. Her father, King Cosmos, wants to sell her—all women on the moon can be sold.

XL

This is not unusual, this woman-market, this lunar stock-market, you know you can find it anywhere, this *bourse*, not only on the moon. It is an exchange and it is a nice fat leather purse or a scandalous reticule, representing a body, a woman's body into which things can be put, you know what kind of things, and 'Dora' fingered her little purse, her *bourse* (and it mattered there if a room was locked or unlocked, like a jewel-case). It is where value is settled and it is the swollen basal part of a cluster of flowers before fruit swells into fruit, an inflorescence. It is where women go when they cease to please, goods to market, yes, and yes, they could refuse if the goods got together. There are women reserved for reproduction, and others reserved for pleasure. They are either housewives or luxury objects. There is either a shortage or a surplus, and if the latter, lovely accumulation, lovely trading, lovely profits. Caprice will buy her, he promises. There is the chorus of the market: *C'est le marché.* Then, in the fourth tableau of the act, there is the marvellous *Grand Ballet of the Snow Flakes*. It is fifty degrees below zero. After that, all the lunar women discover love but the king does not know anything about it. The apple-bearers are imprisoned, and so on, and so on. At the end of the nineteenth century there was a vogue for snow scenes, for snow dances, danced by women who took the forms of glittering snowflakes.

XLI

Anna K. was prescribed heroin for a sports injury, so they said. Heroin used to come in a neat glass bottle with an attractive label, containing grains or compressed tablets or liquid, diluted with chloroform and alcohol. Heroin was criminalised in the 1950s, so there were no more dear little flasks with pretty labels dispensed under the 'British System'. The German company Bayer made its first fortune with the commercialisation of heroin as a remedy for coughs and colds and pain—it was also very good for children who were suffering 'irritation'. It replaced morphine as a safe, non-addictive substitute. Morphine was boiled for several hours to produce diacetylmorphine. Heroin was the trade-marked name. Later it had other names: snow, snowball, white girl, white lady, white nurse, white horse, china white, white. It was the sedative for coughs; it cured bronchitis, tuberculosis (they said), and was used to wean patients from dependency on cocaine. Anna K.'s doctor gave it to her; they wrote a dream story together with a horse, Kathbar, an amalgam of their names.

XLII

Anna K. was very anxious about running out of her supply of heroin. She stockpiled it. They said there was enough heroin in her flat when her body was found there in 1968 to kill the entire street. They said she killed herself; it was heart failure, for hearts do fail, give out, give up, break. Her depressions caused her to spend time in asylums, in and out, in and out. Anna K. believed the drug allowed her to write. She thought writing helped her to endure her illness. Anna K. tried to kill herself three times. She underwent treatment in a Swiss sanatorium. She went in as Helen Ferguson and came out as Anna K. She bleached her hair. She became a glass girl, a white girl. She tried to write from her unconscious and from the events of her life: controlling husbands, a cruel mother, a dead son. She lost her name, no, her narrator lost her name, becoming Lazarus. It was, she said, how she saw the world. The brain-fever birds of a story called *Who-are-you? Who-are-you? Who-are-you?*

XLIII

Loe Kann was analysed by Freud as a favour, for women, you know, are often traded between men. She did not believe in psychoanalysis, yet said she would do anything, as long as ideas were not forced upon her against her will. She was definite that she would rather be treated by Freud than by anyone else. She reduced her daily dosage of morphine in preparation for her analysis. Her husband was advised by Freud that it would be better if he were out of the way. He travelled for three months in Italy. Letters circulated; they read each other's, and then the letters on Loe's side stopped. Her pains disappeared; her morphine use was diminishing, all good progress, in her husband's absence, making way for the confrontation with her sexual anaesthesia. The husband wondered if they would fuck on his return to Vienna; he anticipated that she would desire this, but he would leave it to her. He fucked her maid, Lina, in any case, who had developed the same symptoms of kidney stones as her mistress. Masters can always fuck the maids, *that is a fact*. Loe's pains returned with the return of her husband; she had to raise the morphia from 1.2 to 4. She renounced treatment. Freud persuaded her to continue; the morphia went down to 0.8 and there were no pains at all. She met a man who had the same name as her husband, with whom she was happy, though she did not know if there was any future for them. She was convinced that she would kill herself, for she had lost her taste for life. She wrote to Freud that she took morphine and had never tried to hide it from anyone. She wrote that she had done what she could without it, and anyway, she took only the smallest dose required, though the smallest doses had no effect. She was, she wrote, not ashamed, *not at all*.

Morpheus, the fashioner, μορφή, was one of the Oneiroi, sometimes the son of Nyx, sometimes the son of Pasithea and Hypnos, sometimes the brother or nephew of Thanatos. Morpheus could assume any guise to enter human dreams, delivering messages from the Gods. There was a beautiful garden of poppies at the entrance of his palace in the underworld. The son of sleep, shaping dreams, is winged. The dreamer is held in the arms of Morpheus. The wingspan of the Morpheus moth is between 32 and 38 millimetres. Its forewings are between 13 and 16 millimetres long, their colour fuscous with a grey tinge, inner and outer lines obscured, doubled, the arms far apart. A reddish streak, running through orbicular and reniform spots, is most distinctive. The hindwing is a dull white with a fine dark terminal line and dark discal spot. It has dark stigmata, dark lunules between the veining, a glossy appearance. It feeds on dandelions and nettles. Nocturnal, it comes to light. It flies in one generation. Morphine is produced from poppy straw of the opium poppy. Everyone knows this, but it not does not come from every poppy. The pharmacist Friedrich Sertürner, who first isolated it in 1805, named it morphium, after Morpheus, for it induced sleep as well as relieving pain. [I did not know why Johann Siegfried Hufnagel named the moth Morpheus in 1766. I wondered about this for a long time, but I did not know whom to ask.] Anna K. said that heroin made her eyes beautiful, that she watched herself in the mirror for a long time, which gave her real pleasure.

XLV

Anna F. described her main feeling in a dream was that she was wandering about (on top of mountains, hills) while she was doing other things. At the same time, she had an inner restlessness, a feeling that she should stop whatever she was doing and go walking with her father. Eventually he called her to him and demanded this of her himself. She was very relieved and leaned herself against him, crying in a way that was very familiar to both of them. Her thoughts were troubled: he should not have called her—it was as if a renunciation or a form of progress had been undone because he called. She was puzzled by her dream. In the dream the feeling was very strong that he was wandering around alone and lost. 'Sympathy and bad conscience', she wrote. Odysseus, she noted. Penelope, she noted. The significance did not escape her.

XLVI

Eugen Bleuler became director of the Burghölzli clinic in Zurich in 1899, the year that Freud's own dream-book was published. Bleuler applied hypnotic suggestion and association in treating his patients, and introduced the new method of psychoanalysis, which for many was synonymous with hypnosis (in the *Zeitschrift für Hypnotismus*, a professional journal to which Freud contributed, the editor, Oskar Vogt, called the therapy he conducted under hypnosis 'psychoanalysis'). Bleuler corresponded with Freud, sending some of his analyses of his own dreams for interpretation, though he did not feel he had dreamt anything reproducible. It was, one might say, a self-analysis. He wished he could write more unconsciously. Sabina Spielrein entered into treatment with Carl Gustav Jung at the Burghölzli in 1904; nothing would curb the frankness produced by free association; nothing would check the wild analysis that spread like a contagion among the women patients; nothing would deter their amorous transference. Jung told Sabina Spielrein that it was as if he had a necklace in which all his other admirers were pearls, and she was the medallion. Yes, a jewel. And a jewel often needs a jewel case. When she left the clinic, they continued to meet; it was complicated. It's complicated. LOL.

[I would name every place and each condition of confinement, at least, I repeat, every place, if not each condition: asylum, sanatorium, clinic, hospital, spa, sickroom, classroom, prison, bedroom, studio, study, *chambre de bonne*...but it is too great a task, and I am inaccurate. Yet, someone must say it, surely?] For Anna F., there were the mountains, Merano, *paradiso del benessere*, a boarding-house, a benign rest cure, despite her exile from home, writing to her father every day (for they had no secrets from each other); where she was bidden to think about her future and to gain weight; where a healthful juice was made with radioactive grapes. For Anna K., a Swiss sanatorium, paid for by her mother; then another clinic in Switzerland, the Bellevue Hospital at Kreuzlingen, directed by Ludwig Binswanger who trained at Burghölzli, where Anna O. was treated by Robert Binswanger, the father of Ludwig, where Aby Warburg was treated, speaking with butterflies, the messengers of the Greek gods, and in the particularly refined atmosphere of the clinic, he was received for tea in her salon by Madame Binswanger. For Anna (Asja) L. [I remembered. I only just remembered, and cannot understand why I should forget, how could I have forgotten this? Why am I constantly forgetting what I should have remembered, what I wanted so much to tell you? When I have so much to tell you?], there was imprisonment at the Butyrka prison in Moscow, a hellish place, where Evgenia or Yevgenia Ginzburg, incarcerated in 1937, could hear over and through the screams of the tortured, the shouts and curses of the torturers, the noise of chairs being hurled about, fists banging on tables, and some other unidentifiable sounds; then there was exile to forced labour in Kazakhstan in 1938.

XLVIII

In a letter to Wilhelm Fliess, Freud wondered if ever there might be a marble plaque on the house, 'this house', inscribed with the words that here the secret of dreams was revealed to him. The house was Schloss Bellevue, on the Bellevue-Hohe, near Grinzing, once a sanatorium where Freud had been assistant doctor, then a hotel, now demolished. From Vienna, one must take the bus 38A to Parkplatz am Cobenzl, then turn right onto Himmelstrasse, right again, and finally walk up a concrete stairway and alongside an old path of trees. At the far end of the path there is a small memorial to Freud. The revealing dream, the historical moment, the specimen dream (he had always been a good dreamer) was that of Irma's injection: the revelation of a structure and message hitherto obscure. It was his first complete analysis of a dream, dreamed during the night of Wednesday 23/24 July 1895. He had learnt how to interpret dreams: there was a hall, there were many guests; there was 'Irma', a woman he had treated who had not accepted his solution, and oh, she had such pains, stomach, throat, abdomen, they were choking her. By the light of the window he looked into her mouth. In the dream, he looked into the mouth of a woman who may have been Anna Hammerschlag *née* Lichtheim, the daughter of his old Hebrew teacher, and certainly was not the woman many thought to be behind the pseudonym. Didier Anzieu, Aimée's son, insists it is this Anna, and he uncovered a great deal of sexual content in the dream. Freud named his daughter after this Anna; she was his Anna's godmother. He had never had any occasion to examine Anna H-L.'s mouth during her treatment. She was a disobedient patient, even though one of his favourites. If she had pains, it was her own fault; it was nothing to do with a failure of the treatment or a fault in the diagnosis. He had never done any harm with his injections, no, no, *certainly he had not.*

There was no name and no grave for Walter Benjamin in Portbou, as Hannah A. discovered. It was not to be found. His name was not written anywhere. It was odd, as two days after his death, a niche in the cemetery had been rented for five years and a cloth-lined coffin paid for, and a mass was said —there was a receipt from the priest, and only a few months or maybe a year had passed. Hannah A. wrote to Gershom Scholem that it was one of the most beautiful places she had ever seen. Oh, yes, Scholem wrote, the spot was beautiful, very beautiful, and there was a grave, but it was a fake grave, nothing more than a wooden enclosure with a name scrawled on it, an invention of the greedy attendants who sought a tip in response to so many enquiries. It is, of course, quite different now, though there is still no body, unless it is in a common grave, and that is what everyone thinks. Walter Benjamin became Benjamin Walter—the Spanish police assumed Benjamin was his first name: it was written like this on the hotel receipt, the hotel where he made four telephone calls and ordered five sodas with lemon and left a note that said there was no way out and he did not have the time to write all the letters he would have liked to write and took fifteen morphine tablets, enough to take his life several times over, said Lisa Fittko, his guide over the mountains to the border, the border where he was halted, the border where his papers were found not to be in order, the border from which he was not allowed to continue further into Spain, the border where he was not given the permits to proceed, the border from which he would be sent back to France, the border where he was permitted to stay one night in the Hotel França (taking a room on the second floor), due to the late hour and his exhaustion, the border from where a day or two later his travelling companions continued their journey to board a ship to America.

L

Scholem had expected his friend to emigrate to Palestine, as
he had done, but Asja L., who cut a path, no, a street, a one-
way street (Asja Lacis street, he wrote), through Benjamin
(he wrote), told Benjamin that the path of the progressive
person, in his right senses, led not to Palestine but to Moscow
(she said), and in 1926 he went to Moscow for a rendezvous
with her, staying for two months. She was in a sanatorium,
the Rott Sanatorium; they saw each other in her sick room
and during a few visits to his hotel, the Hotel Tyrol, when
she called by and he gave her presents and showed her the
dedication to her in his book; he showed her its dustjacket,
and sometimes they went shopping or dined out, though he
could not even order a bowl of soup on his own. They did
nothing but quarrel, everyone remarked on this; she eluded
his clumsy courtship. But sometimes he thought she looked at
him very affectionately. They played dominoes, reluctantly.
He bought her halvah. He gave her more presents, a blouse,
stockings. He read to her about wrinkles and helped her into
her galoshes. Asja bought some rubber galoshes for him.
They planned to buy material for a dress for her. It became
more difficult for her to leave the sanatorium. It became
harder for him to see her, to spend time alone with her.
At times, she appeared terrified of spending any time in his
hotel room. Often he could not hear what she said for he was
looking at her so intently. They were constantly interrupted;
there was no hope of clarifying their relationship; there
seemed always to be three or four others present. The only
moment in the dark that they shared in Moscow was in the
middle of the street, on the narrow seat of a sleigh. Taking a
sleigh through the streets felt like a child gliding through the
house on its little chair (he wrote).

LI

Ada, huntress of butterflies and rare words, and Lucette, who like all the Lucettes (such is the name) is lost in advance, kissed Van, kissed each other, one in silence, the other with squeals of delight, and these children, not *les enfants maudits*, might have been filmed if a kitchen boy were to have a camera, their twenty ticklish fingers cramming Van's erect penis back into his black swimming trunks in their dangerous game, dangerous and at the same time inept, and then the governess, their learned governess, who monitored all of Ada's reading, arrived, just as he walked away on his hands, a black mask over his nose, and she was shouting, shouting and panting, crying out *'Mais qu'est-ce qu'il t'a fait, ton cousin',* what had their cousin done to her, though it is clear that the relationship is not simply dangerous *cousinage* but one that is prohibited, and she keeps asking this anxiously, as Lucette, that far more ordinary girl, far more ordinary than Ada (Hell, *muki ada,* the torments of hell, that cunning wordsmith in the depths, *moego ada,* of her Hades, that truly unusual *gamine*), Lucette, weeping, tears pouring down her little pretty but ordinary cheeks, rushed into her mauve-winged arms, in delicate pictorial detail, in butterfly groves and heraldic stained glass windows, with that sweet scent of innocence and cold tea that happy childhoods leave behind.

LII

Girls once learnt to read and write through embroidering, as art or craft or labour, women's work in any case, where the skill of the needlework was more important that the mastery of cursive script. There was a time that only the catechism and needlework were taught to girls. There was little need for anything more than these. They were taught backstitch in red thread, because backstitch was simple to execute and the red dye was fast, and outlines were easier, quick to complete. A woman could earn her living from her red piece-work. Jean-Jacques Rousseau once knew a girl (he calls her a young person) who learned to write before learning to read. She began to write with her needle before she wrote with a quill. She made only Os, nothing but, large and small, inside each other, nestling Os, os, one inside the other, always in reverse, he said, but how could that be for O is the same backwards, oh, he must mean that her os incline to the left: O is a mirror. O is one inside the Other: little o, big O. Lacanians say *petit a*, little other, g*rand A*, big Other. One day she looked at herself in the mirror and though how ungraceful she looked in this constrained attitude of making her Os and threw away her quill. She no longer wanted to make Os. Her brother did not like to write either, but it was the constraint he disliked, not the ungraceful air writing gave him. They tried to bring her back to writing by a trick. She was delicate and vain. She did not like to have her linen used by her sisters. Linen had to be marked, to show to whom it belonged, and no one would mark hers anymore. They said she had to learn to do it herself. It was a matter of possession, ownership. It is always a matter of this.

LIII

Anne B. said that Rousseau's little girl did not stop writing because she could not tolerate her unlovely reflection; no, she stopped because in the mirror she saw a message she had written to herself in code, a set of practical instructions telling her throw down the pen that was her needle, to refuse to write again unless to mark what was hers. Anne B. said the girl had already written her revolutionary letters in her code of Os, every letter, every word, an opening, a ring, a planet, a grammar, a mouth, an eye, a bruise. She, herself, not Rousseau's girl [who was not so little, I think, not really], wrote complicated sentences that seemed quite simple at first reading. She said it was easy to imagine not writing, the manufacture of impossible desire. The wild child of Aveyron, the boy Victor, found wandering in the forest, naked, bent, mute and fearful, his skin white and fine yet criss-crossed by many small scars, could only pronounce the letter O, but the good doctor Itard persevered in his lessons and the child learnt to trace letters spelling milk and soup on a board, *lait, soupe,* and then every day acquired a new word that was connected to his needs, distinguishing the letters of the alphabet with grammatical exactitude.

[Were we all reading Rousseau at the same time, I wondered, at the time when we did not know each other, but in truth we hardly know each other now.] Lisa R. wrote about the anonymous girl, abject, depraved, invisible, and read in Rousseau what she called an inadvertent formula for a solution that she had only found for herself in a more arduous manner, piece by piece, through the rooms, the many rooms, the inhabitations and seductions, what she called the mistaken fucks [as though they are not all mistakes in their way]. She told her reader, who might have been anyone (except Rousseau), me, for example, that depraved anonymity must be turned into a décor, a baroque device of Os within Os within Os, a carapace, exuded stitch by stitch [for which I read: letter by letter], in which the drama of mortal self-invention would advance. She wrote that she would be schooled in the ornament of excess. She wrote that girlhood was in itself a baroque condition. [Girlhood, then, which I never felt myself though I saw it in others, even at an early age, would be infinite, theatrical, ostentatious, elaborate (elaborated), ornate (the same thing), opulent and grandiose, extravagant, absurd, misshapen, diseased. It would be an odd, imperfect, irregular pearl.]

Under the name of Anna O. there was Bertha, who was not the madwoman in the attic, the one who was Bertha Antoinette, who bit, who scratched, who started fires, who had no voice but laughed demonically, who was savage, a German vampire, red-eyed and black-haired (such wild unlovely hair). This was a Bertha who did not want anyone to know that once she had been Anna O. It was a private matter, the thorough chimney-sweeping that rid her of the snakes, the blurred vision, the partial paralysis, the contractures, the hallucinations, the *ramonage* that restored speech to her. She never started talking to Breuer until she had felt his hands carefully, satisfying herself of his identity. He did not mention her addiction to chloral, then later to morphine. Neither did he mention the episode in which she told him his child was coming, nor how he fled in horror from the scene. It caused a marital crisis; he had no desire for a symbolic child and he wished that she would die. She worked in a soup kitchen, then a nursery school, teaching sewing. She formed a girls' club. She wrote a pamphlet on the education of young bourgeois women, advocating an entry into independent life, a knowledge of the world. She translated Mary Wollstonecraft's *Vindication of the Rights of Women*. She wrote that poor education kept girls in poverty and led them to vice. She founded a home for vulnerable girls and illegitimate children. A volcano lived in her, but love did not come to her; she lived like the plants, in the cellar, without light, she wrote, and thought of death as a friendly face. She devoted herself to her wretched sisters, martyrs of men. She wrote that if the father asked what the child was after a successful birth, the answer would be the satisfied report of a boy, or else it would be, nothing, a girl, or, only a girl. She belonged, she said, to a chain of daughters, daughter of her father Sigmund, who was neither Sigmund O. nor Sigmund F., but in fact, was Sigmund P.

LVI

Annie E. said that sometimes she had secrets but they were not secrets for she did not want to speak about them, and in any case, they were things one could not say to anyone for they were too strange. She saw herself reflected in a shop window, the window of a shoe-shop, and thought how ugly she looked. In her family, they said she looked like a schoolteacher; well, it was because of her glasses, which she stopped wearing and then could not recognise anyone she crossed on the pavement, so she could not say hello to them. Lying under the lime trees in June she thought if she did not pass her exams, she would sleep with a boy, she did not want to live until then, all her ugly childhood, having thought about it all the time for, *crac*, nothing. Later, with the black cat with green eyes purring on her pillow, she wondered if she really thought that if she did not pass she would sleep with a boy. Her father hardly ever called her Anne now, only the girl, *la fille*, in fact he barely spoke to her at all except to grumble at her for sleeping with the cat, because one should not allow cats in the bed, it was unhealthy. In July, she discovered that she had no need of her mother, who had nothing to teach her, who did not talk to her about anything, who did not laugh with her. She closed the shutters of her bedroom; she spent the days in shadow. When her parents argued about her, it was as if they were speaking about another Anne, the good little girl, the good little daughter. Her mother told her father she had spent the day reading when he complained but she knew there was something a bit dirty about that, to read all day, especially those kinds of books that stayed with her, not like the magazines of her mother, and that reading was dangerous.

Of Anne S.'s governesses, there was Inès, sent across the
road to look after the old gentleman, the one with the
telescope, there was Eléonore, there was Laura. They were
the governesses, appointed as the mistresses of games and
pleasure. They shut themselves up in their rooms, they
had fainting fits and palpitations, vapours and rashes.
They discussed men; they were experienced. Standing at
the gate, they offered a breast, a bottom, a mouth, to men
who came in their cars, sometimes as many as fifteen,
milling about in the lane in the grey twilight. They had
no friends, no family, and not much of a past either,
everything was swallowed up in their current situation, all
the other gardens, trees, châteaux, by Monsieur Austeur's
château, his enchanted garden. They wore yellow dresses,
covering their buttercup-coloured legs—the little boys,
the unexplained little boys, so many of them, saw that, and
that they wore no stockings—and they slipped out into the
night, under the trees, disappearing into them. They went
hunting, their skirts caught on brambles, their bare arms
were covered in scratches. They tackled head on, licked,
bit, devoured, in quite a lady-like manner nonetheless,
such dainty white pointed teeth; the handsome stranger
could not take it anymore. They loved him, oh yes, but
only when he was inside them. He was bled dry, left lifeless.
He was cold, he did not move, they put his clothes back on
and walked back to the house. Anne S. will not give up her
vigilance. Anne S. will not relinquish her solitude. Anne
S. is economic, controlled, but a little savage, a little cruel.
She remembered a dream she had one night: she was in a
lecture hall, which was also a refugee centre, and somebody
outside tried to shoot her. But he made a mistake: he fired at
her reflection in a mirror. And so she emerged unscathed.

LVIII

Anna F. wrote to Marie B. in 1946 that she had been ill again during the winter, so ill that she went to bed with the flu, then had five weeks incapacitated by pneumonia. She was so ill that she had to stop her work, a new experience for her. While she was ill she thought about the past and her father's illnesses. That was the winter when she learnt that her brother's daughter Eva had died from influenza in Nice. Oliver and his wife Henny had escaped from France to America. None in the family knew of Eva's death. Anna also received the first report about her four great-aunts, the worst possible report, and Anna felt guilty, for herself, for her father, for the decision to leave the aunts in Vienna. She felt that she must tell Marie B. a dream which she had on her last night in Walberswick. That night she was very depressed; she only slept a very little. In the short time that she was able to sleep, she dreamed that she was in Palestine. It was all very interesting. She visited all sorts of places and met many people whom she half seemed to know. A woman invited her to eat goose with them. Anna F. cried and the woman asked if she was ill, and Anna replied that she was not, but she had been. She saw a modern school and looked at the faces of the pupils, who looked very alert. However, there was one very disturbing factor throughout the whole dream, which was very vivid. She could not understand a word of anyone's language and they could not understand her. She did not understand about the eating of the goose and thought perhaps it was to do with being killed, and after all, in truth, they had left the aunts to be killed. She wrote that she was too old, that it was too late, that her paradise would come only after her death.

LIX

Discharged from the hospital of Sainte-Anne, where she had held the post of assistant librarian, Aimée lived with a sister, a second sister, not the one who had stolen her child, and her husband in the countryside. After the war, she became the cook of some rich Parisians who had a country home in her village; she went to Boulogne to work for them. They had been impressed by her culinary skills. In fact, Aimée, by a strange coincidence, was working for Jacques Lacan's father, Alfred, who was the wealthy Parisian, a sales representative. At the same time, and it was even more strange, her son from whom she was estranged was in analysis with Lacan. Aimée and Didier were reunited; he realised his mother was the subject of Lacan's thesis, that Lacan had stolen her story, that he had made her a myth, that she had been observed, ransacked, fabricated, and travestied, that is what his mother said, that is what was done to her. She had no authority over her writing. Her name came from her own novel, that of her heroine, but it was taken from her, like her writing. She was made anonymous, 'A', by Gaston Ferdière, as author and character under the same initial, but Paul Éluard preferred to use Lacan's name for her. Joë Bousquet said she was unconscious of her unconscious, rewriting her, assimilating her, and as for André Breton, he classed her work among the art of madness, *l'art des fous*. That certainly kept her in her place, under the sign of 'A'. Madwomen were segregated at the Salpêtrière: on one side, *les folles* who might be cured, on the other, *les aliénées*, who had given up everything, without hope.

In another dream, Anna F. had a baby. Often women have babies in their dreams, even when they do not have them in their waking life. For unknown reasons, someone threw the baby onto the ground from above. Suddenly it was dead. Anna wept, full of despair. Suddenly she said or thought reproachfully: you people have killed it by dropping it. She wrote that one comes out of illness empty-handed, like a stillborn child, like Marianne who almost lost her daughter, Annerl, from bleeding after birth, and oh, the dead Annerl was her, lamenting her own death. Annerl, Anna, was named after Anna F., one Anna for another, helpless children. Annerl did not die; she became a psychoanalyst, as did her brother, Anton. There were dreams in which a child was not properly taken care of, in which the poor children were neglected by self-absorbed women. Dreams might overcome mourning, she wrote, as one remains loyal to the dead while turning to the living. H. D. had a nightmare in which an enormous bull, or a bison or buffalo, whatever, it was huge in any case, a great bull-like creature pursued a crowded cart or carriage; she was uncertain if the cart or carriage or car plunged over a cliff. She was uncertain if they were in it. Some of them, a group of six or eight, were then seated on a mountain slope. They asked, are we dead? The week before the dream, Freud placed the small statue of Athene in her hand. He did this very gently. He told her Athene was the veiled Isis, or Neith, the warrior-goddess. He said she was perfect even though her spear was broken.

LXI

Mathilde Breuer
Sophie Schwab-Paneth
Anna Hammerschlag-Lichtheim

In a letter dated 9 January, 1908, Freud wrote to Karl Abraham, hurriedly, formlessly, impersonally (he said), in order to offer technical information. Behind the dream, the dream of Irma's injection, was sexual megalomania. The three women were his daughters' three godmothers ... and he had them all. He added an exclamation mark. Who would not! Of course, naturally, he added an exclamation mark! There would be all sorts of intimate things, naturally, and an exclamation mark was necessary, of course! He posted his letter at the main post office so it would arrive more quickly at its destination! The letter arrived at its destination, which one might say was the sender himself, or one might say the destination was where it arrived, or one might add, on reflection, that while it might be possible for a letter to go astray, the message it contained had been sent, including the exclamation mark, indicating strong feelings or excitement, as though a voice were raised! Once it was the sign of emphasis, then of joy! Hooray! Huzzah! Later it became a sign of admiration, of wonderment! Now it is a warning, a command, a screamer, a gasper, a slammer, a startler, a pling, a bang, a shriek!

LXII

Sophie Freud
Mathilde Freud
Anna Freud

The choice was between three women. Three was always the number of Freud's desire. Three essays on sexuality, for instance; and another thing, there are the three levels of consciousness, or the Id, the Ego, the Superego, all busily at work, criticising and moralising, organising and rationalising, seeking pleasure and destroying. One is a chaos, a cauldron of seething excitations; one stores up experiences, brings about changes to its own advantages, poised uneasily between three agencies; one is a third power, prohibiting, judging, a nasty voice of conscience. Jacques liked three as well: real, symbolic, and imaginary, and followed the father's orders, to the letter, to the register. He knotted them together, entwined them in a beautiful Borromean knot, and what was excluded from sense-making made sense hang together; no two things could be coupled or contrasted without a mediating third. Everything that exists *ex-sists*, Jacques said, and has its being in relation to what lies outside it. There is no exception to the rule. *Jamais deux sans trois*, as the saying goes. Things come and go in threes. A magic number, a charm. Three's a charm, a crowd. Neither the first time nor the second. Never two without three. Never thou without thee. Never you without me. NEVER.

Anne S. did not hold back. There was no mincing of words. One sister told the story of the unusual (perhaps it was not so unusual) sex life of her family, for she imagined that was of greatest interest to her reader, rather than other aspects of their existence, such as the charmless courtyard, the short flight of stairs opening onto a dark hallway, the coat-rack, the marble-topped mahogany sideboard, and the armoire, with a mirror in which their mother looked at herself [the word the narrator used was 'inspect', if I remembered correctly, but of course it was in translation, the first time of my reading], regarding her naked reflection, combing her hair. And then there was the dining-room, which had an enormous polished table. It was there, as she had said, that they went about their affairs, where the mother was thrown down, for example, by the doctor Mars, who thrust himself violently inside her on the shining disc of the table like a frozen pool, and Ingrid and Chloë and the girl who told the story might have been lending a hand, though normally the doctor did not need any help, or they were under the table or offering themselves to him. There were a few chairs scattered around the edges of the room. There was the mother's sewing table in the window and her armchair, and sometimes the mother put on a dress and sat sewing in the poor light of the window, but it was not often and then they were all bored or fretful or in despair and they turned into wild beasts, she said, searching a wrist to lick or a sex to devour. The father's study was next to the dining-room, so much more comfortable, even gracious, with thick rugs, many books, a great many books, and the light from the windows was much better here, but of course he would usually draw the curtains when the sisters, one of them or all of them, were in there with him, and for a long time, Ingrid was his favourite, though he pounded away at them all and they were enchanted.

LXIV

Once when Anna F. went for a walk with her father after dinner one evening, as they passed the lovely houses near the Prater, he told her to look at those beautiful homes with their lovely façades. He said that things were not so lovely behind those lovely façades, not necessarily. He said those lovely houses with their beautiful façades were like human beings, that things were not necessarily so lovely behind their faces. Behind the façade, well, there are many things going on about which one does not know, about which one cannot tell from the outside, even if one tells oneself nice stories and does not want to think about a child being beaten, even if one wants to be good, even if one surrenders oneself in an altruistic manner, living the life of other people instead of one's own, instead of dancing, say, or being generous, or achieving like a man.

There were matters that Anna recounted to her father, in his study, his consulting-room, which Sergei Pankejeff, the 'Wolf Man', felt was not like a doctor's office but like an archivist's, with its statuettes and other unusual objects producing a sense of sanctuary, a 'feeling of sacred peace and quiet'. Anna preferred to give and serve, she wrote to Lou, rather than to demand and acquire, but once in a while she would have liked to dance, perhaps, and she wrote to Eva that Eva was her and she was Eva and Eva could take anything from her, Anna, because it was rightfully hers. But then Anna met Dorothy and Eva became jealous until she made friends with Dorothy herself. Anna arranged Dorothy's analysis with her father, so he knew about their friendship with her American friend and Anna did not have to tell him anything about it, because Dorothy was speaking about it already to him in her house in the Vienna woods. Anna and Dorothy were like twins, twins for each other, Freud's daughter and her American friend, which gave Dorothy great pleasure to read in Anna's letter about their lovely friendship, their ideal friendship, for they were such very good friends.

LXVI

The studies of the papas were very lovely. There were oriental rugs in one and a pretty rug with bright flowers in the other. There were books: for one papa, nothing improper, nothing racy, while the other papa had a passion for collecting and owning books. This papa remembered—and it was one of the few memories from his early childhood—that his own papa had given a book with coloured plates to him and his sister for them to destroy, and they pulled the book to pieces blissfully to the amusement of their papa. This memory was, he thought, a screen memory for his later bibliophile propensities, what a bookworm he was! There were large desks, and on one of them, the one in Vienna with the semi-circle of little *objets d'art* or at the summer house in Dölbing, with a careful arrangement of small vases holding a spray of orchids or a single flower, or later, the desk was in London, with statuettes but fewer, in a room that was rather like the summer room in Dölbing, the papa had written a paper with his daughter. The desk was dark wood, with a red felt or velvet top, a nineteenth century-style pedestal desk. There was a shallow drawer in the centre and three heavy drawers to each side, supporting the desk. It was made by Siegmund Spitz in his workshop in Garningsongasse. On the desk, among the figures of, say, Athene, Eros, Venus, and the baboon Thoth, the lunar god of writing, who created language, were ashtrays, cigar boxes, a marble letter opener, pens, and there the papa would lay down his spectacles. This papa wrote about masturbation and phantasy, and his daughter told her papa about a dream in which she tried to defend a dairy farm from attack but her sword was broken, and it was, she said, like she had not lain in bed with her hands at the seam of her nightgown, as the rules required. She dreamed her papa was a king.

LXVII

The three sisters never tired of entering the other papa's
study, so comfortable, so well-lit, so cheerful. They would
stand outside the door, barefoot, knocking softly, hoping he
would let them in. This papa would take Ingrid to his study
and close the door.

LXVIII

Then there was that papa's study in America; this one was another papa with mysterious habits which the daughter did not understand, constantly coming and going, sleeping on his couch in the day and going out at night. He went outside, commanded by the stars, she thought. He was not to be disturbed while he was working at his desk, this papa, this professor, but the daughter could come in as she pleased, as long as she was quiet, and sometimes he let her play with his Chinese paper-knife, which was a grotesque thing like a figure with a squat body decorated with delicate tendrils for its handle and a pot on its head that held the blade of the knife. He allowed her to cut his uncut books and journals but the brother was not allowed to touch them or the knife. The son could not touch the knife of the papa, only the daughter, who knew just how to run the blade under the edge of the page. It had to be done carefully, never with a finger or a pencil, for example, or especially not a ruler, and never should it be ripped wildly, never, even if one wanted to get to the inside with great impatience. The blade of the knife had to be slipped into the fold at the edge of the page, the blade held flat against the surface, and a dull blade was best for cutting out, away from the book. The blade had to move away from the body of the daughter, whose hand had to apply gentle pressure to the page, cutting as the blade drew out of the book. This was an unopened book, not simply uncut, until the paper knife severed the top and fore-edge; unopened is the correct term, but the preferred term, figurative, from the Italian, *intonso*, is untouched, unread. A *barba intonsa* might be an unshaven beard in Italian, but the papa's beard was neatly trimmed.

LXIX

Where were the mothers? Where were they while the papa and the daughter, the papa and the sisters, were in the lovely studies? One mother was keeping a meticulous household; how furious this mother was when the daughter or the papa fed their dogs scraps from the table. She was being an admirable manager, of the children, the servants, the house. She was admired by others. She was maintaining domestic order; however, the housework did not come first, but rather her family; that is to say, there were maids and the housework was their work, performed under her directions. She was reading a great deal in the evenings. She was appearing humble and unobtrusive (and it was true that there was not much to be said about her except how admirable she was), but the daughter felt she was being strict and domineering, saying that her mother made her own rules, observing no other rules than her own. The mother was deceiving, hiding the daughter's school examination schedules and the reason why the daughter was going to hospital: it was, she said, so the daughter would not be anxious, but the daughter was surprised to have her appendix removed when she went there and it was a great deception.

LXX

The other mother was being idle, without anything to occupy her outside the house or the daughters, whom she kept by her side, calling them to her so she might fondle them in various ways, *les gamahucher.* That is an old verb, 'to excite an erogenous zone with the tongue': Sade used it, as one might expect, and Baudelaire, speaking about his mother, according to the Goncourts, used it as an apology for his lateness, and Verlaine used it in a poem, in which he called for all his courage to descend into the pit that had a smell between shit and cheese. Anyway, this mother was waiting for a visitor to call. She did not care about housework though the dining-room table was without a speck of dust. She was sewing badly; she was flitting restlessly about the house; she was looking at her soft white body in the mirror. She was staying by the window, not even looking out at the garden. Never was she reading, but she was speaking well and the daughter thought she could have made a book of all her words, strung together like an oracle. This mother was not a mystery to her daughter.

LXXI

Aucassine had flashes. They became thicker and thicker. She no longer saw things or objects. She was very scared. She did not want this to be noticed. She held on as long as she could, then oh God, for she hurt everywhere, it burst and it was over and she was empty. She did not sleep, remembering a time when she kissed a boy and their mouths were like wide caverns, they were so very dark. She screamed, she burst her lungs, she said that she was dead. She told them she was a foetus. She told them that her mother had abandoned her, but her mother was her friend Monique, who put saliva into her mouth. She screamed when she saw a boy in the bed. And then there was the time she was in hell, when she did not see the walls any more. Her psychoanalyst said that she was not mad, that she might have been pretending to be mad. She was studying Hebrew, English, and German; she had a job looking after two children. She had a generous allowance from her father, which allowed her to live comfortably. Her father was a lawyer. Her mother had received a message from God; he told her that she needed twelve children who would be twelve prophets, and the mother organised her children in couples. It was not entirely clear in the analyst's account if the delusion was Aucassine's or her mother's. Aucassine wrote poems. Once her younger sister came to stay with her in Paris, bringing a 'message', 'dictated' to her, she said, which no publisher in the country would take, despite its urgency. The message said that she was Christ and had been commanded to save humankind. The sister wrote the text in three days and night, without any sleep. She sought a publisher in Paris, that was why she was there, visiting her sister Aucassine.

LXXII

There were the stern mothers, the perverse mothers, the crazy mothers. There were so many crazy mothers. There were the mothers who made their own rules and often these were the worst kind of mothers. There were the strict Moravian mothers whose daughters cried 'My mother, my mother' while they sobbed violently, tears, tears, tears. That mother liked the brother better and the daughter could not get near her. There were the dying mothers, who were losing their minds. There were the mothers who were losing their minds but refused to die. There were the mothers against whom one slept, pressed closely to their warm backs. Sometimes one read while leaning against these kinds of mothers. There were the mothers in hospital who no longer knew who one was and these mothers were crying and turning the sheets over and over in their ugly twisted hands. There were the mothers who did not answer the telephone, while other mothers called all the time. There were the mothers whose mothers were dead, and these mothers talked incessantly about those mothers. There were the mothers who left their children and their children were alone and some died or felt as if they were dead. There were mothers who were beloved by their sons even though the sons were not free to live until those mothers died or the sons were not free to die as long as those mothers were alive. There were the mothers found on free porn hashtag, *do not go there, no*. There were the mothers who slept peacefully as they were carried into a room by two or three people with bird's beaks who laid them on the bed. There were the mothers who could not come out from their darkness and these mothers were tied to their chairs. There were the mothers whom one became without knowing it. These were the mothers who spoke through one's mouth. These were all the same mothers, that's obvious, don't you see? There were too many mothers and it made the daughters breathless. Actually, it made the daughters crazy.

LXXIII

Aimée sent a sonnet every week to the Prince of Wales, but he never replied, not once did he reply to her beseeching poetry. Princes do not reply to poems they did not ask to receive, but how was Aimée to know that? It was very hard for a woman to be heard, especially by royalty. It was very hard for a woman to be published, especially in the literary world, unless she wrote under another name, as a man, as did Amandine-Aurore or Alice or Angélique or Marie-Anne or Anna, or sometimes under the name of a husband or a child, or a woman might write under an aristocratic pseudonym, feminine, *La Comtesse* or *La Vicomtesse*, though usually the masculine name will triumph in this ennoblement, *Le Chevalier* or *Le Baron*; or conversely a common man might take a name of the nobility, another vicomtesse, for example. Stéphane M. did not hesitate to write both as an English governess and as a lady of the *noblesse*. A common woman, Aimée did not stop writing for all that, and what a *cause célèbre* she became, thanks to Jacques L. and his poetic voice, speaking for her, including her writings when no-one else would publish them; he did the same for the Papin sisters, speaking for them, that is, for they did not write— though they did dream with considerable elaboration—in *Minotaure,* that lavish, extravagant publication named by Georges Bataille and André Masson after the monster of Greek mythology, you know, the one with the body of a man and the head of a bull, named Asterios (a star) by his mother Pasiphae. A witch herself, Pasiphae was Circe's sister, Medea's aunt, Ariadne's mother, what a family romance. Bewitched, she fell in love with a bull as white as snow, sent to be sacrificed to her husband Minos by Poseidon. He kept it alive instead, the stupid man, and the god cursed them. Later, the sister of Asterios, Ariadne, betrayed her monstrous brother.

LXXIV

Aimée dreamt and wrote of bulls, which would not stop appearing as evil omens in her dreams and her writing. It is not true that dreaming or writing do not place one in any real danger of being gored, or of absented, annihilated under a letter. A to O. A/O. *Autre,* Other. Nothing. It always comes back to this O/A.

LXXV

Ariadne was both *fille* and *fil*, daughter and thread, unravelling and ravelling. She gave the Athenian Theseus a clew of red thread and a sword so he might find his way out of her labyrinth (she was, after all, its mistress) after killing her poor monstrous brother. This is a long story cut short. The details are missing. Her cleverness must be imagined, as well as his stupidity. Thread, red or otherwise, pebbles, preferably white so they shine in the moonlight; everyone knows these must be carried into the labyrinth, the maze, or the deep dark forest, if one is ever to return. Breadcrumbs are no good at all, absolutely useless, the birds swoop down to eat them and there is nothing left shining on the path in the darkness. The red thread was another matter. It led to their departure from Crete, over the dead body of a brother. Ungrateful, after fleeing with her, Theseus abandoned Ariadne on Naxos, and it was clear, Athenians were never to be trusted. She fell asleep on the beach and when she awoke, she longed for death. The opera, *Ariadne auf Naxos*, is both *opera buffa* and *opera seria*. An opera within an opera, a band of merry travellers play, well, a band of merry travellers who—happy coincidence—come upon a sleeping woman on a lonely desert isle who has been abandoned by her lover. Hugo von Hofmannstahl wrote of his libretto for the opera, the music composed by his friend Richard Strauss, that it was a question of holding fast to what was lost, clinging to it even unto death, or if to live on, to transform. The Composer sings that Ariadne, the matchless woman in a million, one who is really true for she cannot forget, wraps death around her, her soul is void, wiped away. The nymphs (Naiad, Dryad, and Echo, hah! echo...) who guard her, see her sighing and crying in her sleep. When Ariadne awakes, her mind is deranged, but she is only mad, not foolish, and she knows what truth is when not distorted by ill-fated passion.

LXXVI

[D. told me today that she had a dream before Christmas in which I was drawing a red line on a map—I think she said it was a map, but I could not hear her properly and felt I could not ask her to repeat what she had said, even though we had been speaking about repetition in Homeric poetry, about the ring-composition used to keep a grip on the story-line, the recurring patterns of action, the ways of getting the poet back to the place he had started, usually in three rings, repeated in reverse order, repeated patterns of form and content, containing what is unnarrated or unnarratable in the drive towards death and destruction. It goes ABCCBA. It goes in threes. ABCDDCBA. ABXBA. Entrance. Coda. Exit. First last, last first. *Hysteron-proton*. Abracadabra. *Sauve qui peut,* for it is marked by digression. In some stories, there is a bull at the beginning and a bull at the end. D. said that in her dream, the one in which I was drawing a red line on something, I said: 'The story-teller hasn't arrived yet'. I was holding the place of the story-teller in the dream of another. This was not my dream yet I was obliged to inhabit it, waiting for the arrival of someone who would tell the story or telling D. there would be a delay in telling the story. Anne C. wrote that sometimes she dreamt a sentence and wrote it down. Sometimes it was only nonsense. This sentence dreamt by another, I said it sounded liked something I might say, and so I wrote it down, but it is the X between AB and BA. I was surprised to recount this today, in the middle of mythology. In his account of his voyage, Odysseus/Ulysses said it was inadvisable to 're-tell a story already told'; I am told, in Greek, that is to 'mythologise' (*muthologeuin*).]

Aracelis G. wrote that her mother had told her that death
and life was in the power of the tongue. Her mother said that
death and life about any number of things and in any number
of ways. Aracelis G. understood that language could help
them to live and to die. She understood that 'rebuking Satan
and anointing our heads and house with oil actually meant
something'. The point was not if Satan endured, though
it was true they all wanted Satan gone. She understood
that the point was that her mother was teaching her to fight.
[I thought about how one is brought, pulled, into the world.
I thought that a red thread can keep one in the world and
lead one out into it. A skein of thread is called a clew, I told
you this once, and then H. reminded me of it, and from this
comes the word clue, which is a way of solving the mystery,
understanding the puzzle, yes, getting out of the labyrinth,
finding the way, getting answers. I thought that one did not
have to remain in the dark, unless of course one was a monster,
a poor old ugly monster with the head of bull, blind-horned,
snuffling in the shadows. I thought it might be possible to
spin a story or a story from it (what was 'it'?). I thought I
might be confusing Ariadne with Arachne, but then, they are
both weaving goddesses, though one is beaten to death with
her shuttle because there are some dreams girls must not have.
I thought of Ariadne's beautiful braids of hair, described by
Homer in *The Iliad*, in an ornamental epitaph he gives only
to goddesses. She is the fair-tressed. I thought of Freud talking
and writing and even dreaming about women and plaiting
and weaving: that nature gave the model this achievement
imitates through the growth at maturity of the pubic hair
that conceals the genitals. There was, he said, shame, and that
was why the genitals had to be hidden, such an old story, such
a silly tale. He said that the step remaining to be taken lay in
making the threads adhere to one another, because on the
body they stick to the skin and are only matted together.]

LXXVIII

In Catullus's labyrinthine epyllion Ariadne became a stone
sculpture of a bacchante. She was frozen in frenzy. She could
not believe Theseus had sailed away, that thoughtless,
treacherous, fleeing, and forgetful man: *indomitos in corde
gerens Ariadna furores, necdum etiam sese quae visit visere
credit*. Yes, she could not believe her eyes. He had just sailed
away. When she spoke, she raged. Love tore at her like a wild
beast. Her hair escaped from her headdress, her breasts were
exposed, no longer constrained by her bodice nor concealed
by her fine-textured cloak. Her garments fell to the seashore.
She cursed Theseus with all the coldness of heart with which
he had left her, she wished that he would destroy himself and
his family. He did, of course, for he forgot to raise the white
sails to replace the black sails of his departure as he promised
his father, to signal that he had survived the labyrinth.
He forgot, so forgetful, ah, but that was the wish of Ariadne.
In terrible grief, his father threw himself from the cliffs into
the sea, or he fell, his body dashed against the rocks. The
son Theseus killed the father Aegeus. The son has to kill the
father (or often, if he does not, the father will kill the son).
Then Theseus married Phaedra, his father's wife, Ariadne's
sister, daughter of King Minos, sister of the minotaur, but she
would betray him for his own son, Hippolytus. The accounts
differ: in one, Theseus killed his son by using one of the three
wishes given to him by Poseidon; or Theseus cursed him and
the son's horses were frightened by a bull and dragged him
to death; or a bull came from the sea and dragged him and
his horses to drown, and so really, in truth, in justice, in all
fairness, served as just desserts, you reap what you sow, and
what goes around comes around.

Hephaestus repaid Thetis (lovely-haired, golden-haired or
ashen-haired) for her kindness to him by making armour,
a shield and helmet, and leg-guards for her beloved son
Achilles. Hephaestus decorated the shield with consummate
skill, with the constellations, with scenes of marriage, a court
case, siege and ambush, ploughing, reaping, the grape harvest,
cattle-herding, flocks of sheep, and the ocean flowed around
the rim of the shield, oh, and there was dancing: a dancing-
floor like the one Daedalus designed in Knossos for lovely-
haired Ariadne. There were young men and women dancing,
holding each other by the wrist; the girls had lovely garlands
on their heads (golden-haired or ashen-haired), the boys had
lovely golden daggers hanging from their lovely silver belts
They circled lightly around each other and ran in lines to
meet. It was a delightful dance. A fresco at Knossos depicts
three people leaping over a bull. The animal is charging with
such force that its legs are in mid-air. The leapers, the bull
dancers, may be both men and women, for they have signs of
both, delicately articulated. It is not a bullfight, though there
may be the same dances and leaps performed in both. The
bull is always vanquished; that is the dictate of common sense,
though bull and dancer or *toro* and *torero* may be enjoined in
a perilous embrace on the terrain of truth, which, as Michel
Leiris related, is the bullfighting term for the site of combat.

LXXX

In the confessional auto-biographic mode of *L'Age d'Homme*, Leiris felt he suffered the same risk as the matador, the fatal penetration by the horn, that is, the shadow of the horn, for he could not narrate his own death, and anyway, writing did not really place him in mortal danger, for goodness sake. So then, happily, or unhappily depending on the ending, Dionysus or Bacchus, the bull-horned or bull-faced, came to the aid of Ariadne on Naxos. The opera ends as a canopy enclosed them: her pain had made him rich indeed; his body was bathed in immortal desire and death would extinguish the stars in the heavens, ere she perish in his embrace. In another account Ariadne became a constellation of stars; Ariadne in the night sky, a new configuration. Myths, certainly, manage unknown quantities through narrative measures, like women and stars, death: the symbolic work of redeciphering.

LXXXI

Anna P. formed her own company after she resigned from the Imperial Ballet. She moved to Golders Green. In her garden at Ivy House, there was a pond with swans; she studied them carefully in preparation for the Dying Swan, her most famous role. As she was dying from pneumonia, she asked her dresser to prepare her Swan costume. It had always been a choice between dancing or dying. In St Petersburg that night, the violins of the orchestra played the music of the Dying Swan before an empty stage, lit only by a single spotlight. She, *la muse*, prima ballerina, *prima donna*, feuded with her partner, Mikhael Mordkin; once she slapped his face because she thought he had received more applause during a curtain call. They took ten curtain calls for their *pas de deux* at the Palace Theatre in 1910, then returned to the stage, tutu and costume and *pointe* shoes abandoned for Greek tunics and bare feet in the 'Autumn Bacchanal', the fourth tableau of *La Grande Bacchanale des Saisons*. Anna first danced the Bacchante in 1907, a role first taken by the choreographer's daughter, Marie, in the performance of 1901 when Anna danced Frost. There was no plot, just weather, wind, leaves, wildness, abandon. Anna danced as if possessed, intoxicated; she crouched over grapes, her filmy tunic falling from her shoulders, her lovely hair [her lovely hair] held back by a garland of vines and grapes, Mordkin was barefoot, bare-chested. She threw back her head ecstatically, frenziedly, closing her eyes as though they had rolled back in her head. Her frenzy transmitted itself to the audience; they shouted to her as though they were participating in an ancient rite; approach, rejection, submission, exhausted and sublime, collapsing in a heap at her conqueror's feet. She caused a sensation. Her teacher, Enrico Cecchetti, said he could teach everything connected with dancing, but Pavlova had that which can only be taught by God. The gods, the gods.

LXXXII

The bronze by Malvina Cornell Hoffman, *Bacchanale Russe*, is thirty centimetres high. Malvina wrote that she was out of her head during the performances of Anna and Mikhail, unapproachable miracles; oh God, she wrote, to be free. In New York, she threw a fancy-dress party, performing 'Autumn Bacchanale', or something like it, with a partner, in the joyous sensation of having forgotten everything, to have danced and become a Bacchic spirit. Otto Kahn introduced her to Anna: Mrs Kahn arranged a tea-party in their apartment on Fifth Avenue. Anna entered, dressed in black, fragile, pallid. Malvina watched her, as a panther must crouch in a thicket, every gesture recording its line on her sensitive plate, and she felt she must become a reel to register the endless fleeting impressions and characteristic movements. Each night she went to watch Anna dance, prowling about in the shadows, and the scene shifting went to her head like wine. Later, in London at Ivy House, she drew Anna practicing in her studio, that living, fluttering piece of antique beauty, willing, keen, responsive, a quivering body panting and bending. She photographed Anna and other dancers in New York, working on studies for her *Bacchanale* frieze, never realised other than as a plaster cast from a model in clay. In the photographs, the bruises on Anna's thighs are not concealed. It was good business for both women, these images. In 1949 Malvina begged Anna to stop dancing, to arrest her crazy unremitting schedule. In her diary, she described the first 'Bacchanale,' when the first wild rush of beauty grabbed her so tightly and her heart swelled and her entire being throbbed with a new-born consciousness.

LXXXIII

The raving ones, the raging ones, bacchantes, maenads, called also *mimallones* and *klodones*, names derived from the spinning of wool, tore men and animals apart; they ripped off the heads of their own sons. Fire did not burn them. No weapon could wound them. Snakes licked the sweat from their cheeks. They suckled wolf cubs and fawns indiscriminately. Fierce bulls fell to the ground, torn apart by their strong relentless hands.

LXXXIV

In *The Awakening of Flora* in 1900, Anna P. danced the role of the Goddess of the Flowers, lightly, gracefully, roses in her hair, flowers scattered on her tutu. There were many gods: Zephyrus, the west wind, Selene, the moon, Eos, dawn, Eros, love, oh, so many, many gods. Boreos, the north wind, woke the nymph Chloris from sleep. Chloris was so cold and begged Eos for her help, but Eos was not much use, save to tell her that Helios, the sun, would arrive soon, though Eos did offer tender caresses, and they did all manage in the end, the dawn, Chloris, and the other nymphs, to dance a little waltz together. Somehow, Zephyrus became her husband, or perhaps he was already her husband, having abducted her while she was wandering about in a field [stupid nymph, what an idiot, to wander alone in a field, simply asking for trouble], because the librettist confused his Greek and Roman myths. Everyone was delighted, however; everyone was smitten by the beauty of Chloris. Hermes announced the arrival of Hebe and Ganymede, who brought a cup of nectar to Chloris and Zephyrus which gave them eternal youth, and then Chloris became an immortal goddess, Flora. There was a rousing finale, an apotheosis in which Olympus was revealed and all the gods appeared, even Athene, *et cetera*, *und so weiter* [and to be honest, I am becoming bored with Greek mythology now, as is my editor]. Hmm, then Flora ruled the trees, the orchards, the plants, and the flowers, *hmm hmm*, *et cetera*, *und so weiter.*

LXXXV

Anna F. had a good knowledge of botanical Latin for many of her psychoanalytic circle were passionate gardeners; yet she was ignorant of the rest of Latin and all of Greek, for as she did not have a classical education, classical allusions escaped her, despite her *sehr gut* notes at the Lyceum where she was not taught Greek or Latin but instead a rather basic curriculum which included penmanship. She was allowed to sit on a little ladder in her father's study when his psychoanalytic circle met on Wednesday evenings. As a young man, her father became an expert on wild flowers, the grasses of the field, and the herbs of the wood. He had enjoyed tasting all sorts of greenery. Nothing pleased him quite so much as the spicy acrid taste of the small twigs and needles of a certain kind of cypress or *arbor vitae.*

LXXXVI

Freud dreamed he had written a monograph on a certain (indistinct) plant. The book lay before him and he was turning over a folded colour plate. Bound in each copy there was a dried specimen of the plant, as though it had been taken from a herbarium. That morning he had seen a new book in the window of a book shop, a monograph entitled *The Genus Cyclamen*. The cyclamen was his wife's favourite flower, though he rarely remembered to bring her flowers. The cyclamen was associated with both Hecate and the Virgin Mary; both were enchanters and witches. It incited voluptuous desires, while it was also used as a contraceptive or to provoke abortion. Freud and Martha abandoned their sexual relations after the birth of their sixth child. They lived in abstinence, 'amorticised', as he wrote to Emma Jung.

LXXXVII

Martha liked nothing better than to receive flowers, yet he always forgot [oh lord, another forgetful man], his pleasures limited, her pleasures forgotten. Freud recalled the evidence he presented to his psychoanalytic circle to demonstrate that forgetting was determined by an unconscious purpose, from which the hidden intention of the person who forgot might be deduced. A long chain of associations, including Freud's work on cocaine, ended, more or less, with the incredible appearance of a Professor Gärtner and his wife who had interrupted a conversation with the surgeon Dr Königstein the previous evening and he had congratulated Frau Gärtner on her blooming looks. The man called a gardener had a wife who was blooming. Obviously, Freud noted this, certainly he did. The interrupted conversation—at that point, for the crucial topic of the rest of the conversation was withheld—concerned a patient with the so charming name of Flora, to add to the botanical group of ideas. He wondered what would have occurred in the chain of associations if the patient had been called Anna rather than Flora. It was a 'factory of thoughts', like the weaver's masterpiece in Goethe's *Faust*, in which a treadle throws a thousand threads and unseen, the shuttles tie the threads together in an infinite combination. For Diderot, however, the loom was like an argument whose conclusion was the textile. Description after description might be added, a wealth of scenes, from a cyclamen to a gardenia, from a forgotten bouquet to a buttonhole.

LXXXVIII

There are choices between symbols and they are individual, particular. One psychoanalyst, Ella F-S., after Freud, before Lacan (overlapping, cited by him), described the significance of thread, silk, cotton, and string in her patient's dreams. A weaver's loom became a bed, the shuttle, a penis, thread, semen: the making of material from the thread, a child. But this was not any loom or bed, not any shuttle or penis, not any thread or semen. Nor was the child any child. This one, when tiny, no more than a baby, she had slept with her father and mother in a four-poster bed on frequent visits to an aunt in the countryside, in a district noted for its silk-weaving looms. Later she recalled her fascination as an adolescent with the flying of the shuttle, the weaver sitting over his loom; bound into the machinery, alternate movement, up and down, in and out, of feet and hands, pedals and shuttles, an intimacy between body and process, the scene entwined with the intimacies of the four-poster bed, a child between bodies. The psychoanalyst was certain of it, that the external environment gave a special stimulus (there was a memory, there was a place), that there was no operation relevant to this work of weaving that did not symbolise unconscious phantasies: shuttle/penis, thread/semen, woven material/child, and then the snapping of the thread in the shuttle, why of course, castration: either the temporary cessation of work, or an ultimate limit, accepted or denied. It was the weaving of the dream-work, and could only be unravelled through interpretation, from manifest to latent content. Yarn to yarn, a good yarn. The shuttle is a *navette* in French, and it was made to dance, *danser la navette*, thrown or passed between two weavers to make a textile wider than arm's length, until the invention of the flying shuttle allowed the work to a single weaver, cutting costs, dancing now on his own, alone, for the benefit of capital.

A and X were close to each other, dancing and talking in a crowd of dancers, though the couples were not in each other's way. A said that she would love to and asked if the hotel held many secrets. The music was very gentle. X lowered his voice and said she hardly seemed to remember him. Other dancers came between them and the camera and A looked at X in astonishment. The camera shot was held for a few seconds after they disappeared from the screen. There was a view of the room and the crowd of dancers from high up. The dance was old-fashioned [the writer preferred a waltz], worldly, slow, rhythmic, orderly [the writer suggested Brownian movements, the exact motion of pollen grains in water, the zig zag pattern of particles, small, random fluctuations, named after the botanist Robert Brown]. There was a general hubbub of the dance floor, without disorder, however, as the music became louder, more insistent [what the writer described as a somewhat grandiloquent and stilted waltz with many strings playing together]. A waltzing couple, embracing, holding fast, revolves: step, slide, step, rise and fall, in triple time. The origin lies in fertility dances, in rituals of courtship. One, two, three, one, two, three, seductive, vulgar, and sinful, like *La Ronde, la ronde d'amour*, the turbulence of libertine passions, ah, the Viennese waltz whirls, yes, whirls, giddily, at a hundred and eighty beats per minute. The waltzing couple do not look into each other's eyes unless in the *Pendel Schrift*, the back and forth holding pattern like a pendulum adopted when the crowd makes it difficult to turn or when dancers are flustered, dizzy. When turning, the leading man must build momentum between two beats, then he must release it slowly.

XC

The Freud sisters, Anna, Rosa, Mitzi, Dolfi, and Pauli loved to dance. [I thought that they would have loved to dance, in any case, given the opportunity, the right partners, those who donned black tails and white kid gloves and had both pleased and pleasing expressions.] They took dancing lessons with Gisela Fluss and her younger sister Sidonia, the examples they desired to emulate. But to be clear, quite clear, they did not give themselves to wild dancing; they were not Veronicas, not at all, the genus *Ehrenpreis*, 'price of virtue', easy virtue—that would not have been permitted by mothers or brothers or other chaperones. A woman had to be protected from public trouble, observed during social occasions for incidence of impropriety even when she was on a dance-floor, especially when she was on a dance-floor. A reputation could be tarnished all too easily, with a single wrong move, a misstep. Consider what happened to *le Petit Chaperon rouge*, whose mother was crazy, her grandmother even crazier, and there was the mouth of the wolf, not so lucky after all, *in bocca al lupo* to which the reply is 'may the wolf die', all the better to eat her with, *rat-tat-tat* at the door, yet at times it was hard to tell who was who, who was what, whose fur was on the inside or whose fur was on the outside, whose body belonged to whom. That is why there had to be guidelines for correct behaviour, proper surveillance, for it was never certain what form the wolf might take or when it would show its teeth, its forty-two teeth, its sharp teeth, its fangs, its incisors, its molars, which grip and nibble, puncture and shear, grind and crush, all the better to eat you with, my dear, my darling, *ma chérie, dans la gueule du loup.*

XCI

Anne S.'s governesses did not devour every stranger, however, not at once in any case—sometimes they kept them alive for days. It seemed that they had ordinary love affairs, but of these, little was written, though there was mention of future sweethearts, a future, that is, even if all that was left of them at the end of the book was two pebbles with a small flower between them. Suitors were summoned but it was just play acting and nothing came of it, for their ties were just too great to break. They led everyone on a mad dance, that much was clear, while the old gentleman next door watched over them, watched them through his telescope between drawn curtains, and when he ceased to observe them, they faded, every bit of them, their brightly polished ankle boots, their blond legs, their gleaming teeth, and all the books they had read. But they never really learnt anything, despite their attempts at Latin and Hebrew, at botany and wildlife. They were very restless. When they resumed their wild excursions, they frightened their employer, Madame Austeur. She hid herself in her salon during their returns, for it seemed as though they might have thought nothing of tearing her to pieces with their teeth. Until he became bored with the three governesses, the old gentleman could only think of women in threes. He would have liked to merge three women into a single woman, who would call him 'darling'. Freud wrote to Ferenczi that the 'subjective condition' he was in when writing the essay entitled 'The Theme of the Three Caskets', was occasioned by the fact that his third child, Anna, was taking a unique place in his life. Anna was making up nice stories. They had complicated plots and many characters. She was the only girl at home then. The house was very still, three lonely ladies (he said), Anna, Martha, and Tante Minna: daughter, mother, aunt and sister.

XCII

In 1923, Anna F. officially renounced marriage. To Lou Andreas-Salomé, Freud confided his dismay. He feared that Anna's genitality would play a trick on her and he confessed that he was not able to separate her from him, nor himself from her. Her father called her his Antigone and bought her a lovely dog, a beautiful black dog, an Alsatian, a German Shepherd, *berger allemand*, *Deutscher Schäferhund*. It was even mentioned in the newspaper. Dogs like this, noble, of fine character, courageous and steady, often are called Prince or Rex. The dogs do not lend themselves to indiscriminate friendships, no, they have a certain aloofness. It was then a modern breed. Anna F.'s dog was called Wolf or Wolfi. Each morning Anna walked with the obedient Wolf to the Prater. Once, frightened by the sound of a squad of soldiers on exercise firing a blank salvo, Wolf ran away and Anna could not find him anywhere. Clever Wolf, he had mounted into a taxi and refused to leave: the cabbie read the name tag on his collar. Freud paid the taxi fare. Anna wrote birthday poems in Wolf's name, of course she did, a woman speaking for a dog, and they were delivered by him tied with a ribbon to his collar, lovely Wolf or Dog, tail-bearing beast, poem-bearing beast, following a trail, wagging his tail, crowned for the feast.

XCIII

There was animal comfort. Freud had chows, while Anna favoured her Alsatian, wrote her brother Martin; he said they had unconsciously become a household of dog-lovers. The dogs had the freedom of the apartment in Berggasse. They met all who visited and were selective. Judicious in their reception, their opinions were respected. A dog that resembles a wolf, named as a wolf, even a little wolf, 'wolfy', may be as alarming as a wolf for some, certainly for those who reject the comfort of beasts or consider them unclean. The wolf is the enemy of shepherds. The *Schäferhund* is the protector of the flock. One must be able to tell the difference, for wolves, unlike wolf-dogs who tend to retain their dogginess, are masters of disguise. It is a matter of safety, of protecting oneself, from wolves, from men, and for that, for protection, a dog, a big doggy, a faithful black shepherd, say, is useful.

XCIV

On Anna F.'s part, she felt her attraction to women arising once again and confided in Lou. She dreamed a dream with a woman protagonist and it was a story of love of which she could not cease to think. She was tempted at once to write to her father about it, but decided to let it drop in order to concentrate on a paper she was writing. The paper 'Beating Phantasies and Day-Dreams' encompassed the dream. It was a paper about beating in young children, and it follows the famous paper of her father, written in 1919, 'A Child is Being Beaten', in which the phantasies recounted by a little girl resemble strongly those of his daughter's. Her father described the daydream of 'a girl of about fifteen, whose fantasy life, in spite of its abundance, had never come into conflict with reality. The origin, evolution, and termination of this daydream could be established with certainty, and its derivation from dependence on a beating fantasy of long standing were proved in a rather thoroughgoing analysis'. There was an incestuous father-daughter scene. There was masturbatory gratification. There was a scene of beating. In her paper, her first paper, Anna analysed phantasies as though they were not her own, explaining that the dreamer had substituted a lovely story in the place of the memory of a scene. However, oddly, her nice stories were very like her nasty stories. The nice stories, she thought, were an advance, however, a sublimation. She knew that what she did was really very shameful, but it was really very beautiful.

How do wolves appear? How do they seem? Some have their fur on the inside, the *loup garou*, for instance. For Angela C., the wolf took many forms. A grandmother was a werewolf (the grand-daughter did not know this until she saw a severed hand in place of a severed paw—it was a long story so here it is cut short). There was a company of wolves, once a wedding party, whose members had eyes like sequins and candle-flames [I remember liking that part]. There were wolf-men, and then there were just men, but overall, truly there was not a great deal of difference between them in their beastly behaviour. There was a man, a very charming man, a very handsome man, very well-dressed, in the forest, with flashing wet teeth that he tried to hide, and he offered a kiss with his wet mouth with its white teeth to the girl in exchange for her basket (the girl wanted the kiss, there was no doubt about it, she was asking for it and there is nothing that could save her from it, her small breasts gleaming in the fire-light). There were tender wolves, and then so happily, so safely, so cosily, a child could sleep between the paws of the wolf. A child was wolf-prey, in a scabby coat of sheepskin, *Schafsfell* [said Rosa, my nanny in Nuremburg, telling me a cautionary tale when I was four years old, when my mother was in hospital giving birth to my sister, and the boy, the big boy, from the apartment below us, gave me a *Gummibär* and showed me his penis]. A child was raised by wolves, and that is a popular story, and for a long time the child thought she was a wolf. She was a wolf-girl, a wolf-daughter.

The wolves suckled the sons of saints [Saint Eustache], and some saints made the wolves give the piglets they had captured to the poor widows [Saint Blaise], and a priest gave communion to a female wolf who was sick when the male wolf requested it, for they had been good Christians, the male wolf explained, until they had been cursed and changed into wolves, an animal form they had to retain for seven years. Wolf was the word howled by the child, Robert, in the story Rosine Lefort told to Jacques L.: *The Wolf! The Wolf!* This child could not bear that a door should be open. This lupine child opened doors so that they might be closed, shouting *Wolf*. This child had only two words, this wolf-word and Miss! This damaged child yelled *Wolf* throughout the day, he screamed *Wolf* all the time. This child flattened himself behind the door, howling *Wolf*. This possessed child shouted *Wolf* out of the window. This child tried to cut off his penis with a pair of plastic scissors. This terrified child yelled *Wolf* at his reflection in the mirror. This child howled *Wolf* at the psychoanalyst and made her swallow dirty water. This child covered himself with milk from a feeding bottle; he poured milk over the analyst, falling, rolling down the stairs, unconscious and blind. It was as if he had swallowed the destruction. This child stopped saying *Wolf* when he spoke his name, baptising himself first with water, then with milk, exorcising the ferocious figure who threatened to eat him up, or had eaten him, or who had starved him, or had made him and everything else into a wolf, but with the word, the wolf-word after the wolf-mother, he could move, construct, reveal, for he also had a second word, his name, Robert, Robert, which he said softly. He became attached to something living, no longer to death. He could receive and he could give. This child was no longer a wolf-child but simply a child.

Martha Freud certainly knew how to manage servants; she had been obliged to learn to do so, and with a firm hand, an iron hand. She employed a wet-nurse for her first-born son; this wet-nurse was well-paid and well-fed, but what a liar this wet-nurse was, for this woman, this wicked woman, this so-called wet-nurse, had no milk; she was a dry-nurse and the child might have starved to death. Martha was firm, insisting on punctuality for mealtimes, no-one ever waited, seated at the stroke of one and then the maid would enter with the soup, and there was always a cook, and a housemaid who waited at the table and received the patients and a nanny who cared for the younger children and a daily charwoman for the rough work. Nourishing food was prepared, excellent food, boiled beef, delicious puddings, oh, such superb puddings. Martha never served chicken except when the Freuds entertained guests, for her husband did not like it, no, he was not fond of it, though usually he was not fussy. She would lay the table beautifully. There were three courses at every lunch, always soup, always meat and vegetables, the sweet, *Mehlspiese*, and in summer another course of asparagus, sweetcorn, or artichokes. Freud loved Italian artichokes, the bud of a thistle, a flower eaten before it blooms, leaf by leaf stripped to reach the bare heart, the tender heart at the core, the sweet protected vulnerable centre. The first artichoke was a girl. She was walking on the shore when Zeus seduced her and made her a goddess but this girl kept returning home to her mother so the irritated god transformed her into a vegetable, in the careless way gods did transform girls who annoyed or escaped them. She became a delicacy and an aphrodisiac, making the blood warm, stimulating the will to engage in the amorous game of Venus, said a king's physician. She secured the birth of boy-children.

XCVIII

When the writer Tom Wolfe visited Hugh Hefner at his Playboy mansion, he wrote that the latter was living in a prison that was as soft as an artichoke heart. Hefner lay on a circular bed mounted on wheels, a platform over two metres in diameter that turned slowly like a clock, fifty metres an hour. Old magazines and papers littered the floor and the bed, covered with a kilim. He would masturbate on the bed as the Bunny Playmates danced around him. There were dirty carpets on the floor, brown and curling. The stamens of the artichoke, dried and ground to a fine powder, may be used to curdle milk for cheese-making. It imparts a sweet flavour, unlike the rennet extracted from the stomach of a baby ruminant. The texture is gentle, soft. [*Ecco come arrivare al cuore*: this is how to reach the heart, cut off leaves in a spiral movement until you reach the soft bud inside, then trim off the soft bud so you are left with only the heart.]

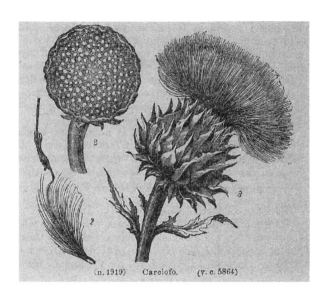

(n. 1919)   Carciofo.   (v. c. 5864)

Freud never had an especially intimate contact with botany. He failed to identity a crucifer in an examination, but was aided by his theoretical knowledge, and went on from the *Cruciferae*, the mustards, the cabbages, radishes, cresses, with terminal inflorescences without bracts, to the *Compositae*, lettuces, asters, sunflowers, daisies, tumbleweeds, dense-headed, their capitula surrounded by bracts; and of course, the artichoke, which he might in all fairness, in all honesty, call his favourite flower, which often his generous wife, more generous than he, brought back from the market, while he forgot to bring her a cyclamen. He and his little sister (he was five years old, she was three) tore apart the book of coloured plates their father gave them, leaf by leaf, delighted, in bliss, like eating an artichoke, pulling it to pieces. In the dream of the botanical monograph, he went from the cyclamen to the artichoke and this led him to a scene with his sister from their childhood, haunted by the latent presence of Flora perhaps, but certainly there was more present than met the eye, inevitably, where there are supressed wishes and desires, where there are wishes that must not be disclosed to others or which one cannot admit even to oneself, where there is censorship and distortion and repugnance, where a point is reached when interpretative work cannot be pursued, the tangle of dream-thoughts which cannot be unravelled and which moreover adds nothing to knowledge of the content of the dream. This is the dream's navel, reaching down into the unknown. The sister is frequently forgotten in the commentaries on this dream: it is as though she was not there beside her brother, dismembering the book, leaf by leaf, his sister Anna.

C

In Titian's painting, *Bacchus and Ariadne,* the abandoned woman, the distraught woman, turns from her sad gazing out to sea, searching for the ship of the forgetful Theseus on the far horizon, Theseus who left her while she slept, Theseus who betrayed her. She is taken by surprise as Bacchus, the god of wine, enters right, flies down, youthful, a red cloak covering his genitals. She appears a little shocked, a little fearful, but also a little interested. One of his followers is naked, muscular, bearded; he is horned, naturally he is. Snakes coil around his body, wrapping his sturdy left leg, weaving around his chest and stomach, from his hand to his upper arm. The god is determined that she should love him instead of the forgetful Theseus, the hastily departing Theseus, Theseus who left while she was sleeping, who did not even wait for her to wake to tell her that he was leaving her. Catullus described the god as followed by a noisy throng of revellers beating cymbals and drums, some girded with mangled serpents, and hurling the limbs of a dismembered bullock. They appear in the painting, as well as a chariot pulled by two rather unconcerned cheetahs. Ovid describes Ariadne as clad in an ungirt tunic, barefoot, golden hair unbound [her lovely hair]. The head of a calf lies on the ground; it is dragged along by a little child, a baby satyr, a chubby faun. A little dog barks and capers. In the foreground, there is a caper flower, a symbol of love, some say. In Ecclesiastes it represents the brevity of human life, for it scatters its seeds and then withers. There is some doubt about the caper, whether it is a tree or a vegetable: if the law of Orlah should apply, it is uncertain which blessing should be said over it. The rabbis noted that its ovary, from which the fruit develops, is carried on a long style protruding from the flower.

The cyclamen is a plant of sincere affection in the language of flowers. Or of maternal affection. Or of sincerity. Or of empathy. Or of devotion. Or of lasting feelings. Or of profound love. Or of happiness. Or of timid hope. Or of diffidence. Or of resignation. Or of *adieux*. Or of departures. Or of death. Or of endings. Or it is the flowering love-child of Eros. Or of fertility. Or of abortion. Or of poison. Or of libido. Or of strong effects on women. Or strong effects on young girls. Or on agitated children, to calm them. Or the cyclamen is food for pigs, called sow bread, a flower thrown down before swine.

1. SOW BREAD   2. SEA MILKWORT
    Cyclamen hederæfolium   Glaux maritima
           3. CHICKWEED WINTER GREEN
                  Trientalis europœa

Pl. 178.

CII

Cyclamen, Solomon's Crown, the lilies of the field, were painted scattered on the meadows where Christ had picked flowers under the gaze of angels. They were painted by Brueghel, the son, in a wreath of flowers surrounding the Holy family, the family painted by Franken, the garland by Brueghel, in the division of labour common in the Flemish workshops. There are anemones, narcissi, roses, peonies, lilies of the valley, marigolds, tiny jasmine flowers, each making reference to an attribute of the Virgin, Holy Mother, Queen of Heaven, Star of the Sea, Cause of our Joy, Mystical Rose, to her grief, her humility, her purity, her chastity, her virtue. At Mary's foot, at her Son's foot, there is a serpent, and neither mother nor son crushes it. Neither tramples it down, neither beats nor enslaves it.

The cyclamen became most fashionable in France in the eighteenth century, cultivated in the nurseries of Grenelle. [I read this, but cannot ascertain if this could be the Grenelle that was once Beau-Grenelle, annexed to Paris 1860, where after reading, after dinner, Samuel Beckett would walk with James Joyce on the Allée des Cygnes, on the isle of swans, the artificial island, the narrow strip of land in the Seine under the Pont de Grenelle, the Pont Rouelle, and the Pont de Bir-Hakeim, and then Joyce would start tippling, but only in the evenings, and Beckett had to bring him home drunk at least once. Joyce was living near the École Militaire, off the rue de Grenelle, an impasse that is now the square Roubiac. My son's first Parisian apartment, his *chambre de bonne*, was nearby, a tiny garret room on the seventh floor of the building with service stairs from the sixth floor, a lavatory on the landing shared with three others. These were once the rooms for the maidservants, the domestics who served the bourgeois inhabitants of the more luxurious apartments below. It is not far from where the Vel d'Hiv once stood, where in 1942 thousands of Jews, rounded up in raids by the police and the gendarmes, were held until being taken to the camp at Drancy, and then to the east. The Vel d'Hiv was demolished after a fire, and the site is not easy to find. Among those deported were R.'s uncles, strong lads who escaped from the train, helped by the *cheminots.*]

It is more likely that the nurseries of Grenelle were in the Eure-et-Loir, for the land in Paris was marshy, uncultivated, and nothing was grown *intra-muros*, though there is a vineyard in Montmartre, planted in 1933 to stop property developers taking over the land, and there are many *jardins partagés*, tended collectively. The fifteenth novel in Émile Zola's *Rougon-Macquart* series is set in the Eure; it follows the misfortunes, the disintegration, of a family of agricultural workers. One sister, the bad sister, held down another, the good sister, while she was raped by her brother-in-law, then pushed her onto a sickle, causing her to lose her unborn child. The bad sister and her husband then set fire to the father, when their attempt to smother him failed. Death, seed, and bread grew from the earth. Zola's book was translated by Ann L. in 1954, who changed her name from D to L, who died after surgery to remove her ovaries.

CV

Jean-Jacques Rousseau, on his seventh promenade in his reverie, now sixty-five years old, his strength declining, his memory failing, without books, without a garden, describes one of his botanical walks on the plateau de Jura: he was alone, exploring the mountain's chasm, woods, rocks, and he came upon a concealed retreat, the wildest romantic scene. The firs and beeches made an impenetrable barrier; there were high peaks and fearsome precipices that filled him with horror, tempered only by the song of small birds. There he found the cyclamen, among other plants, which delighted and amused him, until he forgot his botany and then, seated on a bed of *lycopodium* and moss, began to contemplate at his ease, for he was in a retreat unknown to the whole world, where his persecutors would never find him. Rousseau was joyful, even proud, thinking himself to be the first to have penetrated this mountainous retreat. Then he heard a strange clattering noise, *clack clack*, which repeated and increased, and when he crept through the bushes in the direction from which the sound came, on the very edge of the cliff he perceived a stocking manufactory.

Diderot includes the stocking-making loom in his great encyclopaedia, his systematic dictionary of the sciences, arts, and crafts, the mechanical arts, to which Rousseau contributed on music and political theory. Good minds put each thing in its place. Under the article BAS, that is, the garment covering foot and leg, the hosiery loom is described in great detail and amply illustrated as a complicated and rational machine, a single and unique reasoning that concluded with the fabrication of the piece of work, boasting a rapidity of execution. If stockings are knitted, the worker's hands are seen, flexible, dextrous, one stocking at a time, while the loom makes hundreds of stitches at once, performing many different movements. Little springs pull the silk thread, then let it go, then pick it up again to thread it through another—in inexplicable fashion, and the worker does not understand anything about it, does not know anything about it, and does not even think about it. It is, in short, a most excellent machine, one that may be compared with the most excellent machine God ever made, *et cetera*. Roland Barthes took it as a most admirable metaphor, a metaphor, of illumination, a maquette (the simulation of an object for the purpose of reflection, of analysis), in fact, for expressing the psyche in the many elements including the varied, even extraordinary movements, the pulling and then the letting go, the inexplicable fashion of threading the thread. Roland B. made a little dossier (he said) of maquette-works, which slipped into *mise-en-abyme*, which include *In Search of Lost Time* and a pornographic film (he does not, of course, specify which film), moving between the screen, the cinema, and the spectator, who reproduces the gestures of the scene in an erotic partnership.

Later, the following year (two or three years had passed since his mother, so affectionate, so sensitive, who never issued a single reproach to him, died, and he had been a mother to her at the end. She had become his daughter. His mother never made an observation about him. Some said he had never known a woman's body, or he said it to himself, but he knew the body of his mother, sick and then dying. His desires were those of before, anachronistic, but his *maman* left him accessible to desire. He dreamed only of her, of Henriette, and he would not share the photograph of her as a child in the winter garden, standing there with her brother. He studied the picture of the little girl, rediscovering his mother. He remembered the mornings when he was sick and did not go to school, so had the joy of staying with her. He would say *voilà* when he brought her something and once, half-conscious, she echoed him), Roland B. wrote how as a child he would see all the women around him obsessed with getting a run in their knitted stockings, that a loose thread would unravel down the length of the stockinged-leg. He could still picture the vulgar gesture, vulgar but of necessity, with which the women would moisten a finger in their mouths and ply it to the loose thread, checking the run by the cement of their saliva. He thought that writing was like this, a finger placed on the culture of the Imaginary to check it, immobilise it, perhaps so it might append itself to it, writing to culture, moistened finger to unravelling stocking.

CVIII

Jean-Jacques's passion for botany arose when he reached fifty. In his *Confessions*, he wrote that the study of plants had the same effect on him as did women, filling the void of his leisure-time without leaving room for the fevered workings of the imagination or the boredom of total inactivity. He found botany restful; instead of sad bookishness, he would fill his room with the smell of flowers and grasses. On his seventh promenade, he noted that plants seemed to have been sown in profusion on the earth like the stars in the sky. The *philosophe* became *herboriste*. Between 1771 and 1773 he sent eight letters to Madame Marie-Catherine Delessert. The former, a friend of longstanding, whom he addressed as '*cousine*', desired that he should initiate her four-year-old daughter, Madelon, into botany, to entertain her, yes, but also to draw her attention to things as pleasant and various as plants, the essential beneath one's eyes that one does not see, as he wrote several years earlier to a woman he loved, the countess d'Houdetot. Imparting the principles of botany, he would teach her how to educate her daughter; she would be their *chère petite botaniste*, their *petite botanophile*. The countryside was, of course, his study. The systematic epistolary introductions to plant anatomy were written between long intervals, sometimes following Linnaeus's classification based on the sexuality of the plants though he preferred a less artificial approach, that of Bernard and Antoine Laurent de Jussieu, considering that Linnaeus spent too much time in his room with dried plants and not enough in Nature; he extorted his 'pupil', his *chère cousine*, to go out, to walk, to smell, to 'herbalise'.

CIX

Jean-Jacques reminded Marie-Catherine that a perfect plant is composed of root, stalk, branch, leaves, flowers, and fruits. He described a lily in great detail, for it was the season and because of the sensitive size of its flowers and its parts. Then he took hyacinths, tulips, narcissi, lilies of the valley: they deserved greater examination, as did wallflowers, pansies, and violas. He wrote that when he had time he would recommend some books, though he would be jealous to be no longer her sole guide. He passed on to the pea, the lentil, the milk vetch, leguminous plants, then became most excited about the acacia. He described the labiates, face flowers split into two lips, called 'helmet' and 'beard', whose opening, either naturally or by pressing lightly with the fingers, resembles a gaping mouth. There was the little marguerite, so small and dainty and perfectly surprising for it is comprised of two or three hundred flowers, each with its own pistil, stamen, seeds, corolla, germ. He advised how to identify hemlock, so it would not be confused with chervil or parsley, how to rub its foliage lightly and sniff it, distinguishing its stinking, bitter odour. Take a breath, he wrote, he requested, for this was a demanding letter, yet he could not promise more discretion in what was to come, though they would later take a path bordered by flowers and she deserved a crown or wreath for the sweetness and constancy with which she deigned to follow him through these brambles without being put off by their thorns. Everyone who met her spoke of her sweetness.

CX

In his final letter, Jean-Jacques instructed Marie-Catherine in the art of drying flowers; he asked her to make two samples, a large one to keep herself, a small one to send to him, to number them, and when she had a dozen, to send them numbered in the pages of a little notebook, and he would return it to her with the name and description, so she would have her *herbier*, even though she was far from her guide, her teacher. It was in the end Madame Delessert's son, Benjamin, a banker, who became the keen botanist, the *botanophile*, with a fine botanical library and a renowned herbarium, publishing cheap books on botany and financing the explorations to the Americas of the naturalist and geographer Alexander von Humboldt and the botanist Aimé Jacques Alexandre Goujaud *dit* Bonpland. Annabel D. wrote that Anna A., the English botanist and photographer, followed the binomial nomenclature of Linnaeus, that of genus name and specific name, an orderly system. Plants belonged to a family, there were mothers and fathers and siblings. Linnaeus introduced a sexual system as well, the naming of flower parts, identifying them as female or male. Annabel D. noted that Anna A. wrote in her album that *algae* might come from the Latin *alliga*, meaning to bind, to entwine, to bandage, to fetter or fasten; it also means to hold fast, hinder, detain, or to oblige, to lay under obligation.

CXI

[G. sent me a poem by D. H. Lawrence after we had talked about cyclamens and Rousseau's adventure. At first she had thought it was by another writer. Lawrence's cyclamens are Sicilian, and in the poem, there was (because this is Lawrence) a man and a woman, who came out from the undergrowth of their own hair and they saw tiny rose cyclamens growing between their toes, the leaves of the plants sticky, earth-iridescent, toad-filmy, and other such Lawrentian tropes. There are greyhound bitches, a hare, the cyclamens are ruddy-muzzled like a group of hares fostered in the Parthenon marbles, there are violets—the cyclamen is sometimes called the Persian violet—sprinkling the unborn Erechtheoin marbles.]

In French, the cyclamen was feminine for a long time, but then became male, *la* to *le*. The tuber of the cyclamen allows it to withstand difficult conditions. The stem from its flowers bends elegantly to lead the fruit toward the ground during its setting; this is the formation of the fruit. It is shallow rooting. The flowers are delicate, five united petals, white, red, purple, but most commonly pink. The five-chambered fruits contain sticky seeds, attractive to ants. Its leaves are heart-shaped, green and variegated The cyclamen is a source of food for the larvae of the Silvery Moth, the Small Mottled Willow moth, the Cabbage moth, the Tomato moth, and the Gothic moth, for thrips [I have nothing to say about these nasty little creatures, their vile sucking mouths, their wanton destruction of the plant, curse them, kill them], hoverflies (the *Syrphidae*, friends of the gardener with their appetite for aphids), and small solitary bees (collecting pollen on their legs or under the abdomen on fine hairs, the scopa, or in the case of the yellow-faced bee, swallowing the pollen and regurgitating it). The Silvery moth has light brown back wings, darkening at the edges. The Small Mottled Willow moth has bean-shaped yellow markings on its back wings. The Cabbage moth has a white oval patch on its forewings. The Tomato moth has a wide white stripe on its red-brown forewings. The Gothic moth has broad wings and a dark patch between its forewing stigmata. None are readily attracted to light. Their caterpillars are voracious feeders. Other noctuids may be found on cyclamen, even though this is not their primary host, like the Turnip moth. [That is quite enough about moths, and to be quite honest, frankly, there has been more than enough about cyclamens too.]

CXIII

X said to A, of A, that she always stayed at a certain distance, as if on the threshold, as if at the entrance, to a place that was too dark or strange... A said to X, of X, that he was like a shadow—and he was waiting for her to come closer—she begged him to leave her alone, leave her alone, leave her alone. He said it was as if she were dead. He asked her to remember. It was evening, probably the last one. It was almost dark. A faint shadow was advancing through the darkness and long before he was able to distinguish the features of her face, he knew it was her. They stood like that, they did not say a word. She stood in front of him, waiting perhaps, as if she could not take another step nor turn back. She was straight, motionless, her arms alongside her body. She looked at him, her eyes were wide open, too wide, her lips were parted as if she was going to speak, or groan or scream. She was afraid, he said.

CXIV

Anne G. allowed no linguistic marker of gender. There was A*** and a narrator, I, we... who saw A*** in a mirror, as if a mirror. There were no shes or hes, but instead there were gestures, desires, traits, tendencies, a face, *son visage*, and limbs. There were many ways to avoid identifying logically coherent attributes. There was a love affair, languid nights, ennui (there was always ennui). There was self-restraint and the seeking of pleasure. It was baroque, a procession of corpses dancing in a macabre ball of drives and desires, a dance that dissolved into an amorous waltz of syncopated rhythms and fleeting pulses, the smooth inside of a whirlwind, deformed images, ecstatic bodies, the slow, hoarse death rattle of tortured flesh, oh, those arms, the intense sweetness, a carnal flame in memory, and it was never revealed if either were man or woman, always indirect, through relation to a body, a part of a body, not a person, a whole thing, unless a spirit, a being, a strange character, a beautiful creature, a child, a vision, a parasitic body, a cadaver, a living cadaver, a phantom, an other, a beloved body, a body, an inanimate body, a sphinx. That one did not speak or hardly spoke, a silent life of scent, hair, thighs, a curved neck, skin, an arm, a shoulder, dancing divinely, drunkenly, asking the narrator to dance a waltz, to the long-playing album of Viennese waltzes that would serve as a charming exit, in a carefree lightness of being, in perfect execution of the steps, so perfect that there were no others on the dance floor, intimidated by the perfection of this couple who danced when no-one any longer danced as a couple. The syncopated rhythms produced new bodies, new forms. The sphinx was human-headed, once male, then female, but it was also lion, sheep, falcon, cat, eagle. There was an important encounter, but there is no time to explain.

Later Anne G. wrote a memoir, in which she determined to write every day for a month, five hours a day, recalling each time a woman she desired or whom desired her, and then, she said, she would place the entries in alphabetical order, and it would be, she said, a stammering alphabet of desire. It would, she said, spell out desire in her life. But it was not, she said, a writing of desire, but something that shared the structure of desire, and like desire, there would always be an omission, unnoticed, something that was unwritten or unspoken, and she wanted that tiny nuances, gestures, movements, should be observed with keen attention, with flair, sniffed out, and she thought that writing could do that, that writing could bring their interpretation to the foreground. She said there were threads between people, spider webs, the threads of desire, tugging at extreme attention. It was, she said, like hunting or being prey, being both, and it should not be a narrow pursuit or endeavour, but one of curiosity. In the end, there were twelve vignettes, memory-images, not one day without a woman, she wrote, archivist, she said, neutral, she said, but sometimes she felt like a character, speaking in the phrases of old dramas or romantic comedies, the tired clichés of films, though she delighted in the exchanges outside the radical disenchantment of normative codes, public languages, codified protocols. It was a novel, a *roman*, made up of what she claimed were true stories, then she said one was a fiction, but she did not say which one, and so one would be obliged to guess, in the tangle of the plans of seduction, a woman's face in the dark, the shadows of spider webs against it. She appeared to slip up once, writing *I* instead of *you*, then stopped, caught herself, and for a moment, one might have believed her.

H. D. loved so much the family dog, with his gold-brown coat, his great collar, with the little barrel, which she said was of course none other than her old friend Ammon-Ra, whose avenue of horned sphinxes ran along the sand from the old landing-stage of the Nile barges to the wide portals of the temple at Karnak. She visited Egypt in 1923, stayed at Shepheards Hotel in Cairo, drove or was driven to the pyramids, saw the Sphinx, had lunch at Mena House. There was her Helen in Egypt, which does go on and on so, and where her Helen, by the way, encountered Theseus, and Achilles nearly choked her to death, and his mother Thetis saved her. She said she was part of a composite beast with three faces, but that came later. Sometimes the dogs, the chows, got into fights during her sessions with Freud, and when Yo-fi flew at Lun, he flung himself on the floor between them, and she thought he would be torn to pieces. Anna tore in, screaming that her papa dearest should not have done that, and H. D. had to grab Lun by the fur, and the maid rushed in, the pretty little Viennese maid, Paula, intervened. Freud was sitting on the floor with his money rolling in all directions under the orchids. Anna was so upset, but finally she left H. D. with her papa, taking Jo-Fi with her, Jo-Fi who snapped, who was very difficult with strangers, but H. D. felt that she was not a stranger, not at all, certainly not to the little golden dog. She thought of Freud as a little-papa, *Papalie*, the grandfather. Once he showed her a little clay dog, which resembled Jo-Fi. Then he showed her another little dog, a broken wooden toy from a tomb in Egypt, and she remembered an Egyptian dog in a painting in the Louvre, that looked like Wolf, Anna's dog, exactly like him. She wrote that Freud was midwife to the soul, that he was himself the soul, that thought of him bashed across her forehead, like a death-head moth. He was not the sphinx but the sphinx-moth, the death-head moth.

CXVII

On a ship Annie D. watched a sphinx-moth preparing to fly. Heavy-bodied, it was panting, trying to raise its temperature so it could take off. She was trying to find the strength to write. Its body vibrated and its wings trembled. The sphinx-moth feeds on nectar and honey; it drinks the tears of people and horses and cattle. It pollinates the ghost orchid with its proboscis nearly twice as long as its body. Expert at finding fragrant flowers in the dark, its long tongue probes deeply into the flower. The orchid is white, its flower growing on a thin spike from its root, the long lateral tendrils from its lower petals look like the legs of frogs; it lacks stem and foliage, it has scales; it attaches itself to trees by its roots, appearing to hover. The orchid smells like apples. The moth pollinates the Queen-of the-night cactus; it pollinates the sacred Datura, a plant that produces atropine, like the belladonna, and a few drops in the eye dilates the pupils, oh, so beautiful in women. The moth mimics bees, hummingbirds. It rests with its thorax raised in the air, its head tilted downwards. It takes the posture of the sphinx. There are many in the family; they have many names, including that of *Acherontia Atropos*, Atropos, inflexible, unalterable, the goddess of fate, one of the three sisters called the Morai, then *morta* in Latin, sphinx, *tête de mort,* death's head-hawk. The moth crawls around the face; it places its proboscis on the eye; its long hollow tongue causes the eye to water, to produce tears. Almost all moths observed drinking tears are males. The moth took off from the ship's rail finally. Annie D. felt she was the moth, that the ship's rail was the tiny cabin in which she was trying to write. The moth gained height but then fell, rising again only to fall. This moth drowned. Another moth burned in the flame of a candle, a female, for what seemed like hours. [They are no more than dust.]

CXVIII

Annie E. often dreamt of her mother, as she was before her illness, alive while she had been dead. On waking, she was certain for a few moments that her mother was still living in a dual form, alive and dead, like those who were ferried twice across the Styx. Charon, the son of Erebus and Nyx, the son of darkness and night, took his fee as a coin. He took the coin, *obolos*, from the mouths of the dead, where it was placed for that final payment; in Latin, *viaticum*, sustenance for the journey, is also the term for an allowance that permits one stripped of everything, condemned to exile, to live a life of sorts. The bank of the river—where a whirlpool spews its sand into the deep pool of Cocytus and the marsh of Styx—was crowded with those who could not pass over, the destitute, the unburied, condemned to wait for a hundred years, grieving, lacking honour in death. It was a place of shadows, of uneasy sleep and drowsy night. The living were separated from the dead, yet nonetheless there were revenants. Advised by the sibyl, Aeneas had to take a branch, a golden bough, from a sacred tree in a shadowy valley to hand to Proserpina (it was, of course, more complicated than that). It gave him passage; the ferryman agreed to take the living Aeneas, accompanied by the sibyl. It was easy enough to cross the river, then to descend to Hades, but the hard task, the challenge, was to return, to retrace steps. Only a few ever achieved this.

CXIX

A said that it was impossible that she had never even been to Frederiksbad. She said, no, she had not been waiting for X—why should she have been waiting for him? She said that she did not understand a thing he said. She said with irony that X should continue, tell her the rest of their story. She was alarmed, exasperated, almost supplicant. She begged X to leave her alone, but then said she would meet X later for dinner, and then they entered the theatre together. And there was complete silence until the beginning of the piece the orchestra played, a small orchestra, decorative, unusual, of remarkable appearance, a grand piano, a flute, a set of kettledrums, harp, contrabassoon, slide trombone, playing twelve-tone music, notes separated by silences. She begged him to leave her alone, and her words fell into a silence of the music.

Symptoms: Manipulations of clothing. Tunes hummed
to oneself. Sending the maid on indifferent errands.
The inability to walk across squares or wide streets.
The stopping of clocks. The collection of vases and
flowerpots on the writing-table so they do not fall over in the
night. Placing objects in the open doorway to one's parents'
bedroom. Not allowing the pillow to touch the wooden
back of the bedhead. Lining up one's head exactly with the
diamond shape on the head of the bed. Shaking out the
eiderdown so the bottom end becomes extremely thick, then
pressing apart the accumulation of feather to even it out.
The refusal to sign one's name. Hysterical vomiting.
The clacking of the tongue. *Une attaque de sommeil*.
Frenzied rage. Day-dreaming. Somnambulism. *Tussis
nervosa*. Squinting. Paraphasia. Loss of speech. Writing in
a peculiar fashion, using Roman printed letters. Refusing
nourishment. Never consenting to eat bread. Contractures
and anaesthesias. Seeing a death's head instead of a father.
Seeing snakes at the end of the fingers. The inability to read.
Deafness and deafness and deafness. Animal hallucinations
(white rats and mice, and American Indians dressed up as
animals). The constant fear of surprises. Fearful dreams.
Animal deliria, zoöpsia. Seeing bloody heads on every wave
of the sea. A painful coldness in the extremities. Frightening
ideas. The story of the mouse. Dreadful animals. Fear of
worms. The inability to say the word 'toad'. Storms in the
head. Railway inhibition. The smell of burnt pudding.
Breathlessness. Fainting fits. *Belle indifférence*. Weeping at
leisure. *Taedium vitae*. A disagreeable pricking sensation
in the fingertips. *Délire ecmnésique*. An aura in the throat.
Laughter, chattering, and shuffling of the feet (but that was
someone else, you know). Disturbances of vision. Absences.
Confusion. Unsociability. Possibly migraines.

CXXI

More symptoms: The unwillingness to walk past a man in eager or affectionate conversation with a woman. Somatic compliance. Sensual sucking. The craving for revenge. An excessively intense train of thought. The avoidance of the normal course of a woman's life.

CXXII

This is what Jean-François Lyotard wrote: the voice is deaf, even dumb (silence is a voice). It can sound with all the tones that connote, in Indo-European, the root *mu* (*mut*), which indicates the sound obtained by closed lips: to moan, to mutter, *murmeln, murmurer, mugir* (in French, even the word for word, *mot*, comes from this root, *muttum*). The voice is choked up, it explodes, it is blank, it whines, sighs, yawns, cries, it is thin or thick. [Today I have a thin voice; but yesterday, I had a thick one: there was a bone in my throat. The moths returned: the meconium inside a chrysalis resembles human blood, the remains of a body.] Anna O.'s power of speech was reduced so greatly that she could no longer speak her native language, though she could speak English. She could not understand German either, but she could read French and Italian, and when presented with a book in German, she was able to make and read a correct and fluent translation into English immediately. Another woman made a clacking noise when she was obliged to speak at the times she had resolved to remain silent, such as when she did not want to wake her children or when she should not frighten the horses. *Clack clack*. [I coughed. It was a thin sound, then a thick one. I tried to clear my throat, to dislodge the obstruction. I did not want to wake the sleeping children. I did not want to frighten the horses.]

CXXIII

In the imaginary bedroom, there was a baroque mantelpiece, a real fireplace. There was a large mirror in an elaborate frame over the fireplace. A was alone, sitting on the bed. Her hands rested on the cover at either side of her body. She was unmoving, looking at the floor. X's voice resumed, continuing his earlier speech, speaking faster, tensely, without control, in an excited choppy tone. He was telling her about her husband, then that he had found all the doors ajar, and that he had only to push them open, one after the other, then to close them, one after the other. A's face was frozen, in evident anguish. X told her she knew what happened then, and terribly, her face distorted and her mouth opened and she began screaming, but the strident sound had scarcely time to be produced when it was drowned out by a close violent detonation [...]. Later, a little later, she protested no, no, no. She did not know what happened then, she did not know him nor the ridiculous room. It was all wrong. She did not know any more. There was an intrusion, a disruption by a shot or series of shots. The words sounded to a greater or lesser degree, intricate, wandering. It might be said they were waiting for their moment; that X was waiting for his moment, but in the end, it would be A who waited, as a clock, unstopped, struck the strokes of midnight.

H. D. asked if she could help Ida wash clothes. She said this was Ida, this was that mountain, this was Greece. What an idiotic refrain. She asked: Helen? Then continued: Helen, Hellas, Helle, Helios, and it seemed that everything was too bright and too fair. Too bright, too fair, sitting in the darkened parlour, feeling the heat: the rival to Helios, to Helle, to Phoebus the sun. The sun was too hot for her mama, who was sitting in the sitting room with her aunt Jennie. The mother and the aunt were whispering, like they did. They hid their sewing. She did not care what they talked about, and anyway, they left her out of everything. But Ida did not leave her out. No, Ida handed her the washing, gave it to her to wring out: take it, she said, squeeze it harder. Ida was the maid, and maids may speak more than governesses under certain circumstances. Maids, in fact, actually, sometimes tear out the eyes from their employers, the rulers of their households brought down like the enemy, laid low, slaughtered, struck down. [*If ever I return, all your cities I will burn, destroying all the ladies in the area-o.* This is a very good song.] They go onto the mountains at night or even in the day, leaving the laundry behind, and there they are not afraid; they will tear apart any man they meet.

CXXV

Artemis prayed for eternal virginity. She prayed for as many names as her brother Apollo. She prayed for a bow and arrow like his. She prayed for the office of bringing light. She prayed for a saffron hunting tunic with a red hem reaching to her knees. She prayed for sixty young ocean nymphs, all of the same age, as her maids of honour. She prayed for twenty river nymphs from Amnisus in Crete to take care of her buskins and to feed her hounds when she was not out hunting. She prayed for all the mountains in the world. Lastly, she prayed for any city that might be chosen for her, but one city would be enough, because actually, she intended to live on mountains most of the time.

CXXVI

Oh, are you a doctor, sir, asked the maid of a guest in the inn, a noted refuge in the mountains of the Höhe Tauern, an inn away from the main road. 'Katharina' had served the meal but was not a really a servant; this could be seen from her dress, from her bearing. She was a rather sulky-looking girl. She has seen his name, his title, in the visitors' book. She told him her nerves were bad. She told him that she got so breathless and sometimes it caught her so much that she thought she would suffocate. It would come on her suddenly, all at once, pressing on her eyes, making her head heavy, and there was a dreadful buzzing. She would get so giddy that she almost fell over, sir. Her throat would squeeze together so she thought she would choke, sir. There would be a hammering, enough to burst her head, sir. It was as if she were about to die, sir. She was brave usually, she said, accustomed to going about everywhere alone, all over the mountain and even into the cellar, but when this came over her, well, she felt there was someone standing behind her, who would catch hold of her. She always saw an awful face, one that looked at her in a frightening way, a dreadful way. It started when she was living on another mountain, sir. It started when she saw her uncle lying on top of the maid who did the cooking, when she looked in through the window in the passage. She came away from the window at once but she could not breathe, everything was blank, buzzing and hammering. It was too dark in the room to see anything through the window and besides, her uncle and the maid both had their clothes on. She told her aunt and there were repercussions; the aunt took her and the other children to a new inn on another mountain.

CXXVII

Later the little country-maid, who was really Aurelia K. at the time, then later Aurelia O., remembered the uncle had once tried to disturb her while she slept, and it wasn't nice. She had felt his body, a part of his body (she was too embarrassed to say which part, but anyone could guess), in her bed, but she had jumped up, stood by the door until he left. She did not like his 'nice things', whatever he was offering her in the dark bedroom, telling her it was nice, that she would like it. The doctor had found that often in girls like Aurelia anxiety was a consequence of the horror by which a virginal mind is overcome when it is faced for the first time with the world of sexuality. Later, it turned out that she was not the niece of the landlady but her daughter, and the uncle with his 'nice things', which were really disgusting things, was really her father—this was not such a matter of indifference as would be shifting the scene from one mountain to another.

Souvenir des Alpes

CXXVIII

Artemis encouraged the girls and the chaste boys to sing. Mothers called out her name when they were in childbirth. She was the goddess of the moon, and she was the goddess of hunting, virginity, labour, vegetation, protecting children. She was the mistress of the beast, of cultivated land, of wilderness, of hills and streams, of woods and glades, the sultry places of *mons, silva virens, saltus,* dark, wet, fertile (Catullus knew what he was doing in his poem). She measured the months, the years. She was the goddess of counterfeit light; the moon does not cast the true light of day: moonlight, pale reflection of the sun; Artemis, reflection of Apollo. Her statue from Lepcis shows her lower body covered by spherical forms, sometimes thought to be breasts or gourds, or (most likely) the testicles of bulls. Her robe is decorated with lions and leopards, with griffins and goats, and again with bulls. The lady of the animals turned Actaeon into a stag and hunted him with his own hounds, his own pack turned against him, his Harpy, Racer, Barker, Towser, Rover, Blackwood, Quicksight, Shepherdess, Savage, Bristle, Blackmane, Tempest, Tiger, Babbler, and Snap. His dogs tore him apart with the frenzy of wolves. They did not know him in the form of the hart, ἔλαφος, *cervus*. The girls and the chaste boys sang in allegiance to Artemis. They were unblemished, without stain, virgin lads and lasses in a mawkish sort of translation. They were whole of heart and oh, they were fair, her hunters. In the magazine *Le Chasseur français* hunters who sought wives through the lonely-hearts column declared they would accept a woman with or without '*tâche*'—that is, with or without stain. They sought women to replace their dead mothers (*ma mère morte*), who were sweet-natured (*douce*) or bosomy (*poitrine énorme uniquement*) or broad-hipped (*hanchée*) or comfortably off (*avec fortune*) or with simple tastes (*goûts simples*) or in good health (*bonne santé*) or nice, even crippled (*gentille, même infirme*).

CXXIX

Anne Lesley S. wrote of a chorus. This chorus sang or recited that forms of pain found the victim, forming rivulets around her eyes, that horns spiralled off her forehead, that each song she sang was sad and there were a hundred pale boys, the devotees of pain. The women came in attitudes of wonder, majestic, god-intoxicated, girded with snakes, fawns at their breast. There was a voice on the telephone; it threatened a girl. Others threatened the same girl or perhaps other girls, but the girls learnt to fight, to tuck jouissance into the coat pockets of history, she said, in her staggering invention, diamond all the way down [her words, her words, not mine, but some words we shared, she and I, and some I stole from her without asking or apology]. The Bacchae will celebrate with proper custom. They will adorn themselves with the sacred dappled skins of fawns and the fleece of white sheep. They will garland themselves with oak and yew and ivy and flowering convolvulus. They will hunt for snakes to twine in their hair. They will be agitated, dancing and rejoicing. They will be joined in their hunting by the Maenads, the possessed. These women will be goaded away from their weaving. Together they will perform incredible feats. They will perform miracles. No weapon will harm them. They will roam freely. They will drag wild bulls to the ground and strip the flesh from the bones. They will carry fire in their hair and it will not burn them. They will put men to flight. They will descend on the plain like birds, like doves, they will skim the air. They will snatch children from their homes. They will immerse their hands in the blood of the sons and the fathers and the so-called uncles.

CXXX

Freud decreed that he would let Martha rule the household as much as she wished, and she would reward him with her intimate love and by rising above all those weaknesses that make for a contemptuous judgment of women. Fully formed, Athena sprang from the head of her father, Zeus. He swallowed her mother Metis, her name meaning wisdom or magical cunning or craft, as he feared she would bear a son who would strike him down; he turned her into a fly, devoured her whole when she was pregnant with their daughter and buzzing around his head. Metis remained imprisoned inside his belly. Some might admire this arrangement.

CXXXI

Miss Lucy smelled burnt pudding, the odour of charred pastry, when she was agitated, but otherwise she could not smell, could not sniff out a thing, not even her own desire for her employer, a factory superintendent. It was irksome, it was tormenting. Miss Lucy, Miss Lucy R., was not a maid, but a governess, a British governess to Austrian children; her job was to govern, to educate, not to serve. Her job was not to let lady visitors kiss the children, especially not on their lips; it was her duty not to tolerate that, a duty she was neglecting if she allowed it, a duty that would go to another if it occurred again, for she was responsible, her angry employer, whom she desired but did not at that time know she desired, told her, very angry, very annoyed. Because of her job, she could not be treated for her depression, her other symptoms of a loss of appetite, a heavy head, weakness, and an incapacity for work, save for outside her hours of work, work for which she felt incapable. In consequence, the conversations with her doctor were short; the thread of conversation would often break, to be taken up at the next appointment. She resisted hypnosis; she never fell into the state of somnambulism. Only concentration was required of her, to close her eyes when lying down on the couch, as her doctor placed his hands on her forehead or took her head between his hands, so she would feel the pressure of his hands on her, and she would think of something under the pressure of his hands, and she would see something in front of her or it would come into her head, and she would catch hold of it, for it would be what they sought, the information would be extracted from her from the pressure of his hands on her head, on her forehead, to be precise.

CXXXII

Later, a little time later, the English governess smelled the smoke of a cigar. It was irksome. It had been there all along but masked by the smell of the pudding. Now it emerged by itself. She felt a stab in her heart: the gentlemen were smoking and the cigar-smoke stuck in her memory. Although everybody smoked in her house, everyone but the children and the dead mother—the father, the visiting gentlemen, at lunch, at dinner, the cook, the other servants, all smoked incessantly—the smell still bothered her.

CXXXIII

You see, don't you, what employers do to governesses, as they do to maids? You see what they do in their comfortable well-appointed houses in the suburbs of Vienna or in the small towns in France or in the suburbs of London or on the moors of Yorkshire? It does not matter where they work, despite the lovely little writing desk lined in pink velvet, the governesses, the maids, or where they live (daughters, too, you see?). The employers (the fathers, too, you see?) will smoke their cigars and the women, the governesses, the maids, will smell them, sniff them out. And then the tenderness will be taken away.

Oh, what larks Anna F. had when she was a little girl, beautified by naughtiness, her father said of her, and how she was loved, how she was cared for by Josefine, her nursemaid. This, by the way, to avoid any confusion, was not Josefine Stross, Anna's friend, Anna's doctor, her father's doctor, the doctor who may have given her father, Anna's father, the final injection of morphine on his death-bed, though no-one, certainly not Anna, mentioned it, and Josefine was omitted from the account until she told it herself when she was a very old woman. This one, this Catholic nursemaid, was Josefine Cihlarz. Josefine came to the family when Anna was a baby to look after the three youngest children and stayed with them until Anna finished her first year at school. Anna knew that she was Josefine's favourite, her best-beloved. Anna knew they were very close, that they were always united. Why, it was obvious! After all, it was Josefine who rescued Anna from her crib when there was a gas explosion in the watchmaker's apartment below. Josefine went to Anna first, not to the other children! Anna's brothers told her the story when she was older; they asked Josefine whom she would save first from a fire, and why, of course she answered that she would save Anna. In the park one day Anna lost sight of Josefine, and even though her mother was there, she ran to search for her and was lost herself. Everyone had to look for her. Later Anna wrote that when the mother's emotions are engaged elsewhere, the child not only feels lost, but in fact, gets lost.

CXXXV

Josefine loved Anna and Josefine loved animals. Josefine loved dogs and she did not mind when they barked because they could not help it, they were dogs after all, but she did not love people arrested by the police, like the dishevelled students who made political protests in the streets, or poor people, those without decent pride, who ate at the cheap canteens because they were destitute. Josefine left to get married when Anna was six. Josefine died while Anna was in analysis with her papa in 1924. Anna wrote to Lou that Josefine had not much left to give any more, but still it was sad to lose an old relation. Women, nursemaids, servants, disappear, they are dismissed or they are dead. Beloved figures are missed but not always as much as one might think. Nana or Anna: Anna became Nana. Anna was at her father's death-bed with Doctor Josefine, but of course that was quite another Josefine, the woman who was the doctor, not the one who was the nursemaid.

CXXXVI

Anna F.'s father also had a Catholic nursemaid until he was two or three; he even retained an obscure conscious memory of her. He supposed he had loved her. She took him to mass with her in Freiberg. The woman was dismissed suddenly, for she turned out to be a thief, stealing *Kreuzers* and *Zehners* and the children's toys when his mother was in bed with his new-born sister Anna. They found them hidden among her things. Once he dreamt or remembered that his nursemaid washed him in reddish water in which she had previously washed herself, red threads floating, as though washed in the blood of the lamb. He dreamt that his nursemaid was his teacher in sexual matters and she complained because he was clumsy, unable to do anything, such a little blockhead. There was a long chain, a thread, from the red water to the shiny silver coins to the heap of paper ten-florin notes he was accustomed to give to Martha for her excellent housekeeping. The nursemaid was the prime originator of his neuroses, he remarked to his friend W., and everyone knew how women servants, even the ugly elderly maids, delighted in seducing the young boys, the very young boys. In fact, if it is fact, he had three nursemaids, who were condensed into one: Monika and Magdalena and Resi. The one called Magdalena may have wet nurse to him or to his brother Julius, the little younger brother who died, or it may have been the one called Monika or the one called Resi. He thought the one called Resi made him steal coins for her, but really it was she who did it, and his half-brother Philipp accused her, the brother whom he thought had taken his father's place and given his mother the child that was Anna. His mother told him Resi was sent to prison for ten months, that she was a clever woman, but cleverness did not get her anywhere, except locked up, his thieving *Amme*.

CXXXVII

Later the boy dreamed or remembered a scene where he could not find his lovely mother and he begged his brother Philipp to open the cupboard but his mother was not there, not in the cupboard after all, and he thought then she must have disappeared like the nursemaid, that his lovely mama Amalia, the only woman he ever kissed in public, had been boxed-up as well, another woman who is a casket of gold, silver, or lead.

CXXXVIII

Follow the bloody threads of a nursemaid, the bloody threads of maids, the bloody threads of governesses, the red threads reeled out by women, from women, these interior scrolls. Follow the threads from the end of Bendlerstrasse, where the labyrinth began, W. B. wrote, a labyrinth that was not without its Ariadne (because it was never without her invisible presence, even if the boy cannot reach her). He attached a particular significance to the maze surrounding Frederick William III and Queen Louise on their plinths, rising from the shrubbery at the entrance to the strangest part of the Tiergarten. At that time, it was true, he felt, it must have corresponded closely to what was waiting behind it. Here, or not far away, were the haunts of that Ariadne from whom he learnt for the first time (and was never entirely to forget) something that was to make instantly comprehensible a word that at scarcely three he could not have known (it was love, he wrote, vaguely). However, something intervened, a cold shadow, an icy shadow, driving away what he loved or would come to love. Whose was that shadow? Why, naturally it was none other than that of the *Fraulein* who intervened before his adventures could properly begin, limiting his sorties, standing at the gate, reducing him to impotence (as did his mother, who did not hesitate to criticise his ineptitude for practical life, the fact that he could not tell left from right— and how then, to get into or out of a labyrinth?); it was not [I think] that of the nursemaid who leant over his bed in the morning, the one who baked an apple for him on the stove by his bed, though she too cast her shadow in her own way, and he hesitated before biting into the apple's shining cheeks.

CXXXIX

It seemed to begin with the boy's nursemaids, his first guides
to the city, but still the nursemaids robbed him of Ariadne,
whom he imagined hovering in the Hohenzollern labyrinth.
The maids were like the robbers in his dream who stole the
silks from his mother's cupboard, and the maid who stood
at the iron gate seemed to be complicit in the theft. The stern
nursemaids sat on the park benches, reading novels, keeping
the children in check by raising their voices, while there
was music in the distance, coming from Rousseau Island.
And then he saw bears, with his nursemaid (or was it with his
French governess?), who looked after him and his brother
Georg and his sister Dora.

CXL

There is a painting by Eva Gonzalès, entitled *La servante* or *À la barrière*. She painted it between 1865 and 1870. She was Manet's only woman student. Her father was a writer, her mother was a musician. She painted her younger sister, Jeanne, her double, her soulmate. She would have liked to be very beautiful like Jeanne. She was more beautiful in Jeanne than in herself, in painting Jeanne. She painted her sister, she painted a milliner, she painted her sister as an artist, she painted a lady with a fan, she painted her sister at the piano, she painted two women reading in a forest, she painted her sister in profile, she painted a woman awakening, and she painted her sister with her husband, Eva's husband, in a box at the Italian Theatre, but it was doubted at first that she painted this work because of its masculine vigour. She died in childbirth and her sister brought up her child, her son, and later Jeanne married her sister's widowed husband. Eva painted a nursemaid with a child. She painted her sister arranging a bouquet of violets in a small blue vase. She painted white shoes, roses in a glass, shiny apples. She left Paris during the siege in 1870 and painted outdoors around Dieppe. Jeanne, too, was a painter. Jeanne painted Eva in Dieppe. Eva painted a woman standing at a gate in a fence, holding a large sunhat decorated with flowers and ribbons. The figure of the maidservant stands out against a background left partly in reserve and on which the artist has intervened with lively touches to suggest the vegetation. The face, the clothing, and the environment of the figure are treated with a fine and light material, in a harmony of blues and greens punctuated only by the yellow of the hat and the red of the flowers on it and in the background. [I read in the newspaper that the painting was acquired by the Musée de Petit Palais at a sale at Christies, Paris, in March 2021.]

Dora/Ida dreamed that the house, a house, a dream-house, was on fire. She did not know what caused the fire and no-one thought to ask, and certainly she did not appear to wonder why the house, a house, a dream-house was on fire. Her papa was standing by her bed; he woke her, and they hurried outside, but her mama was saving her jewel-case, and the papa was very annoyed. She dreamt this on three successive nights. It would recur later. Her mother would clean and clean; she cleaned the furniture, the utensils, all day long, and it was impossible to enjoy using anything in the house. They did not get on, mother and daughter; they were estranged. Dora/Ida coughed, all the time, she lost her voice, she did not want to eat. She became hostile to her governess, a well-read woman with advanced views, for she saw that the governess was in love with her papa, becoming quite amusing and obliging in his company despite the criticisms the governess made of him to her in private. Oh, indeed, she saw quite clearly that she was an object of indifference to her governess, who only had affection for her father. When the father was away, the governess was attentive, but that fell away when the father returned. That woman, well, she read every sort of book on sexual life and talked quite frankly, quite improperly, about them. Dora/Ida would faint; sometimes she would wet her bed. She masturbated. For a time, after an operation, she dragged her right foot. She dragged it on occasion still, walking as if she had twisted her foot. She would always drag that foot, always. She told her doctor, Anna F.'s papa, that she would see him no longer; she had decided this a fortnight before she told him, and he said it sounded like the notice given by a governess or a maid, characteristic of a person in service. There was a great deal more to follow, about another governess, one who also was obliged to give notice.

CXLII

[I have written about that whole affair, that whole sorry business, in fact, I have written at length in a largely ignored or forgotten book, a bloody big red book, in fact; to continue here would be bloody boring, it would such a bloody drag, to keep repeating myself, to keep reminding others that I wrote this big book, a bloody good book.]

The child, the boy, a belated child, a child hiding, pilfering, untidy, dreaming, reading, was prevented from following the labyrinthine itinerary of his desire, but later, as a man, he was enraptured by the mere unravelling of a skein of thread. Nothing, nothing at all, compared with it, not the sounds of Africa, not the ornament, not even the ecstasy of the trance. He was smoking hashish and found the joy of intoxication very like the joy of unravelling the artful clew. He felt that he went forwards in the rhythmic bliss of unwinding, as in the twists and turns of venturing into a cave. He became, he felt, an enraptured prose-lover. Once, his walking-stick gave him special pleasure. At the door of a dance hall girls displayed themselves, but he felt free from all desire, despite his earlier amorous joy in a café, eating oysters, though the music rose and fell, and he marked the beat with his foot. Once, he felt the most passionate love for a woman as he watched her dance and he tried to describe her dance to her, the dance of extravagant figures that gave him a red Ariadne-thread to find his way out of the labyrinth. Her movements took up a destiny, he told her, or let it fall or she wound it around her, became enmeshed or strained after it or let it lie or looked upon it kindly, until she opened her mouth and shouted the most abusive language until she mastered herself (or so he thought). He remembered: the children used to draw Ariadne Puzzles on blotting paper or in the margins of their school-books, strange, meandering, zigzag lines. He drew three houses built into a wall, enclosed. There were three wells, three neighbours who hated each other so much that they sought not to cross each other's path on the way to get water. It was possible, of course, but how? Lines had to be drawn but nor crossed. In some myths, Bacchus saved Ariadne and gave her a constellation only to leave her for another lover. Such star-crossed, malign influences.

CXLIV

Freud heard his patient's step on the stairs. He wrote her case history from memory and it was not phonographically correct (wrote the man who confessed to a tin ear, who was nevertheless a listening ear, an '*auditif*', a phrase his famous ears overheard muttered in a muted voice from the mouth of Charcot, his *maître*). But he was trustworthy, in his listening and in his account of hysterical phantasies arising from things heard but only understood later; for example, he could be trusted when he said that the usual sexual attraction had drawn together the girl and her father on one side, and the mother and the son on the other. Oh, that girl was a heavy trial, refusing to take up her share of housework, intermittently attending lectures for women, though writing came specially easily to her. That girl was appealing, intelligent, troubled, *et cetera*, *et cetera*. She dragged her leg, and from one false step on the stairs, slipped, fell down the stairs, her foot swelled up, had to be bandaged, she had to stay in bed for weeks, but that was when she was a child, before she was eight years old and had her first attack of asthma that left her so breathless, so out of breath, unable to breathe, a bone in her throat making her hoarse, making her cough, preventing her from speaking, though, as noted, she could write, it came easily, one word after another. She did not like all the questions he asked her, not at all, but Anna, his daughter Anna, did not mind the same sort of questions, those elegant questions he asked her six days a week for an hour in the autumn of 1918, sometimes at 10 o'clock at night, and she would not leave him under the circumstances. She still felt envious, she wrote to Lou, pulled in two directions: either to achieve like a man or to dance like a woman. But if one looked like she did, with her heavy ankles, how could one dance, elegantly, stepping lightly, like a ballerina? And in any case, her father did not like music to be played at home.

There was no dancing for Anne when her ankle was locked, the foot and leg at right angles, her feet were useless. She jumped from a window to escape prison, smashed the bone, the talus, the astragalus that holds the entire weight of the body. Without muscles, without a good blood supply, the healing takes a long time and she was on the lam, *en cavale,* like Albertine S. herself, who wrote the story of her life, romantic, romanesque, like a novel (and it is a novel, certainly). She died after surgery, the third operation in a year. Professor Merle d'Aubigné had operated on her famous astragalus, the romantic bone, then she had appendicitis, they thought, but it was in fact renal tuberculosis. A diseased kidney is not at all romantic, it is not like the tuberculosis of the lungs from which it may originate, which at least has a certain cachet, a certain romance, you know, caused by too much mental exertion or too much dancing, leading to the Swiss mountains, the sanatoriums, and then there was the white skin, the rosy cheeks, the red lips, the bright sparkling eyes (a flattering malady, as Emily B. remarked), fainting, breathlessness, the weariness, the fever, the fret, the blood that came from the mouth like displacement of menstruation, the pallid cheek that came from an excess of passion, the stooped posture, the wasting away that produced a lovely corpse: in the last stage of consumption, a lady might exhibit the roses and lilies of youth and health, and be admired for her complexion—the day she is to be buried. Renal tuberculosis may spread from the bone, with lesions that necrotise, unlike roses, which came from the blood of Adonis, born from incest between a father and daughter, unlike lilies, which came from the milk of Hera, the drops spilling from her breasts when she refused to nurse the child of another. An embolism, a foreign body, clot or bubble, blocking an artery, finished her off.

CXLVI

Julien carried Anne through the forest from the road and their romance began there. 'I'll be back to get you, wait for me,' he said, when she could only crawl. He returned with a motorcycle to take her away and at the end, she was taken away to prison. It was tender and it was brutal; it was like Anne, like Albertine.

CXLVII

[I was not that interested in Anne, another Anne, Anne B., another Anne B., and then I remembered the nature of her death and remarked upon it.] Anne B. died, like her sister, the sister who overshadowed her, from tuberculosis. She had been a governess, for five years working for the Robinson family—her second post, for she had been dismissed from her first—and she wrote about a governess in her first book. Her brother, who said Anne was nothing, absolutely nothing, had a secret affair with Anne's employer, Mrs Robinson, a bad woman, said Elizabeth G., who corrupted him. Mrs Robinson's maid Ann M. saw him with her mistress, saw him do enough with her—enough, he said, to hang him. The children in Anne's charge gave her a spaniel dog, Flossy, and the little dog outlived her mistress. She wrote in the evenings in her neat, elegant handwriting, she wrote on her neat portable writing desk, she wrote about a governess called Agnes, but she did not yet name her work after her character, and she wrote in her prayer book that she was sick of mankind and their disgusting ways. She wrote about the unpleasant and undreamed-of experiences of human nature. When her book was published, it was seen as inferior to her sister's book about a governess, even though it was not known that they were sisters, for they wrote under the names of men. The critics wrote that her books were coarse and vulgar. She wrote that in her own mind she was satisfied that if a book was good, it was so whatever the sex of its author. Her brother died of tuberculosis, then a sister, and then Anne. The remaining sister, by her own admission, culled some of Anne's papers, though she claimed it was only a little poem, here and there, *snip snip*, so to speak, and another little poem was gone.

CXLVIII

Anne's ankle pounded heavily, bursting into incandescent waves at each beat of her heart. Anne had a new heart in her leg, still irregular. The pain had grown familiar, it wandered through her body, visiting every recess and numbing it, it spread out and settled down, making incessant little stabs. The blown-up foot would not bend any more, killing her at the slightest touch. The pain gathered into a ball above her heel, slowly twisting and winding itself up, and when the ball was finished—she could tell the precise moment—it would burst with a sensation of light, and the flashes shot through her foot and exploded, in stars that quickly went out, in her toes. The bones formed a vice which tightened itself, a big cube of iron clamping shut. Her leg was dying. Her foot was black and ghastly. The doctor said—what did he say?—he said that her name was the name of her fracture, an astralagus, and her face, too, was an astralagus. She passed over unsuspected thresholds of dizzying pain. She learnt new words: resection, abrasion, astragalectomy, arthrodesis. She dribbled scent into her cast, eau de cologne, cypress, lavender, poked knives and knitting needles down into it. Later she danced on her crutches, swinging like a puppet. She curled up around her rage. She dragged her foot like a turtle drags its shell. She wondered when she would be able to walk, to get away. She pretended to walk again at night, pushing against the sheet with her toes. She was wounded and begging. She said her name was not Anne. She could no longer walk without shoes, the least little pebble pierced her foot with pain. Every step was a pretence, a rectified fall; if she stopped thinking about her walk, she found herself limping, putting her foot down crookedly in the angle learnt in the slightly equine cast. She went down the stairs, hardly limping at all.

CXLIX

The astragalus bones of deer were used as dice: knucklebones, snobs, tali, jacks—Plato said Thoth invented the game. It was no game for Anne, but then everything was a bit of a gamble, a punt, a risk: to shoot the moon, to buck the odds, to tempt fortune (lady luck, but there is room for doubt), to chance your arm or stick your neck out, to go for broke or take a shot in the dark, to roll the dice. Jacques L. said that the enjoyment of gambling places subjectivity in doubt. He told the story of the three prisoners, a parable with consequences for all. Only one would be freed, yet each deserved liberty. There was a rhythm in the game, evens and odds, but it could not be determined by the means of logic. A symbol will never abolish the symptom. Bones, tombstones, ivories, shakers: they will make snake eyes, the lowest possible roll, and if you remember, if you go back, the black snake came out from the wall towards the sick father, the feverish father, Anna O. saw it, quite clearly, but she could not move, her arm was paralysed, no choice there, no throw (except earlier in the day, the quoit into the bushes), only *la dame chanceuse.* A lady does not leave her escort, it is not fair, it is not nice, a lady does not wander all over the room and blow on some other man's dice. Let us keep the party polite, but no, Tyche was capricious, and although Palamedes (ingenious inventor of eleven letters, eleven consonants added to the five vowels of the three Fates, sixteen sounds turned into symbols by Hermes) dedicated the dice of his invention to her, she did not intervene to save him and he was stoned to death or he was drowned or he died in a well where he was crushed by stones and drowned. It was his fate, already written, too bad, a mystery. Even in attempting to make sense of chance, the throw of the dice will never abolish chance.

CL

'The faun in the afternoon' was written by an anxious man, who suffered from insomnia, who had problems with women, who had a complicated family, whose son died, who had a drab lineage, who was a corpse in his own life. He was a bit facetious, and he enjoyed that. His poems could be ambiguous, and he took pleasure in that, too. He liked reading the novels of Zola. He knew all about fashion; he wrote about the kingdom of the ephemeral and feminine elegance, in the eight issues of his magazine, to be exact; he wrote as a French aristocratic lady, as a Creole lady, as an English governess. He exalted trinkets and artificial flowers, described two threads crossing, silk and gold (for example), listened attentively to the siren song of frivolous things, while elsewhere he sought an Orphic explanation of the world. He scribbled notes at the theatre, writing that ballet gave but little, that it was an imaginative genre, allegorical, in which signs (of scattered beauty: wave, jewel, cloud, *et cetera*) could only be known through juxtaposition with his spiritual nakedness so it was felt as analogous, adapted in a (exquisite) confusion of himself with this (fluttering) form, even though it was a rite, an uttering of an idea (he placed a capital on the I, of course, as he did for Dance, for Music, Work, or Beauty, where, he said, he stood like a holy spider, weaving the threads of his soul with those at the heart of Beauty, and so on). His ballet dancer was a woman, or at least had a female appearance, her writing of pirouettes extended towards another motif, her whirling illustrating the meaning of his ecstasies, his melancholy incantations, his quivering nerves. The pastoral monologue of the faun in the afternoon was broken by dramatic silences, cued by capitalised instructions, woven with italicised addresses to the audience, set in alexandrine rhyming couplets, allusive, alliterated: twelve syllables with a caesura, the metre of tragedy usually, but this afternoon everything was bright, even jaunty.

The faun's costume caused a sensation: black spots were scattered on the clinging costume, painted on his bare arms and hands. The difference between flesh and material was imperceptible, it could not be seen where the human ended and the animal began. He had a goat's tail, tiny horns rising from a little wig of golden coils, and pointed ears, his own ears extended with wax. There were, reported *Le Figaro, réalités animals*, vile movements of erotic bestiality and shameless gestures performed by an unseemly faun in Dionysian ravishment. The journalist entitled his review '*Un faux pas*', such a misstep. The faun evoked scenes from the friezes painted on the vases of antiquity. Seven girls, the seven nymphs the faun encountered as he awakened, were chosen for him, all the same height as the staging was composed like a bas-relief. The faun leapt high into the air, near the stars, one woman who loved him said, and another said he was virile and powerful. Auguste Rodin wrote in *Le Matin* of the faun's attitudes and gestures of a half-conscious animality: the dancer crouched, straightened, moved forward and backward with nervous angular, arms outstretched, hands and fingers opening and closing, his head turned with a deliberate clumsy covetousness, with the beauty of fresco and statuary, the ideal model Rodin desired to draw or sculpt. At the end, the faun sank to the ground, rubbing himself like an animal on the veil dropped by the loveliest, the most desirable nymph, danced by his sister, as she fled from him in panic. The police were brought in for the sold-out second performance. The faun was the dancer's favourite role, but it dropped from the repertoire and by the time it was revived, years later, the dancer was dead from renal failure. Diagnosed with schizophrenia, in and out of asylums since 1919, including the Burghölzli, committed by Bleuer, and then the Bellevue, under Binswanger's direction, the dancer ceased to dance. Tamara, his second daughter, never saw her father dance.

CLII

In the Louvre, an Athenian red-figure terracotta *oenoche*, a pitcher used to pour wine at banquets, painted around 410 BCE, was exhibited. The body of the vase was decorated with a dance scene in which a naked, crowned young man appeared to be preparing to leap into the air, while a young girl, dressed in a short tunic, sketching a dance step, perched on tiptoe, one arm extended, the other folded; she was standing in front of a naked young man holding a branch of leaves, followed by another naked young man. Her attitude was known from many representations on bas-reliefs and terracotta plaques. The male nudity, as well as the floral crowns or the branch held by one of the protagonists, indicated a religious dance in honour of Apollo and also of Leto and Artemis. The dancer visited the Louvre, seeking inspiration for his choreography. In 1911 he danced *Giselle* in St Petersburg, and his costume, designed by Alexandre Benois, caused a scandal, as he danced in revealing tights rather than the trousers or modesty skirt mandatory for male dancers. He refused to apologise. Later, he would be silent for long periods. He danced like a girl, they said, *en pointe*, or with feet turned out, hammering the stage. There is a painting by Jules Léon Flandrin of the dancer (like a black and white butterfly, said Flandrin) and Anna P., she wearing a long white tutu, in *Les Sylphides*, a romantic reverie without a plot to the music of Chopin. The dancer became afraid of other dancers, he feared that a trapdoor on the stage would open to swallow him. He wrote that he danced frightening things and that everyone was afraid of him. He wrote that words were not speech and that he knew all languages. He tried to patent a perfect fountain pen, a pen he named God. He wrote that he was his own but also that he was another's, which may be the truth for many.

CLIII

Stage traps are elaborate and ingenious, allowing appearance, disappearance, the transformation of characters and objects: the grave trap, downstage centre, is an open grave, the cauldron an opening through which items may be passed, the star a series of sprung flaps, triangular, through which an actor (or a leaping dancer) may be propelled; the vampire, with two sprung leaves, gives the impression a figure is passing through solid matter; the ghost glide, a sliding arrangement, allows a phantom to rise or sink through the floor. Jean-Jacques escaped unwelcome visitors, the '*importuns*', through a trapdoor in his bedroom in the farmhouse on the île St Pierre on the lake Bienne, where he had retreated from persecutions and exiles. The trapdoor was first mentioned in Monsieur Desjobert's account of 1777. It led to the ground floor, where he took refuge, or he would escape to the woods, where often an admirer would try to accost him. He was not able to shelter for long on the island where amid the wind and ice of winter he had hoped to find the peace he required: the prefect of the government in Berne ordered him to leave, with the greatest regret, with painful bitterness. He left the island with a sore throat, fever, and death in his heart, wandering and sick, accompanied only by his beloved curly-tailed little dog Sultan, his sole comfort. He would never return to Switzerland. The island was the place he had been happiest; he could have spent two years, twenty years, or all eternity there without becoming bored; the happiest time of his life, those two months of precious *farniente* on the island where he filled his room with flowers and grasses instead of books and papers, where he delighted in refraining from unpacking his library and hardly writing, save for a few unhappy letters that obliged him to take up his *plume*, where he indulged his botanical fervour, going out with magnifying glass in hand, where he experienced delight and ecstasy on each observation of the structure, organisation, and action of the sexual parts in the fructification of vegetables.

Filming in the forest, a mournful wood, the film director Robert Bresson sent out men with guns to silence the birds, putting an end to their cheerful jarring song. He liked silence in his films, writing in capital letters that the soundtrack invented silence, using a loud voice to do so. He sought immobility and silence. He met Anne W. when she was seventeen. Anne W. came to his apartment on the île St Louis, introduced by Florence Carrez-Delay, who played the role of Joan of Arc in Bresson's film. He asked Anne how old she was. He asked Anne to read for him. (He wrote that the voices of his models—he would never call them actors—drew for him their mouths, their eyes, their faces, made for him their complete portraits, outer and inner, better than if they were in front of him; the best deciphering achieved by the ear alone. The eye was too frivolous, too easily satisfied, while the ear was profound. He wrote that his models should not think what they said or did, nor think about what they said or did. He would guide them according to his rules, with them letting him act in them, and he letting them act in him.) Anne described him: tall, old, with an understated elegance; he wore beige trousers, a light-coloured shirt, a sweater of grey-blue cashmere; he had lovely white hair, his skin was tanned, his voice was pleasant with a slight speech impediment. Despite the season, he wore espadrilles, his feet bare. She started to read and he stopped, saying *non*, no, no, that she must listen to him read then read exactly like him. She could not get it right, but she wanted to please him. It was a dialogue from his first film, *Les Anges du péché*, which she admitted she had not seen, nor had she seen *Les Dames du Bois de Boulogne*. She read aloud from the script: she did not know a riddle, but she knew a puzzle: was it better to have dust on one's furniture or on one's soul.

CLV

When Anne left *his* apartment, she walked along the Seine with Florence, who invited her to have a coffee in the café where *he* had met her, Florence, for the first time, and Florence would tell Anne everything, about *him*, about the way *he* would behave with her, Anne. She always referred to *him* like this, Anne noted. She felt Florence's warm breath on her neck as she spoke.

Anne W. waited with impatience. There was no sign of *him*, no news at all. Florence said Anne should not be concerned: *he* was hesitating, *he* was taking his time, *he* would be in touch, she was sure. *He* showed up or rather, *he* telephoned, and Anne's mother replied, holding out the receiver to her daughter with a fearful expression Anne did not recognise. Anne turned away so her mother would not see her trembling hands, her impatience, her reddened blushing face. *He* told Anne that *he* missed her, that *he* thought about her, asked her to tell *him* that she was thinking about *him*. *He* said when *he* heard her voice it was as if she were in front of *him*, that *he* needed to hear her voice in order to know her, to know a little more who she was. There were more telephone calls. *He* was both attentive and distracted, asking her many questions, about everything, nothing important. Florence said *he* was testing her voice. Anne felt she could tell *him* anything, which disconcerted her. *He* called usually when she returned home from *lycée*, and suddenly *his* voice would harden, would become brutal and precise, telling her that *he* was wasting *his* time with her, that *he* had found another girl to play the part, and then *his* voice would soften. Anne returned to the apartment on the île St Louis. She read and re-read the same scene as before: faster, slower, without emotion. They adapted to each other's rhythm. *He* put *his* face next to hers, looking at her triumphantly and amazed, caressing her cheek gently. From another room, she heard the clacking of high heels and a woman's voice (Florence had told her *he* had been married for a long time). *He* remarked to Florence, seated on the sofa, that Anne's skin was so soft, so very soft. Florence laughed. It was as if Anne was no longer in the room. It seemed to Anne that Florence was trying to seduce this old man. As Anne put on her coat to leave, *he* caught her by the arm and told her next time to come on her own, squeezing her arm.

CLVII

In *Les Dames du Bois de Boulogne*, a woman took revenge on her former lover. The woman was played by Maria Casarès, steely, venomous, the vengeful Hélène. She played the role of the Princess (a deathly figure with a smooth white face, a ravaging enigmatic beauty, like marble, like ivory, like bone) in Cocteau's film *Orphée,* and Cocteau wrote the dialogue for the ladies and the man of the bois de Boulogne. Cocteau said Bresson was too precise, that everything he included in the film (every door, for example, too many doors, in fact) was there for a purpose, to be seen. Casarès was most reluctant to act without any emotions, impassively, as Bresson demanded of her. She was anxious, very anxious; because, for example, appearing on stage in Julien Green's play *South* (considered to be rather provocative), when she had to say the line, *il pleut* (it is raining), even these simple words were inflected by her tragedian temperament, as she shouted, with great emphasis, separating each syllable, even each letter. In her anxiety about the film she would drink a little glass of cognac before acting to gain courage, and when Bresson discovered this, he made her take a sedative instead, which he said she did willingly, and it started to go better, things improved when he drugged her. It was 1944, but there was nothing of the events of that year in the film, the year Casarès began her love affair with Albert Camus, when they met at the home of Michel Leiris. She said they lived through magnificent hours then, but they were shot through with pride on both sides. Later, Camus said that they loved each other as trains love each other when they cross paths in railway stations. Casarès said, many years later, smoking a cigarette, that Bresson was a tyrant, the actors were exhausted, he killed them, *doucement*, gently, quietly. Killing them softly. Telling their whole lives. Strumming their pain.

CLVII

Hélène realised her lover, Jean, no longer loved her; she was angry, she was wild, full of grief, and she pretended not to love him. He, the idiot, thought they could part as friends. She arranged a meeting, a chance meeting, in the wood: Jean met Agnès in the wood, and he, the idiot, though she was an innocent girl from the countryside. But no, of course not, Agnès was a nightclub dancer, a courtesan, her bare-legged somersaults in a froth of tulle and silk were obvious metaphors. She was leading the hateful debauched life into which her poverty had forced her, fucking horrible lecherous old men, until Hélène, the vengeful, installed Agnès and her mother in an apartment, to help them, the idiots, leave their degrading life. It was a quartet, three women, one man. Her mother said Agnès was her little girl, but Agnès replied no, she was a whore. Agnès tried on earrings, looking at herself in the mirror, watched by her mother. It was heady: the burnished glass, the eroticism in the faces reflected, the jewels. Jean said he loved Agnès, that he was losing his head, that Agnès's face was like a gash across his heart, that he met Agnès in his dreams and dreamt of her in his waking hours, that he walked the streets thinking of ways to break down her door (a precise door, among many). There was a marriage, a society marriage, and then the triumphant, the baleful, Hélène revealed her malicious revenge of social destruction. Standing by the window of Jean's car, with the sound of the windscreen wipers moving back and forth, she told him, the idiot, '*Vous avez epousé une grue* [...] *On dirait que vous ne savez pas ce que c'est qu'une femme qui se venge*', that he had married a whore, a tart, a slut, a hooker, that he did not know what a vengeful woman was capable of. Yet, at the end, Jean's car, its acceleration, wiped Hélène from the screen.

A well-known story: a rich man with fine houses in town and country had a blue beard; he was so ugly no woman would look at him, but nonetheless he had married several wives, all disappeared. His neighbour had two daughters, perfect beauties. He sought to marry one, it did not matter which, the mother could decide, he said, but neither would have him with his nasty blue beard. He engaged their affection by inviting them to his country house with other lively young people; there were lovely parties, there was hunting and shooting and fishing, there was dancing and feasting, a glorious time, and his beard did not look quite so horrible to the youngest daughter after all, not so blue, in fact [the transformative power of wealth] so she married him. Then he went on a journey: he would be away for six weeks, gave her the run of the house in the country, invite all your friends, he said, gave her the keys to the great wardrobes, the strongboxes, the caskets, all his apartments, told her she could enter them all but the closet at the end of the hall, opened by the smallest key. He forbade her to enter it, she promised she would observe his instruction. She and her friends had a grand time in the beauty and richness of the house, the superb furniture, the extravagant mirrors, oh, everything. But all she could think of was the little closet opening with the smallest key, which she must not open, and so she opened it, so impatient to see what it contained that she nearly broke her neck on the stairs. She thought for a moment about her husband's orders; trembling as she opened the little door. Inside it was dark, then she made out the corpses of several women, stacked against the walls; the floor was clotted with their blood (what a bloody chamber), into which the key dropped from her trembling hand. Later, in her own chamber, she tried to wash the key but the blood would not wash off, disappearing from one side, only to reappear on the other. Her husband returned unexpectedly that evening. Husbands always do, unless they are dead.

[I was quite tired; I felt very fatigued by it all; yes, it was true that I thought that there had been too many sessions of writing lately, trying to be brief, to keep the words, those of others, pared down to what seemed to me to be essential, paying attention to the detail, counting words to fit the page while retaining meaning, while my accounts, like symptoms, like analysis, despite my attention, became longer and longer, spilling over the page until I returned later, the following day or the following week, to pare, to peel, to whittle, to skin, turning from one leaf to the next. There was too much reading in between the writing, too much reading of Anne W. and Annie E., for example, who would not leave me, as well as too many other young women's voices, articulated and heard as voices from the past in the present, those voices that kept me awake at night, echoing every moment of failure, of disappointment, of regret, of shame, of loss, of mortification. I did not sleep well, restless, unsettled, waking dry-mouthed or sweating. There were other voices, sometimes, reminding me that once there was a time when I wanted to know everything, while now, this time, in the present, in the day to day, I sought to know nothing. There was nothing to know. This was self-deception. There was too much to know and it was exhausting, it was troubling. This work comes into existence in a contingent way, in flickers of time, in moments when it is possible, when it is inscribed or spoken aloud. There was that which I did not want to know yet I found myself talking about it incessantly to myself.]

CLXI

The setting was vague, remote, scarcely visible... and on these last words the book slipped from A's lap, and a photograph fell out of it. She leant down and, after looking at it, returned it between the pages of the book, which she replaced on her lap, until, thinking better of it, she picked up the book again and leafing through it, found the photograph again and looked at it more carefully. She also looked at the back of the photograph. It is a photograph of herself, in a garden. There was an interruption, then a voice continued... a garden, any garden, the white lace spread, the sea of white lace where her body... but all bodies looked alike, and all white lace, all hotels, all statues, all gardens. It was a quiet place, this garden, often deserted.

CLXII

Anne W. got the part, of course she did, and, to cut a long story short, filming started at Guyancourt. He told her to keep the navy-blue skirt, the Liberty-print blouse from Cacharel with the Claudine collar [why have I not thought of Colette until now?], they would be perfect for the scene with the seed merchant, and they would go to La Samaritaine for other clothes, where the sales assistants, scandalised by their behaviour, the clothes on which he insisted, thought Anne was his grand-daughter. He took her aside under the trees, spoke to her softly, told her that during the filming he wanted her always at his side, always. He pressed her arm, asked her if she understood. He told her he would describe in detail their life together and his pressure on her arm increased. They lived together in the same house, with the owners, a couple with whom they ate, who prepared their meals. Their bedrooms were on the first floor. To get to hers, Anne had to pass through his. They shared a bathroom, where he kept his two Siamese kittens and sometimes she could hear him speaking to them at night. He was anxious; he asked her if this promiscuity troubled her. He told her she was a young girl, fragile, modest. She said that as her room had a door opening to a wooden staircase that led to the garden, she could come and go as she liked, but he said that the door must kept locked at all times.

Every evening after supper he invited her to walk with him in the garden. He would take her by the arm and tell her about the filming; he would interrupt himself to tell her to listen to a bird or the church bell or the distant laughter of children. He would ask her to be nice to him; he would try to kiss her mouth. She found this unbearable. She would push him away and he would release her, regarding her with an expression of immense pain and they would return to the house, in silence, a heavy silence, until he spoke to her in a glacial tone, and she felt responsible, that she should apologise. Ghislain Cloquet, his director of photography, told Anne he would never allow a daughter of his to work with Bresson, never. He said when one spoke of the were-wolf, the *loup-garou*, well, there he was, *le voilà !* They all called her *jeune fille.*

CLXIV

Rosmarie W. refused to accept the opposition of night and day she must pit against others, the subtler periodicities against the emptiness of being an adult. She said that their traces inside her body attempt precariously, like any sign, to produce understanding, but though nothing might come of that, the grass was growing. She asked if words played their parts. [Rosmarie, my dear Rosmarie, they do, they do, I assure you, and you know this as you move between them or step into your mother's room or take a piece of paper, finding it to be already covered in signs. There is, after all, for example, the paternal metaphor, phallic inscription, the subtle body of language, the illness made from truth, the couple as a symptom, the passage between terms, the special relation with lack, the mark in the signifier, the surrender to jouissance in the very articulation of signifiers, and further, moreover, bodily events in the discourse of the master or the discourse of capitalism, and I could go on, relentlessly, insanely, and so on and so on, with yelps of surprise or gasps of horror or wonder.]Words also found their own way to the house next door as rays converge and solve their differences. Or if notes followed because drawn to a conclusion, she wondered. She said that if we do not signal our love, reason will eat our heart out before it can admit its form of mere intention, and we will not know what has happened. [This is true, *è vero*, *c'est ça*, *c'est exactement ça*, *c'est bien ça*, *c'est cela pour moi*. *C'était déjà ça.* Who can know what happened? Precisely, exactly, and hearts will be eaten and cores extracted and there will be blood on a sea of white lace (for instance).]

CLXV

The next morning, he asked her for the keys. He saw the closet key was missing. He told her to get it. He saw there was blood on it. She said she did not know how this could be, but he told her that he knew what she had done and so she must join the dead ladies. She wept and begged his forgiveness for her transgression, for certainly she had no desire to join the women in the cupboard, but he was unmoved. He gave her a little time to say her last prayers. He left her alone to pray. She called for her sister. Sister Anne, she asked, go to the top of the tower. Look out of the window, sister Anne, see if our brothers are coming. They could not save themselves. They had to hope for brothers. Sister Anne saw nothing but a cloud of dust in the sun, the green grass, and no-one was coming. He was shouting with a sword in his hand, shouting for her to come down. She called again to her sister, oh sister Anne, sister Anne, who saw only dust, who saw only a flock of sheep, and he shouted again that she must descend. Anne, sister Anne, she cried, do you see no-one? And then there were two horsemen, the brothers, but a long way off, far away, sister Anne called from the tower. He shouted, he made the house tremble, she came down, she threw herself at his feet, weeping, her hair down, but it meant nothing to him and he readied himself to strike when there was such a loud knocking at the gate that he stopped and the gate opened, and the brothers with swords drawn from their sheaths entered and ran their swords through him as he tried to flee. She became mistress of his estate and sister Anne, dear reader, was married off to a rich man.

Angela C. wrote a version in which a lovely young girl married a wealthy old French Marquis. They met when she was playing the piano at a tea-party. Her governess, although pleased her pupil had made a good match, observed that the Marquis had formerly wed three women, all of whom died in mysterious circumstances. The Marquis gave his bride a choker made of rubies, warning her against ever taking it off, and took her to his château in Brittany. She found his collection of pornographic engravings and paintings. Their bedroom was filled with white lilies and mirrors [obviously]. When he left for urgent business in New York, he too gave her the keys, forbidding her to open his private chamber. Of course, she did, and found the bodies of his wives, *et cetera*, surrounded by white lilies [what else did she expect?]. And of course, he returned, usual story, pressed the bloody key on her forehead, made ready to execute her, there was a blind piano-tuner but he could not save her [did I mention she played the piano?]. Her mother burst in, shot the Marquis, and then the mother, the girl, and the piano tuner left the château to live together, opening a music school near Paris while the château became a school for the blind. She had the red mark on her forehead forever. The piano tuner could not see it, but the mother could. There are many other versions of this story [one is told by mice, in squeaky little voices, and mice are very good storytellers despite their pitch], and some of them are true.

Élisabeth de C-C married a very rich man, a nasty philanderer, and became the countess de Greffuhle. Her famous 'Lily' evening gown, from the Worth fashion house, was made of black silk velvet with pearl embroidery, metal *cannetilles*, and gold sequins. Patterns of lilies in appliqués of ivory silk extended through the body and the flowing train. The bertha collar was of ivory silk satin, also embroidered. It could be turned up to form bat's wings. The gown was tailored to show the countess's tiny waist, at which there were no seams. The lily pattern echoed a tribute to the countess by her relative, the poet Robert de Montesquiou, the last line in his sonnet: *Beau lis qui regardez avec vos pistils noirs.* The countess wore the lily dress when posing for Nadar in 1896. She was photographed from behind, emphasising her slenderness and height. In one photograph the countess arranged white lilies in an elaborate vase in front of a mirror. In another she looked at herself in the mirror. There were pearls in her hair. Sometimes she wore cascades of pearls flowing down her back to her waist. The press observed that her dresses, invented for her or by her, resembled no one else's: she preferred to look bizarre rather than banal. The countess was the model for the duchesse de Guermantes in *Remembrance of Things Past*. Proust saw her in front of the glass playing; each of her dresses seemed like the projection of a particular aspect of her soul. In her correspondence with Montesquiou, the countess confessed that she did not think there was any pleasure in the world comparable with that of a woman who feels she is being looked at by everybody. She did not like Proust and his sticky flattery, always pestering her for photographs; photographs, she said, were intimate things. During the Occupation, although remaining in the *hôtel particulier* of the family, she lived in the maid's room in its attic. For an interview when she was very old, Élisabeth wore a tweed skirt and a green silk scarf, such as a *concierge* or maid might wear.

CLXVIII

Anne W.'s mother called from the île de Ré to tell her that her beloved dog Sary had disappeared. Her mother was astonished by Anne's optimism that the dog would return. She said to Anne as she hung up that she did not recognise her. Later, during a weekend absence from the film, Anne wanted her mother to guess what had happened to her during another weekend away from the film, but she also wanted to recount how she had seduced a man and how delicious it had been. They opened the windows of the car because of the heat, her mother smoking a cigarette, one hand on the steering-wheel, as usual. The conversation was stilted, her mother asking superficial questions about the film, not listening to Anne's replies, then repeating how discreet she had been, how she had not visited Anne on the film set, how she had not asked her to write or telephone often, how she had left her free to live her new life. The dog had never returned, and perhaps the dog too was happier in re-finding his liberty. Anne had almost forgotten about the dog. Her mother remarked dryly that she found her indifferent, that Anne seemed not to care, that she had ceased to love him since the filming, that she ceased to love her family. The next morning, she tried to speak with her mother, but her mother evaded her. Suddenly Anne told her mother that she was no longer a virgin and her mother was furious, livid with rage, a grimace of disgust distorting her mouth, looking at Anne as if she were a hideous, contemptible object. Anne wanted her mother to hold her, to forgive her, to console her, to speak to her, anything that would take them back to before, but her mother pushed her away, saying that she hoped her daughter would not get a taste for it, becoming a *female*, that she hoped her daughter would not tell everyone about it, because, she assured her daughter, it was nothing to boast about, nothing to be proud of. On the train to Versailles Anne thought what a horrible word *female* was. Anne tried to laugh about it, alone on the train.

During her adolescence Annie E. thought it normal to have a father who did the washing-up and a mother behind the cash desk. Cooking, ironing, and sewing had no value for her. She had no interest in dancing either, no time for the little girls in tutus, but she did like to look at herself in the mirror in her Petit Bateau knickers and vest, making *entrechats* in time to her interior music, those weaving or braiding jumps in which the legs cross at lower calf with numerous rapid crossings, *trois*, *quatre*, *cinq*... [Nijinsky could perform an *entrechat-dix*] landing on both feet for an even number of jumps, on one foot for an odd number. Sometimes she felt uneasy, even troubled, that her mother was not a real mother, not like other mothers. The mothers her schoolteacher described did not resemble hers or those in her family or neighbourhood, who complained how much children cost them, who swore, who did not make the beds, and who threw out from the café clients who had drunk too much. But her mother took the time, despite the bills to prepare or pay, the housewives to serve, the goods to unpack, to get up very early at dawn on fine days to weed the rose-beds and the heucheras, and she would wake Annie by rubbing her cheeks with sprig of hawthorn blossom because that would give her a pretty colour, a healthy glow. Her mother preferred to see Annie reading, to see her writing stories in her notebooks rather than tidying her room. Later, her mother would say to her she should leave if she wanted, that a daughter should not stay under the skirts of her mother, should not be tied to her apron strings.

CLXX

Anne W. had to run, then fall, in the scene Bresson called the scene of seduction. Marie stopped the car for she saw the donkey Balthazar, and suddenly, Gérard, the predator, appeared, entered her car, caressed her neck, silent. Marie ran from the car and he chased her, circling around the donkey, incarnation of purity, of innocence. Anne W. had to run and fall, run and fall, take after take, though Cloquet said it was fine, there were three excellent takes, but Bresson said she could do better. Her ex-lover, a young actor, watched as she ran and fell; he watched her without warmth, without complicity, and she asked herself if that was it then, not to be loved, as she ran and fell, her knees grazed. She felt pain everywhere, especially in her right knee, but she was oddly relieved, as though she had ceased to suffer. She had decided to sleep with the young actor, because he pleased her, because he was handsome, because he left notes in her jacket pockets. It was her first time, and she persisted, absolutely, in her desire to please him. In bed with him, she felt as if at last she was breathing, with all her body, drunk with pleasure and with pride. The *beau garçon,* on the other hand, overwhelmed her with reproaches: she should have told him she was a virgin, she had behaved in a brazen way, and in any case, he thought she was sleeping with Bresson, and as she was a minor, did she know what he was risking? She cried and he said she was such a baby, that he had taken her for a woman. He told her he had a girlfriend, who would scratch out her eyes if she found out about their adventure; he told her he slept with men, too, initiated by his philosophy teacher at *lycée* [obviously], but was more discreet about that. He took her to the station the next day, put her on the train to Versailles—for Bresson could not be kept waiting—and from the train window, she watched him on the platform until she lost him from view. She ran and fell, and no longer wanted to die.

CLXXI

Annie E.'s mother took her to the station, insisted on travelling with her because there was a change of trains at Rouen. Then she was still Annie D., with a scar on the side her mouth, short-sighted, her hair in a chignon, wearing a loden coat, a tweed skirt, a striped sweater, and she wanted to forget this girl, a hidden interior presence who had the power to cross fifty years of distance, a girl who was her but who was real in her, a kind of real presence, who together became an 'I', the first dissolving into the second, she and I, but cruelly, as one might hear from behind a door oneself being spoken of and at that moment, feeling that one was dying. That girl was full of desire and pride, waiting for a love affair. It was the first time she had left her parents. She had no clear self, simply one that passed from one book to the next. She had never touched a man's sex. The vacation colony was a château, between that of *Le Grand Meaulnes* and that of *L'Année dernière à Marienbad*, and later she would find it again [as I was to do also, returning from Saint-Malo one late afternoon]. Everything was new to her. She felt his cock press against her, as he pressed her against the wall, and felt subjugated by his desire for her. In her room, she had no time to get used to his nakedness, as he forced himself between her thighs. She was hurt. She told him she was a virgin, either as a defence or as an explanation. She wanted to be elsewhere but could not leave. She was cold. He made her slide down his stomach, take his cock in her mouth, and the greasy explosive spray of his sperm filled her nostrils. She went with him to his room. She felt that she was submitting not to him but to a universal, indisputable masculine law, brutal and dirty. He was twenty-two; he had a fiancée back in the Jura where he was a gym teacher.

CLXXII

She was lost, that girl; she was, *je suis*, she wrote, but 'I am not', *moi je ne suis pas*. She wrote that she was not what they said she was. She wrote that one night she asked herself what she had become. He wrote on the mirror in her room with her red toothpaste (*Email Diamant*, the one with a dashing toreador on the packet, stepping forward, his *montera* under his arm, pointing gaily upwards, the one that contains the natural reflection of light and guarantees the brightness of your teeth and a brilliant smile), *Vive les putains*, long live whores or scrubbers or slappers or sluts, long live the harlots, the fallen women, the tramps, long live the working girls. Fifty years later, writing, she thought of a scene in Barbara Loden's film *Wanda*, the last scene in which Wanda was in a roadhouse, she was on the lam, escaped from the car where a man tried to rape her, running through the woods; then mute, now in the bar between two men, taking a cigarette from one, turning her head to the right, to the left. She was no longer there. Before, she said that she was worth nothing. The camera framed her face, froze it, and little by little, she dissolved. She was lost, another woman who is the same woman, who was but was not, in an apartment in Annécy, which she had to keep in order, beauty and order, Ajax, mop, dusters, where the kitchen sink had to shine, where there must be no traces of the lunch left on the table, where the kid had to sleep, take its nap, where all her agitation since seven o'clock in the morning ended in this emptiness, and it must be the time, the hour that women take pills, or pour themselves a little drink, or take the train to Marseille, and the world stops: she is a frozen woman.

CLXXIII

[Actually, it is not really a toreador on the toothpaste packet but the son of the owners of the shop in rue Lafayette, Paris. The Barreaux proposed a new American tooth powder invented by John Walton, a chemist from Philadelphia, to their clients in 1893. The son, André, was a lyric singer at the Opéra-Comique. He is pictured on the toothpaste packet in the costume he wore for role of Figaro in *The Barber of Seville*. It was his wonderful smile, an important asset in conquering the stage, that gave his parents the idea to make him the emblematic figure of *Email Diamant*. His father, Jean-Baptiste, had been a music teacher, his mother, Annette, a milliner, but seduced by the modern and promising nature of the American product, the couple decided to embark on their enterprise, aware that a hygienic mouth and a brilliant smile is an essential fashion accessory.]

De 1893 à nos jours...

Comme à la belle époque, le charme et l'éclat du sourire sont rehaussés par l'emploi du merveilleux dentifrice rouge de John Walton.

Considéré à juste titre comme produit de PREMIÈRE QUALITÉ, L'ÉMAIL DIAMANT réalise l'hygiène parfaite de la bouche. Son colorant est absolument neutre.

Un Sourire...

EMAIL DIAMANT

AVEC LE MERVEILLEUX

DENTIFRICE ROUGE DE *John Walton*

✳ MÉFIEZ-VOUS DES IMITATEURS ✳

PUB R. JACQUOT

CLXXIV

The filming continued, as did the evening strolls in the garden, and he would enlace his arms with hers. Anne W. could not forget that he had lied to her, denying that he had told François Lafarge to hit her for real, to hurt her, as he had directed her to do to François (a frail little thing, she would not really hurt him), and she had fallen to the ground from the blow—Cloquet refused another take, saying that this was not cinema but sadism. There was a little glimmer in François's eye when Bresson tapped his shoulder, complicit, united, it had been planned between them. Cloquet pointed his finger at them, said this to Anne, but she had seen it already in their faces, their little gestures. Cloquet said Bresson was a circus master, making his animals perform, exhibiting them. Antoine Archimbaud, the sound engineer, said he was a tyrant, a manipulator, who isolated his actors, that he had taken this to the extreme with Anne, making her live with him, drawing a line around her, forbidding her to leave its perimeter. They all said she was in a cage, that he had caged her. He refused that she should see her friends, Thierry, Antoine; he did not even wish to hear their names. She felt mysteriously tied to him, and sometimes he had only to make a gesture with his hand or blink an eye for her to understand what he wanted from her. It was as if he was saying to her that they no longer needed to speak, that his thoughts went directly to hers. Returning at dawn from filming all night, he told her she smelt of alcohol. Gin, she replied, proudly and a little drunk. They walked in silence, his steps were heavy, and at the door that separated their bedrooms, he kissed her cheek and told her she was behaving like a child; he shut the door and she heard him go to bed without first going into the bathroom and playing with his little kittens.

CLXXV

[Perhaps this is enough of Anne W.; nonetheless, I must tell you this story.] The producer, Mag Bodard, came to lunch at Guyancourt with Jean-Luc Godard. Bresson felt he did not have time for this; he insisted Anne came, there was no question of him being left alone with them. Anne had never seen any of Godard's films. Bresson and Cloquet were amazed at her ignorance. The lunch was not amusing and Godard was servile towards Bresson. Anne caught him staring at her on the set, but she was too busy with the film crew to pay much attention to him. A year later he told her his real reason for the visit: he had seen her photograph in *Le Figaro* and meeting Bresson was only a pretext to approach her. She said that was another story. At the end of the filming, Bresson told her that her youth had made him young again. She was astonished. He said that she would understand later, much later. A year later she was married to Godard, just before or after the opening of his film, *La Chinoise*; he called her his *fleur-animal*, his animal-flower. Two years later in 1968 she stood at the crossroads of the boulevard Saint-German and the rue Saint-Jacques, frozen, paralysed by fear, incapable of running, as the students came from everywhere, fleeing from an army of police, helmeted, batons in hand and hitting any young person they could. Already she and Jean-Luc were parting, slowly, definitively, painful for them both though she felt it came from her, the unhappy banal end of their marriage a year later, like the end of a beautiful month of May. There is a photograph of them, taken on 7 May, on the streets of the Latin Quarter, Godard filming the students, while Anne smokes by his side, sullenly. That too was another story. The years passed. She tried to speak to him in Cannes in 1982, and he told her he never wanted to hear from her again, he did not want to move her nor be moved by her. In 1993 she sent him a note, telling him that she loved his old beating heart. He did not reply.

There were times when everyone had to take to the streets, including women; for example, in 1871: Anna, André, Béatrix, Blanche, Elisabeth, Eulalie, Clara, Hortense, Léontine, Louise, Marcelle, Nathalie, Noémi, Paule, Sophie, Victorine... there were thousands. They seized the cannons at the beginning, the women were bolder than the men; they sewed sandbags, piling them on the barricades; they made cartridges; they tended the wounded; they took up arms and fired them. They organised, they affiliated; they restructured education and work; they denounced the enemies of the revolution; they called for rights for women, for equal pay and pensions and the right to divorce husbands and an end to marriage. They talked and they talked and they talked. They acted. They lobbied against senseless exclusion, there were to be no masters, no slaves. They were laundresses, seamstresses, bookbinders, and milliners. Some dressed in trousers. They established a new organisation, the Union of Women, and to hell with Proudhon and Michelet, to hell with them all. They reorganised the social life of the city, and for that, they were called *pétroleuses* and wealthy women lined up to abuse them, to beat them with parasols when those who did not die, those who were not shot in the street, against walls, on the barricades, were taken to prison. They called evil; they were called jackals; they were called furies intoxicated by the fumes of wine and blood, hideous viragoes who had un-sexed themselves. It was reported that they had burnt down buildings, pasting small tickets, the size of postage stamps, upon walls, with the letters B.P.B., *bon pour brûler*, good / voucher for burning. It was reported that the tickets were fixed on places designated by their leaders, and a *pétroleuse* would receive ten francs for every house fired. Square or oval, each ticket had the head of a bacchante, devotee of frenzy and chaos, printed on its centre. They were called amazons. They were myths. They were legend.

An *amazone* is or was a superior kind of prostitute, a woman who picked up her clients from the street in her own car; the clients did not pick her up from the *trottoir* in their cars. The *amazone* waited by arrangement at the steering wheel of her car, on the Champs-Élysées or on the *grands boulevards*, near to the opera or in the bois de Boulogne, a *femme galante* (for gallantry does not belong only to men), elegant, dressed in *haute couture*, the upper-crust of prostitution, the *crème de la crème*, perhaps only with a few serious clients. In Heinrich von Kleist's tragedy *Penthesilea*, the Amazon queen was overcome by her desire for Achilles; she had to follow the law of her people that a man must be conquered before love was admissible. She killed him, tearing open his body with her teeth: kisses and bites, *Küsse* and *Bisse,* and there was no difference between these, she said. She hunted him down like a bitch with her dogs (he said), a dog among dogs, slaying him and devouring him. She had killed her sister, Hippolyta, wife of the treacherous Theseus, shot her with her bow and arrow; it was, she said, an accident. Anne W., this time accepting the director's instructions to be naked in a scene, acted in the play in Strasbourg, with Anne Alvaro, the other Anne, newly arrived from Oran, in the title role. The set was spectacular, magnificent: there were snow-covered mountains; dogs were barking in the distance, they came out of the mist. The mist filled the orchestra pit.

CLXXVIII

There is a photograph of Mary Frances and her younger sister Anne on a book cover. The sisters are with their mother, who is veiled. Edith, the mother, looks out of the frame, Mary Frances looks at the camera, Anne looks at her sister. Edith's right hand trails next to the younger daughter's right shoulder, Anne holds a large book of puzzles under her left arm, Mary Frances's left arm and hand drape across her body. Edith's regard is distant, Anne's is sullen, no, Anne is furious, Mary Frances's regard is intense, as she bites her lower lip. Anne was docile, her sister said. Anne hid her flinches, she never revolted, she never kicked, but Mary Frances thought there was scar tissue, nonetheless. How could there not be? Her sister realised that she used Anne like putty as a child, pushing her this way and that. Anne could do no more than nibble at food in public places, asking for something special then pushing it away sneeringly. Anne ate in strange waves and cravings. She starved herself with a small sensual smile or gorged hysterically on what she knew would make her ill. Anne disrupted the lives of others to hold on to their frantic attention. Anne was horrified by animals. Grown up, Anne treated animals as she did men, coolly, with a need for vengeful power, her sister said. Animals and men would bow to one lift of her graceful slender wrist; they would dance when she said to dance. Anne died an ugly painful death from intestinal cancer at fifty-five, after her tortured pattern. Later, Mary Frances knew she deserved Anne's unconscious resentment. She named her daughters Anne and Mary.

CLXXIX

In the childhood house of Anne and Mary Frances, servants passed through, to cook, to sew, to make the beds, to be nannies. Some could not cook at all and some refused to clean. Some were abandoned in a strange country. Some were called 'the girls'. Some were simply baby-sitters, doing their homework while Anne and Mary Frances broke the rules upstairs in their own night world, doing nothing to entertain the children, just checking that teeth were brushed then retreating. Some were nursemaids with crackling uniforms, who did not cook or clean and had nothing to do with the children, attending only to Edith and the new child. Some were the hirelings, who would arrive by train, stay for several weeks, then disappear, leaving a shadow of wretched human misery. These forgettable drabs moved in and out, no more than passing doxies. Others left profound memories. There was Cynthia, who stayed until the loneliness of being the only black woman in the Quaker town became too much for her. There was the hissing Amimoto, far from home, whom Edith could not understand though the children could, who sent tea wafers for Christmas after he left: Edith felt this was unsuitable. He became an admiral of the Japanese fleet. There were the sisters, Blanche, Margaret, Elizabeth, Bertha, whom the children's father, Rex, could not distinguish between. There was Ora, who used her sharp bright French knife as if it were part of her hand, cutting delicate pastry *fleurons*. One day Ora did not return to work from her day off. Mary Frances's grandmother said it was because she was above herself, that she did not want to be in the house with a nursemaid. But it was because Ora had turned her sharp French knife on her own mother after church, slashing her throat, then cutting her into several neat pieces, next slashing the tent (in which they lived on the west side of town) into ribbons, then in a mad slicing arc, she cut her own throat and wrists, expertly, and there was not so much as a nick on the knife, the police said.

CLXXX

In Marseille, Mary Frances read *Le Monde* while sipping a gin-vermouth. (In California, many years later, when she was very old and in bed, she would sip a pink drink through a straw, a drink with the herbal scent of gin; flushed, she whispered that sobriety was a rare and dubious virtue, if it were that at all.) Her sister, the youngest sister Norah, turned up, jauntily, with the excited news that the devout people at the local shrine of Mary Magdalen had told her that the breasts of the saint, when she was very old indeed, had flowed with milk. Artemis has eighteen breasts, and it was Artemis, protector of sailors, who led the Greek sailors of Phocea to what would become Masallia, to a land of salt-gatherers. They arrived during a feast, at which the daughter of the king was to select her husband from her many suitors. Obviously, inevitably, Gyptis chose the Greek captain Protis, and then her father allowed Protis to become ruler of the new city on the northern bank of the Lacydon. That all happened in just a few hours. Protis built a temple to Artemis, installing therein her statue brought from Epheseus with her priestess. The statue of Artemis faced inland. Later there came Mary Magdalen, to replace Artemis as protector of the city; she came with Lazarus and Joseph and Maximus and Martha and Sarah, with Mary Salome and Mary of Clopas, whom some think was the blessed Virgin herself, ferried first to the Camargue, to what is now Saintes-Marie-de-la-mer. They came in in a little boat, a barque, symbolised in the dry little biscuits flavoured with orange flower water and olive oil, fragant and not too sweet, called *navettes*. On 24 May in Saintes-Marie-de-la-mer the statue of Sarah, black Sara, Sara-i-Kali, saint of the Romani, is carried down to the sea as was the statue of Ishtar, called also Astarte and Inanna, long before her.

CLXXXI

W. B. described the hill on which Notre Dame de Garde stands, from which she, Queen of Heaven, Star of the Sea, looks down, as her starry garment, the lamps at night as unnamed constellations. He wrote that the chains of streamers and sails are her earrings. He noted the unfathomable wetness of the shellfish and oyster stalls, the quivering creatures: *oursins*, *portugaises*, *marennes*, *clovisses*, and *moules*. There were discoloured women in pink shifts in the rue Bouterie, which is now the rue Lacydon. It is near the port quarter, and was then a street of miserable dwellings, more noted for prostitution than provisional architecture, though there were a number of *maisons closes*, at least a dozen if those in the rue Lanternie that descended to rue Bouterie were counted. It was called the Quartier d'Amour, and tourists could dream of this captivating Marseillaise *plein air* where there blended, under the control of the Administration, family life, the concerns of hygiene, the purest Orientalism, and the most spiritual French grace. Casanova wrote of Marseille that there was no city in France where the libertinism of women was as great—the women not only refused nothing, but offered men what they did not always dare to ask. The women, the whores, were placed strategically in the narrow streets of the red-light district, called *les bricks*, an agglomeration of alleyways, turrets, bridges, cellars, arches, a refuse heap of houses in which a man (W. B. said), bounced like a ball from one side of the street to the other, might forfeit his hat (lose his head?), the trophies of manhood on consoles or hung on racks, trilbies, boaters, bowler, jockey caps, and ah, yes, hunting caps, and where there are snake-ringed Medusa heads over the doors, as well as high-breasted nymphs, designed by the sculptor Pierre Puget, reflected by the 'caryatids' standing below, captured in a moment of repose.

Hannah A. remembered that W. B. related how once, in the Café Deux Magots in Paris, he drew a diagram of his life, and it was like a labyrinth, each relationship figuring as an entrance. She evoked his recurrent metaphors of diagrams and maps, of dreams and memories, of panoramas and vistas, of arcades and labyrinths. In Paris, he learned the art of straying, errant ways of charting, understanding the lie of the land, getting lost. There were ink stains on the blotting paper, the traces of labyrinths blotting his copybook. In Marseille, taking hashish, space expanded; there was dreaming and waking from the dream. [I fear I am repeating myself, unable to extricate myself from the circles in which I turn, waking and dreaming and waking again]. The street was like a knife cut. He observed the pavements, which could also have been the paving stones of Paris, and one often spoke of stones instead of bread, and these stones were the bread of his imagination, seized by sudden hunger to taste it, like the children abandoned in the forest who, famished, ate their little crust of bread or the birds, always hungry, who ate the crumbs that should have led the children home. Sometimes they used ashes and returning home, the stepmother killed the boy and the girl had to prepare him for supper when the father ate his son. The girl hid her brother's heart in the trunk of a tree. At the start of the story, but not this one and not every story, the children found their way out of the wood once because the clever boy marked the path with pebbles, but the next time he was not so clever, dropping breadcrumbs instead, and they could not find their way. In another story, a true story, in the time of great famine, mothers and fathers abandoned their children or they ate their children, or they opened the graves of their children and stripped scraps of flesh from their skulls. [I do not want to tell this story. I cannot tell this story.]

Jacques L. said that it is not enough to have the blueprints to a reconstructed labyrinth, not even a pile of them already worked up. No, he said, what is needed, above all, is the 'general combinatory', which certainly governs their variety, but which more usefully (for there must be use-value) accounts for the illusions and shifts in the labyrinth that happen right before one's very eyes. He said that in obsessive neurosis there is no shortage of either, for it is an architecture of contrasts, contrasts insufficiently noticed, or at least not yet observed, which cannot simply be attributed to differing façades. His daughter saw him from her window one afternoon when she was ill at home but her papa was not coming to see her, as she thought, as she hoped, as her mother had told her he would, and when he arrived, he would understand her, he would save her where all the stupid doctors could not. From her balcony she saw a woman, walking rapidly, coming out of a *maison de rendez-vous* in the same street, rue Jadin. Then she saw a man come out, following her, and then she saw it was her papa, and she was stupified, indignant that he had the nerve to come to fuck that woman in rue Jadin a step away from the apartment of his children and his ex-wife, furious that he had put her through this ordeal of waiting while satisfying his desire first. But then her papa was a puzzle, and she had grown up in the *l'ombre des glaïeuls*, the shade of gladioli. If she committed suicide, she wanted the circumstances of her death not to be concealed in any way.

CLXXXIV

The corridor that might include columns and pilasters and closed lateral doors was an empty setting, and if a straight trajectory was impossible, this might be replaced by a labyrinthine series of corridors and salons, to give the impression of an unending course. That was the interior, obviously, in which a dark salon was seen, really very dark, and then there was threshold, a door to the garden. Later a voice was heard to ask 'Do you know this story?'. And X told A that behind this hand, pointing towards a balustrade or a statue or a sconce or a sculpted frieze or a column's capital, unseen but in any case, a detail of baroque complexity, she could glimpse the foliage, like the living leaves of the garden that was waiting for them, though this detail, the detail of the leaves was not visible, and in fact, the garden *à la française* had appeared, as though by error, in a very brief shot in this sequence. A garden in this style has statues with mythological themes, topiaries and walkways, pools and fountains, grottos and labyrinths, and order is imposed on nature. There may be a wide ditch dug at the edge of the garden to close off the passage without obscuring the view, called a *saut de loup* in French, and in English, this wolf's leap is called a *ha-ha*. Trees and bushes are trimmed into ornamental shapes; they are usually quick-growing evergreens, with small leaves that can be sheared and with a dense branching pattern. Box, *buxus*, is best for small topiaries. However, it can be disfigured, even defoliated entirely, by the Box-tree moth, *cydalima perspectalis,* a moth with a striking appearance, with white wings with an iridescent border. It spins a cocoon of white webbing in which its caterpillars feed.

CLXXXV

Goethe told the story of botanical forms: the unfolding leaf of the plant contained the germ of its metamorphosis, the true Proteus, hidden or revealed in vegetal forms, writing from Rome to a friend of his discovery in the diverse flora of Italy of the truth of the *how* of the organism. Ah, the leaf, no more or less than floral organs, the refinement of the sap, the cycles of contraction and expansion [as in a diagram, if I may make a perhaps fanciful comparison, in case this is missed] that become enhancement, and above all the truth, though he omitted roots in the plantness of the plant, the leaves dwelling in the realms of the invisible. Hashish, heroin, morphine, and cocaine are derived from plants [as everyone knows, for goodness sake], as Freud knew, experiencing a gorgeous excitement, exhilaration, and lasting euphoria. His biographer mentions only the cocaine he was prescribed for a nasal infection, on which Fliess operated twice. Freud and Fliess shared a keen interest in the state of each other's noses, and it was, of course, that organ which had aroused Fliess's interest in the sexual processes. Freud consented only to take the occasional dose of aspirin for the pain of his cancer until towards the end, when he was given morphine. Aspirin, too, is derived from a plant, first from the bark of willow; the name comes from a combination of acetyl and *Spiraea ulmaria*, meadowsweet, queen of the meadow, bridewort. The contribution of Arthur Eichengrün [oak green, if I may translate, without making too heavy a point, once again in case this is missed] to the development of the drug was erased in the Bayer pharmaceutical company's account, as was his work on a treatment for gonorrhoea. In 1944 he was sent to the camp at Theresienstadt. He wrote to Bayer for help, but received no reply.

CLXXXVI

The last book Freud read before his death was Balzac's *La Peau de chagrin*. He remarked of it that it was just the book for him, for it dealt with starvation. In the novel, a young man found a magical piece of shagreen, the untanned skin of a wild ass, in the shop of an antiques dealer. The skin was embossed with a phrase in Sanskrit, a text of the skin. It would grant him his every wish, but the skin shrank with each wish and eventually consumed him, depleting his life-force as each of his pathetic desires was achieved. He was warned by the mysterious and sardonic merchant but chose not to heed the warning in favour of the skin in his pocket, the gratification of his desires, because he wanted to live now. But the life of the young man shrank with the *chagrin*, as he wished for a good dinner, money, and women. Shagreen has a rough texture, granular, prepared by the embedding of plant seeds in the soft raw hide, trampled into the skin to leave indentations, then shaken off. *Chagrin* is anxiety, grief, suffering, sorrow, pain, vexation, discomfort, heartache, heartbreak. The last fragment of the skin is *fragile et petit comme une feuille de saule*, as fragile and tiny as a willow leaf.

CLXXXVII

Anna M. translated Bresson on Bresson, a collection of interviews. Bresson edited each interview very carefully, fastidiously even, before publication, refining them further, as he had refined his answers. In one interview, he says that the audience, which he says he respects deeply, is always ready to feel before it understands, and that is how it should be. Anna M. also translated a book by Annie E., which began with the death of the father, born from the grief at the loss of her father, told as simply, as emptily of emotion, as coldly as possible, and that is how it should be.

Anna M. wrote about two women: first person and third person, but one may assume they were both her. In a photograph her arm reached across a black surface printed with flowers, peonies or roses. The sleeve of her dress, also black, was scattered with flower-like abstract forms; a slender silver bracelet fell back over the sleeve, catching its edge. Her wrist was exposed: radius, ulna, the carpal joint, the soft tissue under the skin. Sometimes, she wrote, she was a good utopian, at other times, a bad one; she was thinking about divisions of language, possibly, perhaps, maybe, conceivably [it could be, for I could only occasionally gather her meaning, despite my pleasure in the strange intimacy, in the ruptures of narrative cohesion, in the sudden shifting thresholds between a book, its writer, its subject. I remembered reading with her, no, after her, in Cambridge, when she was reading her novel in instalments across Europe, city to city; that was when we could travel, when it was still possible to step out fearlessly into a dark room and read to an audience, even if no-one really knew what was being said, lost in the narrative that was out of earshot]. In the novel, a novel was being written, back and forth, examined, pulled back into itself, then unravelling, spreading. She said that things did not necessarily happen in order. She said that something in her had crossed over, and she could not go back. Rules were often broken, the plot was incidental and fungible (as someone commented, without remarking on the legal or economic aspect of the word, the equivalence between commodities at the same time, in the same place). There seemed to be constant revisions or deletions. Positions or roles did not stay where they started or walked-on briefly with few words (for example, Arthur Rimbaud, followed, as it were, to Ethiopia) if, as if they ever did, and that was how it should be. At the beginning, a woman looked at a bead of blood on her thumb. At the end, a man, Aidan, played with his fingers, and he reminded I of her.

Arthur Rimbaud called his mother *bouche d'ombre*, mouth of darkness. She sent him two pairs of stockings, *bas*. He thanked her; he complained about the pain in his legs, the swelling in his right knee, the horrible suffering, the stretcher he had made to take him from Harar to the European Hospital in Zeilah, a journey of three hundred kilometres that took ten days and sixteen negro porters; he thought he would come home to France to be looked after; better days would come, he wrote, but P. S., as for the stockings, they were useless and he would probably sell them. Madame Rimbaud's hosiery of silk or cotton or even fine merino wool [I imagine] would be sold by her son with the swollen knee. Dying in Marseille, he was given morphine, and death advanced with rapid pace. Isabelle, his sister, was at his bedside. Sometimes he called her 'Djami'. Quickly, quickly, pack the bags and we will leave, he murmured. He was skeletal, with the complexion of a cadaver, his poor limbs mutilated, paralysed, his right leg amputated in May. He had thought to have a wooden leg made. Isabelle wrote to their mother that she would respect her brother's wishes concerning the little that remained to him, that she would be as faithful to him after death as in life, and what he told her to do with his money and his clothes, she would do exactly as he asked, even if it caused her to suffer. It was *la Mother's*, Madame Rimbaud's wish that his body be returned to Charleville-Mézières, the town of his birth that he had described as exceptionally hideous: to *la Mother* who was the man of the house without a man, her name cracking like a whip, *pas drôle*, not funny, these mothers. Eight years after his death she had a hallucination: she saw a young man hobbling in on crutches during a church service and thought she recognised her son.

Kyra N., the daughter who saw her father dance, was a painter as well as a ballet dancer. She liked to use bright colours. Her father was a frequent subject of her paintings, but always as a dancer, in his ballet roles, never as himself. Margot F. met her, describing her as fascinating, sturdily built, full of exuberance, with the most engaging smile and unusual grey-green or grey-brown eyes, the eyes of her father. [*Pupilla*, the little girl reflected in the eye, the hole in the iris, an orphan, an apple, a little doll, a little image.] Kyra N. described a Russian dance, and she made a gesture with her right arm, brushing it across her brow, and Margot F. could see her father exactly in the gesture, in the movement and in the daughter's face, all that could be said in that instant and it was unforgettable. Her mother, Romola [educated by English governesses] said that it seemed they had been one person split apart, father and daughter, constantly wishing to be reunited. Her father taught her how to point her toes like a ballerina when she was very young; he carved little wooden toys for her. For a long time, she thought she had to behave in a crazy manner, falling to the floor, writhing, throwing fits. She thought it was expected of her. Her practice clothes were those of a man, just like her father's: a white shirt rolled at the sleeve, open at the neck, black tights with a leather belt, soft dance shoes. She danced the role of a young girl in in *Le Spectre de la ros*e in London or she danced the role of the Spirit of the rose (the accounts differ, from *Le Monde* to *The New York Times*), who enters through the window, dances with the girl, kisses her, then leaps out of the window again, a famous Nijinskian leap. When Margot F. met her, Kyra N. was working as an interpreter or a saleswoman or the manager (the accounts differ) in a fashion boutique in the via Condotti in Rome: the most exclusive shopping street, luxurious, prestigious, elegant, refined, expensive, very expensive, *chic*, very *chic*, *molto elegante, alla moda*.

In May 1917, the garment workers of *haute couture*, the *midinettes*, went on strike, refusing a reduction in their wages. They were called *midinettes* because living far from their homes, they were obliged to eat rapidly at midday at a diner or on a bench in a park square, sacrificing a proper meal in the service of consumer production. Later the name designated a young *ingénue* with the heart of an artichoke. They worked ten-hour days in the workshops, making clothes for wealthy women. The seamstresses of Jenny and Cheruit downed tools, followed by the seamstresses of Lanvin, Schwob, Brandt, Zimmerman, Deuillet, Premet, Worth. Two thousand women stopped work. They would, they said, accept a reduction in their working week, but not the reduction in their pay. They hung red flags in their showrooms. They marched in their thousands on the *grands boulevards*, in a demonstration at which they sang, laughed, ran, jumped (it was reported). They wore corsages of lily of the valley and lilac. They were joyous. They were a battalion. A journalist from *République française* commented on the grace of these young girls, who were like Parisian sparrows, their clothes fluttering, their songs, their smiles, their gaiety even in the midst of sadness. They should not be taxed with frivolity because they were young and pretty, he wrote, because they wore flowers, because they laughed and sang. None of this protected them from suffering, from pain, from hunger. Their stomachs were not dominated by vanity, by coquetterie or delicacy.

The women garment makers were paid the lowest wages in manufacturing. This did not stop writers comparing them with birds, with bees, with fairies, observing them lasciviously through the rosy lens of the connoisseur, as though the sweatshop were a brothel, as though the women lived for pleasure rather than for food, as though their small statures and narrow waists resulted from fashion rather than from undereating in the filthy economy of the *petit sou*. It did not prevent the eroticisation of their hunger. Their labour militancy was leavened in the nostalgic descriptions of the journalists, calling them *Jenny l'Ouvrière* and *Mimi Pinson*, calling them nothing but birdbrains, even as the striking women were hemmed in by the police. They should remain the charming soul of the street, pleading their cause by staying on their own ground, their ingenuity suggesting more skilful procedures than the rioters of *Germinal* or those women who had made the boulevard their home, whose vice made them the evil soul of the street, advised an article on the front page of *Le Temps* in 1910. The women persisted in strike actions between 1901 and 1919. They mobilised, dropping their needles and taking to the streets, again and again.

L'atout maître
de la Séduction...

un parfum

WORTH

"JE REVIENS" · "DANS LA NUIT"
"VERS TOI" · "IMPRUDENCE"

De la simplicité au grand luxe
les Flacons de 750 f à 70.000 f

[I was tired: the year unfolded, time passed, and I was slowly disappearing. Each day I diminished, shrinking among or into the words of others by my own volition. I found myself digressing as I contracted, as though I were unravelling, led here and there, willy nilly, as some words registered while others did not, as they did not strike their mark, so to speak, or became undone. I knew it was not really haphazard, that a certain logic of association was at work; no, I hoped it was not so: that though it was by compulsion, it was not undertaken helter-skelter, pell-mell, randomly, blindly, erratically, impulsively. Will I nill I? Will ye nill ye? I lost Anna for a while, Anna, my Anna or my Anne, or any other of the women I was not. I lost her, I lost them in the nameless women of the street or the hills or the mountain slopes or the forests, where they gathered together, where they chewed on bones, some with scraps of flesh still clinging to them, with their sharp white teeth. Delicious. Down to the marrow, the soft spongy tissue. I was tender at the bone. I thought the end was approaching, and so I would be obliged to start all over again, in the making of sense, in the clipping and polishing, melting down the hard fat: the ending, the ending, the ending. The weaver sits quietly, faithfully, and throws the shuttle.]

There was a poem by Anne C., in which a wind described as glassy broke on a shore, which was shoutless, and stirred around a—no, *the* rose. Then before a snow, before the emptiness of night, lanterns threw shapes of companions, old companions, and there was a cold pause that followed. What knife skinned off the hour—it was not at all a question. Buoys sank. The wind blew on what had been their house. There was nothing for it but to row.

In chapter 10 of *Capital*, 'The Working Day', Marx calls capital dead labour. Capital lives like a vampire, sucking at living labour; the more labour it sucks, the more it lives. Taking time away to eat or rest deprives the vampire of its sustenance. There were small thefts of capital from workers' meal- and rest-times, a nibbling and cribbling, a petty pilfering of minutes. Moments were the elements of profit. The silk manufacturers spun silk for ten hours a day from the blood of children who had to be elevated on stools to work. The silk manufacturers annulled the education of child-workers, for the delicate nature of the fabric in which they were employed required a lightness of touch, one that could only be acquired by an early introduction to the work, childhood slaughtered for the sake of their delicate fingers. They worked on, laboured ten and a half hours a day, silk-twisting, silk-winding. The rate of death was high in the silk districts, exceedingly high, and among the female part of the workers, higher than even in the cotton mills of Lancashire. In supposedly respectable dress-making establishments women worked sixteen and a half hour days without a break, often up to thirty hours during the season. The flow of their labour power was maintained by occasional supplies of sherry, port, coffee, as they conjured magnificent dresses for the aristocracy. Mary-Anne W., a milliner, worked without rest for over twenty-six hours, with sixty other girls. She fell ill on a Friday, then died on the Saturday, having completed the finery on which she was working. Children and women pined and died.

CXCVI

They were the daughters of night. One was the spinner, one the allotter, drawer of lots, one cut the thread, the inflexible: the end, the end, the end. One sang what had been, one sang what was, one sang what was to be. They were the sisters of death and retribution and decay. They were the sisters of sleep and dreaming, of blame and misery. They were the sisters of peace and justice and order. Their acts were not governed by the gods. They were the daughters of necessity. They span and they bound thread. They read and they wrote the book of fate, but they seldom intervened. Hesiod called them avenging furies, who never ceased from their dread anger, but others said they left punishment to the Erinyes. Sometimes they were beautiful, sometimes they were ugly and old and lame. They were always severe, unyielding, and stern. They led Persephone up to the light; they returned her to the darkness.

Anna F. bought two second-hand looms in 1955. She kept one in London, the other in her house in Suffolk. A picture of Wolf hung behind the first. It was said that she composed her psychoanalytic papers and lectures while weaving. Her father wrote that past, present, and future were strung together on the thread of the wish that ran through them. Good balance was required, thought Anna, the hand had to be kept as busy as the mind. Jacques, another Jacques, called Jackie as a child, wrote that one might dream of taking on a braid or a weave, a warp or a woof, without being sure of the textile to come, if it would deserve the name of text in the figure of the textile. He had a memory from his childhood: the women of his family, raising their eyes from their woollen threads, but without stopping or even slowing the movement of their fingers, saying they had to diminish the stitches, reduce the knit of their work, and their needles and hands had to work with two loops at once, and this was not the ruse of Penelope, he said, who wove a shroud for the father of Odysseus by day and unravelled it at night. Penelope unpicked the threads but Jean L. said she recomposed them. She did not cut them: she wove, hand by hand, thread by thread, then un-wove, hand by hand, thread by thread, then began again, a new shroud, a new work. It took time, like the time of mourning, undoing and then taking it up again, anew. It took great patience. Anna F. compared herself with Penelope, her father with Odysseus: that was the dream in which she was faithful, he was not, but there were two conflicting reproaches, and in another dream, she lost her father and her mother in Paris or Vienna; she looked for them with search parties but only her mother was found and she was in despair. She wondered how then should he find her in her dreams. Anna always unravelled her knitting if she made a mistake, if she dropped a stitch or made an extra one, going back to the place the error was made and beginning again from there.

CXCVIII

The history of psychoanalysis is one of spinning and weaving, of bobbins and threads. (The child threw the cotton reel from his cot.) The woven rug was placed on the couch of the father. But Anna's couch, a flat divan, rather low, with a single pillow and an embroidered antimacassar, described by one analysand, had a hand-knitted blanket. Now there are three little pillows, one with a scrap of rose-coloured silk trimming. She sat at the head of the couch, facing the windows. Her loom was in the corner. She could see the patient but the patient could not see her. She would greet the patient with the words: *well, you know what to do*, or ask what they had for her today. Her weaving had practical outcomes; it should not be taken solely as metaphor, though often Anna used it as such. It was not a work of mourning. At the end of her life, Anna's hands shook. She tried to knit but was discouraged. She felt degraded but she laughed at herself, saying that her hand was angry with her for she had controlled it for so long. But then she said it was bad, very bad, and that she could not stand it anymore. Instead of knitting, she slept or her niece Sophie read detective stories to her. She wanted the name of her dog, her chow, Jo-Fi, to be written as her next of kin. She wondered if it was the end. She asked Manna F. to bring her father's coat to the hospital. Anna wore the heavy loden wool coat when Manna took her in a wheelchair to the lily pond on the Heath, where she fed breadcrumbs to the ducks. Loden is made from carded wool, spun into fine yarn, woven, walked or fulled—hammered in warm water, dyed and dried, napped or shorn (sometimes with a thistle), twice-ironed. She had often worn her father's coat, the coat he had worn to travel from Vienna to London, putting her plastic rain hat and her bus and underground tickets in the pockets.

Lou A.-S. said that psychoanalysis was like following the thread of the left hand with the right hand, that it was a working with knots and loops, although analysis was more creative for it was put into the service of life, while braiding left the maker feeling empty and exhausted. Anna sent Lou parcels of clothes she knitted for her, imagining Lou wearing them. She asked Lou about their elegance, their fit, constantly requesting her measurements, the lower width of her skirt, the minimum width, the size of her waist, the length of her sleeves, the size of her bust, the distance from her shoulder to her waist. Anna covered Lou with wool and love. Self-image. Ravishment. An unfinished heart.

Paula F. was the pretty little maid who worked for the Freuds in Vienna. She came to London with the family. She arranged the new house in Maresfield Gardens, hanging Pirodon's engraving of Brouillet's painting of Charcot's clinical lesson at the Pitié-Salpêtrière over the couch. Paula was interned for nine months as an enemy alien on the Isle of Man, like Anna's nephew Ernst. She worked in the camp's kitchen. She fed the cats. She learnt English. She saved her money to buy herself a black fur jacket. Martha Freud and Paula controlled the household; they gossiped about the patients and Anna did not like this at all. Paula used to say that the *Herr Professor* was a lovely man. She was always breaking the dishes and when she broke the dishes she went to the *Herr Professor* to tell him that she had broken them again. And the *Herr Professor*, he would say to her, courage Paula, that together they would go to Frau Freud and confess. Paula said the house was dominated by the *Herr Professor*, who was often in his study where she dusted the furniture and objects every day with precision, that Frau Freud was self-effacing, that Tante Minna was omnipresent, that Anna became increasingly important. After the death of the *Herr Professor* and his Frau, Paula stayed working for Anna, but was not a *Kinderfrau*; she was a maid, not a companion. She became infirm, she often fell over and had paranoid fits. She spoke plaintively. She used to run rather than walk, but that was all over. She could no longer keep up with the housework, yet guarded her position fiercely should anyone try to help. After Dorothy's death Paula and Anna lived alone with the chow Jo-Fi, until Alice C. and Manna F. came as *Kinderfrauen*, to help with controlling Paula and Jo-Fi, unruly maid and unruly dog. Paula would not admit she was weak, she refused to give up her place; she became a burden to Anna, who could not place her in a home, for then Paula would say that Anna had used her for fifty years, only to throw her out. When Anna died, Paula returned to Austria.

Martha despaired of Anna's drab clothes, her daughter's plainness. She hated the ugly shoes Anna insisted on wearing. It was a source of tension between them, for equally, Anna was impatient with her mother's preoccupation with her elegant dresses, her careful attention to her hair and her makeup. (Some said this was nonsense, of course, that Martha was not all dedicated to her appearance, it was absurd to say this.) The most effort to which Anna would concede was a little rouge on her cheeks when winter colds left her pale. As a woman, she cropped her hair, bobbed it, her fringe held back by a grip such as a little girl might wear, while as a girl, she wore it long, tied back, coiled or braided. She wore wide long dresses, two sizes larger than was necessary. She was a childish slight figure in a pinafore dress with a voluminous ankle-length skirt. Her dress was habitual, hand-sewn with considerable skill, timeless. Her flat shoes had blunt toes. She refused to meet her mother's view of femininity. It was felt that she went out of her way to show off her plainness. However, she always wore the beaded necklaces and jade brooches her dear papa gave her. He gave her a signet ring with an inset semi-precious stone, carved with the image of a goddess. Sometimes Anna dreamed that she was looking for women, for Marie or Dorothy, but she could not find them. Once she dreamed that she followed a serpentine walk, in and out of houses, but through their windows, not their doors, and she thought in her dream that all the houses would be spoilt. When she arrived at the highest point, there, sitting in a room, were her mother and Tante Minna. Minna was sewing, Martha was mending (a doormat, Anna thought). She had the strange feeling that her father was present throughout the twisting walk, in every house, in every room.

CCII

Paula F. helped arrange the furnishing of the house in Maresfield Gardens. A maid in Vienna, she was in fact the housekeeper in London: from *Hausmädchen* to *Hausfrau*. In French, a maid may be called a *femme de ménage*, the woman of the household, implying a great deal of cleaning, of heavy domestic work, while a French maid was a lady's maid, a cut above other servants, skilled in matters of clothing and jewellery and hairdressing. The French maid is subject to frequent eroticisation and fetishistic costumes, appearing in her lively and flirtatious soubrette form as the domestic sexual servant of a bourgeois household, in both phantasy and reality. How might she serve her master? The costume is black and white, with a little ruffled apron. The skirt is short enough so that when the little maid reaches up with her feather duster, to dust, say, the top of an engraving, it will lift to expose her garters, her thighs, her buttocks, *le très-haut, le plus-haut*. *Ooh là là:* cosplay, kinky porn, erotic femdom, slutty fantasy, adult accessories, a variety of styles and materials, conservative or revealing, shocking and full-figure pleasing, sweetheart necklines and puffball sleeves, pearls or chokers, naughty and fun, sultry or traditional, racy and teasing, new and used options. It is a servant text among master narratives, between maids and nurses and governesses (one who gathered up her skirt behind her, crying out *oh do look at my little tail*), between dirty feet and bedwetting: the part played by the servant-girl, what Hélène C. called the hole in the social cell.

CCIII

Oh, the maids, the maids. They drop the fragile objects and they destroy them. The appreciation of art and works of art is completely foreign to them. They are dominated by a mute hostility to the manifestations of art. They do not understand their value. They loathe the fine objects particularly when the objects become a source of work for them, when they require dusting, polishing, and such careful treatment. The maids have their *tâches*, and the maids have their *taches*. As Emily A. pointed out, indicated so clearly, so, rationally, so seductively, the former must efface the latter. And the maids must not play the mistress.

The painting by Brouillet, the engraving of which Paula hung over the couch, depicts a woman falling back into the arms of her doctor, mesmerised, observed by a group of what once were called 'men of science'. Some are students, some are doctors, some are writers. The men of science are observing attentively a tableau of five people to the right of the painting: Dr Charcot, Joseph Babinski, the clinic's chief house officer, Mademoiselle Ecary, a nurse, Marguerite Bottard, the director of nursing, and Blanche (Marie) Wittman, a patient. That is the scene. It was a theatre, some said. Blanche (Marie) was called the queen of the hysterics and there were stories made up about her; there was even one that showed her as a nothing more than a torso, a trunk on a trolley, writing with one hand, and what nonsense that is, what a stupid invention, though it is true that Blanche enjoyed reading romantic fiction, like Emma Bovary, and would often recite scenes from popular novels. There was a certain rivalry among the hysterics, and they were not only women (though many did not want to believe that, not at all, even when Freud took that news back to Vienna, explaining the contractures, the seizures, the *arc de cercle*). Charcot systematically made family trees of his patients, going into their history, their family pathologies. Once he said to Freud, *C'est toujours la chose génitale*, it was always the genital thing, always, always, *toujours, toujours, toujours*. On her deathbed, Blanche said one could not fool Dr Charcot: no, he knew how to recognise those kinds of jokers and would just look them straight in the eye and command them to be still.

The dancer Jane A. was a patient at the Salpêtrière when she was fourteen and then still Jeanne Beaudon, diagnosed with St Vitus's dance, *Sydenham's chorea*, a neurological disorder characterised by rapid, jerky, involuntary movements of the face and limbs and outbursts of crying and laughing. She learnt gymnastics, and later, at the Moulin Rouge and the Divan Japonais, the can-can kick of her legs was one of her signature dance moves. The nurses thought of her as a child of the house, charming and sweet. For Jane/Jeanne, it was an Eden, everything on this earth being relative. At the annual masquerade ball, she dazzled the crowd with her dancing, her leaps and twirls, her high kicks. She noticed the similarities between dancing and her symptoms. She always danced a little madly, with inexpressible strangeness, pale, thin, as though she were fed on flowers. She danced like an orchid in a frenzy, a critic wrote, as though she danced for her own pleasure. They called her *Jeanne La Folle*, mad Jane, which she hated, or *La Mélinite*, after a high-explosive shell. She had the sad face of a fallen angel, they said. But she was refined, with good taste; sophisticated, educated, she knew about art and literature and music. Toulouse-Lautrec designed a poster for her when he was in a sanatorium: in the drawing a snake wrapped around her body, her snake dress, and she liked it very much but her impresario refused it. When she retired to Jouy-en-Josas, she spent her days knitting and embroidering, seldom speaking to anyone of her past. She did not return to Paris until 1941, going to a dinner in her honour at which she improvised a ballet on hearing the music played. She said if dancing was like madness, it had helped her to live and she was its enchanted slave; she said if dancing existed in the next world, it was likely that she would be called upon to interpret a *danse macabre*, a lovely allegorical dance in which the dead are most lively and agile.

Avril Jane

CCVI

Charcot syndrome is a deformity of the foot, a dislocation,
a fracture, which may result in amputation or death; or it is
an amyotrophic lateral sclerosis; or it is hammer toes and the
grinding of teeth and scoliosis and high arched feet. There
may be disintegration of the bones and trauma. The toes may
curve under themselves like claws. A Charcot foot may be
cured at an early stage by the wearing of a cast boot to protect
the foot and ankle.

CCVII

Blanche (who was really Marie) did not escape the hospital, unlike Jane (who was really Jeanne), who was declared cured because of her dancing, unlike the intrepid A or Augustine (who was really Louise), who shimmied down the walls, dressed as a man, and was never seen again (which was not entirely true: after her escape, it was reported that she was living with her lover whom she had met at the Salpêtrière). Augustine had once been a kitchen maid. She was tall and blonde, active, intelligent, affectionate, impressionable, and capricious. They said she was a *coquette*, spending a great deal of time on her appearance, fixing her long full hair in different styles, made happy by brightly coloured ribbons. They felt she was too brazen for her age. When she was about to have an attack, she would gape and cry out, *ah*, *ah*, *ah*. She suffered from trembling, from cramps and muscle contractions, from the paralysis of her right leg, from involuntary movements of her head, torso, her right arm and leg. Her condition was, they said, unstable and mobile, as was the sex it preferred to inflict. She heard voices, experienced an aura of psychic disturbances and somatic sensations. She felt as if she was being embraced, lifted from the ground, and then her cheek was kissed, but she only felt that kiss on her right cheek. She had visions of dirty black rats, of a hirsute man who rolled his eyes at her, of a deathly chariot, and of an invisible lover. The pains started in her right ovary, followed by a *boule hystérique* that blocked her throat, suffocated her; there was ringing in her ears, palpitations of her heart, pressure on her eyes, pounding at her temples, *ah*, *ah*, *ah*. They said she was a good person at heart so she was made a *fille de service*, a ward maid. She refused to name the object of her desire, though she wrote she would speak more openly if she dared. (Jane said some of the patients deceived the doctors to capture attention and gain stardom.)

CCVIII

The dress was black, a bodice and a skirt, and over it, there was a white apron. There was a white cap, which tended to tip back in the displays of muscular hyper-excitability, when she was placed on chair, rigid, inflexible, her body not even bending when a heavy weight was placed on her stomach. The cap would fall back too, at the moments of contracture, induced through hypnosis for she no longer produced contractures as symptoms. Her body could then be bent, moulded, it was remarkably pliable. At her throat a ruff of white collar could be seen, sometimes tied in a bow with a white ribbon, at others, with a black bow that may have been part of the bodice of her dress, on which a row of buttons ran down to her waist. There were black leather boots, of course, *bottines*, exposed when she was laid back across two chairs. Although neat and tidy, the costume was far from *haute couture*, no more than serviceable, but it would serve for a girl of service. Her parents had been domestic servants in a grand house, and she came to work in the same grand house when she was thirteen, the same house where her employer Monsieur C. raped her, threatening her with a razor when she refused him and his offer of beautiful dresses, the same Monsieur C., who was her mother's lover in the same grand house. Her mother made her kiss this gentleman and call him father; she was placed in his house to clean to sew and sing with the children. She would not kiss him at breakfast the morning after he raped her, so Madame C. became suspicious and Monsieur C. turned pale. There was a certain right the masters had over the bodies of those who worked for them, those who kept their grand houses clean in their white aprons, their neat caps, which tended to fall back on the head during a sexual attack, until the servants, the maids, took up a kitchen knife or a hammer, or, why not? a razor and then, then their aprons are not white at all, *ah, ah, ah*.

The French maid was usually no more than a minor character. She hovered in the background, up and down stairs and in her lady's chamber. Or if she was Mademoiselle Hortense, for example [yes, I mean the Hortense who is a minor character upon whose actions the plot turns in part in a web-like novel about decay and corruption, not the Hortense of a musical in the carefree world of the French Riviera], she was proud, she was vain, she was from the south. If she is Hortense, she was murderous. If she is Hortense, she had a lowering energy. If she is Hortense, she was keen and wan in her anatomy, with a feline mouth, a tightness to her face, watchful, very watchful, but without turning her head, from the corner of her eyes, which could be pleasantly dispensed with, especially when she was in an ill humour, especially when she was near knives. Accomplished enough, tasteful enough in dress and adornment, with impeccable comportment (despite her sideways glances), she was like a very neat She-wolf, imperfectly tamed. *Ha ha ha*, she laughed bitterly at the idea a new maid, a pretty English maid, should replace her, that doll, that puppet. Oh, how droll, what grim absurdity, what a joke that would be, one that she had to express repeatedly, further tightening her face, compressing her lips and looking at herself repeatedly in the mirrors of her mistress.

CCX

Joan R. described the mask assumed by women analysands as a trait of deception, concealing despair under feigned compliance and superficial politeness. It was a beautiful illustration, a place-holder for no place at all, or at least, a place that did not as yet exist. It was a hysterical position, as Freud and Breuer's patients demonstrated, though one should not too rapidly conflate hysteria with femininity (but it is done, nonetheless). Joan R. 'discovered' masquerade, writing 'Femininity as a masquerade' in 1929, describing a defensive mask of a particular kind, one that is assumed to hide masculinity. If something was felt to be forbidden—and the psychoanalyst Colette S. said, after Jacques L., that it was phallic jouissance—it was because to take it, to assume it, would lead to loss, which for Joan, was the loss of femininity. In any case, any attempt to find another way of definition other than defining relations with masculinity was really very difficult and often viewed somewhat unfavourably. Jacques said that representation of the Other was lacking between the two opposed worlds designated as the feminine and masculinity, designated, that is by sexuality (which, moreover, is constituted on at least two levels). He was clear that Freud, in setting up the bases of love on a polar reference of activity/passivity, was making a metaphor from what is unfathomable in sexual difference; an opposition that was 'poured, moulded, injected'.

CCXI

The French maid had the look of a woman of the streets in the reign of the Terror. She watched the English maid in a malicious way, and it seemed the pretty maid was her rival for the affection of her mistress. She declared herself to be the true maid, the real attendant, bringing cloaks and shawls and wraps, not the pretty girl, but it was the pretty girl whom the mistress meant, and Hortense looked on, unnoticed, her lips tightly set, as the pretty girl dropped the shawl lightly in place around the slightly stooped shoulders of the mistress, who drove off in her carriage with the pretty girl while Hortense remained standing where she had alighted, the wrappers over her arm. Prideful, imperious, and punished: she stayed perfectly still, rigid, and when the carriage turned, not in the least discomposed, she took off her shoes and walked after it though the wet grass. The onlookers discussed her: one asked if she was mad, but no, replied another, she had as good a head on her as any but was high and passionate, and having given notice, having had others put above her, she had not taken kindly to that. But why did she walk through the water, the wet grass, without her shoes? Was it to cool her anger? No, it was because she fancied it as blood, blood that she would as soon as walk though as anything else, and there would be blood, a man shot through the heart, but that was later, when the man, a lawyer, threatened to have her jailed, when he would not write a reference for her, and what kind of work was there for a French maid without a reference? And later still, she would pant like a tigress. For now, at this moment, she was a steadfast, even peaceful, figure in the landscape, shoeless, quietly walking through wet grass.

In another place, another place entirely, where Hortense might be found, or where one might be asked to find Hortense as a little riddle or a guessing game or an unveiling, there was a bloody floor or a bloody ground, like a battlefield, it might be conjectured, though that would have been a *champ de bataille,* as Alina R. said, adding it might have been a butcher's shop, asking what kind of language was spoken there, and of course it would be *louchébem,* the argot of prisoners and butchers and the French Resistance in which words are camouflaged. Of course, Alina would say that, having made an account of the sexual encounters between a young woman and her butcher employer in a seaside town. (The story began with dismemberment, a knife blade plunging gently into muscle; the butcher began by whispering obscenities into her ear, his fantasies among the carcasses, the body parts, merging human and animal flesh, alive and dead; he would eat her, he said, he would eat her arse and her breasts her shoulders her arms her navel and the small of her back her thighs her legs her knees her toes.) There, all the monstrosities violated Hortense's atrocious gestures, the solitude, her erotic mechanics, the lethargy, her amorous dynamic. There, under the surveillance of childhood, she had been the ardent hygiene of races. There, she was under the letter H. There, her door opened to misery. There, the morality of real beings decorporated in its passion on or in its action. There, in terrible shudders of unskilled loves on the blood-stained floor, and there, by *l'hydrogène clarteux,* bleached, find Hortense: the riddle of the letter, the mystery of the letter, among hygiene, hydrogen, the aspiration of breath that closes one more fairy tale. *Là là.* There there. *Lheretatte lheretatte.* In another place, it might have been evident that 'Hortense' derives from *hortus,* a garden, a gardener.

CCXIII

Oh, the beautiful Hortense. Oh *la belle Hortens*e, a distracted
student of philosophy who appeared outside the grocer's
shop, wearing a tiny mini-dress that barely covered her, but
it was expensive, and all the looks turned to her, and she
had no knickers on under the dress and she was late, as five
pairs of eyes watched her disappear into rue de Citoyens;
the narrator felt the omission of a little slip of cloth might
create an extremely difficult situation for his future. To be
honest, Hortense did not really get much of a look in herself,
though she was ogled endlessly, and then later, in another
book, she was kidnapped and a dog was murdered, and
later still, she was exiled to Queneau'stown and forced to
play the role of Ophelia, and something was certainly amiss.
That is what happened to women in the Oulipo, which has
only ever admitted six women so far. Ciphers. Archetypes.
Same old, same old. In the *ouvroir*, women do what is
appropriate to their sex. So Juliana S. and Stephanie Y. made
their own manifesto, the Foulipo, taking on and off their
clothes as they delivered it amid a great deal of shouting in
the room. They asked what they needed and they asked what
they wanted. They asked if there could be a new formation.
They needed more addition and less constraint. They wanted
complications and interconnections. They did not want to
be caught in the very apparatus they sought to critique.

In Maresfield Gardens, Mary, Mabbie, Dorothy's daughter, took an overdose of sleeping pills. She died in hospital three days later. In Vienna, Anna F. had analysed Mabbie and her brother Robert when they were children, and later, in London, when they were adults. Mary/Mabbie flew from New York asking for analysis once again with Anna, despite Anna's advice to continue with her analyst Marianne Kris in New York. Mabbie was torn, some felt, between two mothers. Mabbie once said that in analysis with Anna, her thoughts fell like Cornflakes. Anna always wanted to change the children in analysis with her. Mabbie used to come to London every year for her summer analyses. Robert was already dead, of a heart attack or suicide (accounts differ), but he had been very sad for a very long time. The other children, Tinky and Mikey, survived their older siblings and their mother. Anna analysed them too (accounts differ). If she did, they survived her. They were all useful for her work. She wrote to Max Eitingon that sometimes she thought she did not only want to make them healthy, but to have them, or something of them, for herself. It was, she felt, a desire that was useful for her work, but sometime or other it would disturb them, really disturb them, and so it was stupid, her need. Mabbie's death was not talked about. That is, it remained mysterious, as the *fiancée* of Robert's son remarked, following a visit to London. She felt Paula implied that she could say more but it seemed as if Paula had been ordered *under no circumstances* to answer certain questions. Paula cooked for her in the kitchen, but would not approach this subject, Mabbie's husband and children were very sad and they were very angry; they were angry that psychoanalysis had not helped Mabbie. They thought that she should have been given chemical treatment. The family would talk about the pain and damage wrought on Dorothy's children by Anna, by psychoanalysis.

This was a ghost story or a fable or a moral tale, which Amina C. wrote sparingly, precisely, sharply, elliptically, archly, or as if it were unfolding like a painting, stretching to its edge, the limit where it met the world. A cleaning woman who worked in a museum of art wanted to write, but she had not published anything, and to say that she was a maid would probably have been a more accurate way to explain who she was, she observed. In the museum, she mopped the floors, she scrubbed the walls, she looked out of the windows where the paintings beside her were reflected in the glass and she saw herself in them. She was often taken in by the scenes of paintings, just as she was taken in by a ballet performance. She was quite invisible until a rich man saw her, until the rich man married her. The woman exchanged one form or labour for another (but the husband always had sex the way she wanted); another woman was obliged to clean for her and there was a combative relation between them. She watched her friend dance the role of a Wili in *Giselle*; her friend danced it mournfully. She wondered if her maid had friends. The maid was beautiful but people do not marry their maids. The maid became her husband's lover and she heard the moaning, the creaking springs of the bed. She left her husband and that brought her closer to writing; he would give her money, enough to live on, and people would be told that she had refused to have a child, that she was unstable. She said that she was not unstable. She thought living in the country would help her to write, to write about paintings. She had her own body, she had her own chair. She took the dog with her. She had everything she wanted. She no longer had to work as a maid or a wife. She looked at paintings with snow in them. She seemed to mirror a black dog running wildly in a landscape.

CCXVI

FIGURES, remembered in order of appearance, subject to inexactitude or error:

1. Huddled together in a barren landscape.
2. Fading into a red background.
3. Setting fire to ships; pointing to the distance.
4. Surprised while reading.
5. Standing by a fringed velvet chair.
6. Lying down, but looking up.
7. Looking at the devil in the form of a goat.
8. Holding a book in pink-and-gold cloth.
9. Carrying a dead man; giving milk from the breast; asking for shelter; clothing the naked; comforting a cripple; drinking water from the jawbone of a donkey.
10. Holding a lamb and a book, in the guise of a saint.
11. Reading a letter by a window.
12. Standing partly in the shadows.
13. Hurrying to another place.
14. Floating in the air.
15. Ascending or falling.
16. Clumped together in a tree, being lectured.
17. Unfinished.
18. Holding back a man at arm's length; covering the mouth in disbelief.
19. Running wildly. Yes.

In the Gemäldegalerie Alte Meister of the Staatliche Kunstsammlungen Dresden, 'Dora'—that is, Ida—stood in front of the Sistine Madonna, a painting that greatly appealed to her. She was enraptured by it, standing in silent admiration. She was not the only person to have been transfixed by it, to have experienced rapid heartbeat, confusion, fainting, or hallucination. These responses were frequent among the painting's viewers. Some felt quite hysterical. For instance, George Eliot's heart swelled too much for her to remain comfortably before the painting. Widely revered, it was infinitely reproduced. Wilhelm Grimm had a copper-plate engraving in his sitting-room. His son, the art historian Herman Grimm, author of *Das Lebens Raffaels*, had a large phototype of the painting that made him feel assailed by the forms of mother and child, their gazes fixed upon him, as if the space in which the framed reproduction hung no longer was his but instead, belonged to the Madonna.

CCXVIII

W. B. wrote a long footnote invoking the history of the Sistine Madonna as instance of two opposed modes of reception and the oscillation between them, quoting Hegel on the work of art as a beautiful image with a spirit, addressing its beholder and incorporating something external: the Madonna steps forward, treading over the clouds, a painted figure entering the space in which the painting is seen, crossing a threshold between the space in the image and the space of its exhibition. 'Dora' saw the Madonna, she said. Freud said she saw the Virgin Mother; he said that she saw herself: there, in her phantasy of defloration, in her phantasy of childbirth, in her motherliness towards the K's children, in the oppression of imputations of sexual guilt, in her longing for a child, in her homosexual love for Frau K. There were other pictures, *Bilder*—a thick wood, nymphs, the views of a town. Freud felt they all depicted the female genitals in one way or another, a neat matter of representation, when all is said and done, eventually, sooner or later, in the long run, broadly speaking, by and large, at the end of the day, of the infinite substitutability of women.

Among everything that is missing, 'the pathos-ridden holes' (as W. K. called the blank unpunished places that artists and writers leave behind), were fifteen sketches of Anna A. by Modigliani. He drew her head bedecked with the jewellery of Egyptian queens and dancers and love curled like a snake in a ball. He gave her sixteen drawings and all disappeared in Tsarskoye Selo, now Pushkin, during the first revolution. He wrote to her all winter in Paris; he told her she was part of him, that she possessed him, that they understood each other. The letters were lost, burnt in the fire, like the drawings. Ten portrait paintings were also lost, but some said Anna had hidden them. One sketch remained, and she said it was an inheritance. She said he did not draw her from life, but alone, in his room, but others said he drew her in the Egyptian galleries of the Louvre. He said that women who were worth painting always looked clumsy with their clothes on. He asked her to have the drawings framed, to hang them in her room. They talked about poetry, about Verlaine, Rimbaud, Baudelaire, Mallarmé, Lautréamont. He always carried about with him *Les Chants de Maldoror*. Once Anna A. threw red roses through his window into his studio when he was absent. He complained that he could not understand her poems. Anna A. asked all the people who came from Paris to Russia for news of him. During a meeting of the Writers' Union she was given a copy of a French art review in which there was a photograph of him and a long obituary; she learnt that he was a great painter of the twentieth century, she learnt that he was dead. Anna A. called the books of her translations of the work of others 'animals', while her own books were 'people'. She declined to translate Baudelaire or Mallarmé, saying she would not dream of translating anyone other than mediocrities.

CCXX

In a play by Apollinaire, Theresa, tired of being a woman, done with submission, became Tiresias when the two birds of her fraility, utterly delicious, good enough to eat, two balloons, one red, one blue, popped out of her blouse, flew up into the air on strings and she pulled the strings down to her, bobbed them about then exploded them with a cigarette lighter, getting rid of her mammaries and her beard, and yes, a moustache too, grew, and she felt devilishly virile, a stallion, a bull, a *torero*. He said there were no symbols in his play, that it was quite transparent. Theresa was fed up with cooking; she wanted to be a soldier, an artist, an MP a barrister a member of the government. She wanted to be a doctor a mathematician a philosopher a chemist a page in a restaurant a little telegraph-boy. In Neu Glück, Apollinaire fell under the charm of Annie P., an English governess. He was crazy about her and mad with love, told her he would jump over a cliff as a token of their passion; the young governess took fright, resigned her employment, fled back to England, leaving for America in 1905. She became Mrs Postings on a ranch in California, and in 1947, twenty-nine years after Apollinaire's death, knew nothing about him, not under that name, nor that she was the amorous heroine of an important French poet. If she remained insensitive to the advances of the young man, she said it was because she was then a stupid little girl who could not let herself love him, mainly because of her puritanical education. She said that those who love his poetry should be grateful to her for not having married him. If she had, who knows, she said, perhaps such poetry would not have been written. She told her interviewer that she would be delighted to read some of his works if they might be sent to her.

FORMS, in no particular order, from memory, subject to inexactitude or error:

1. Alexandrine.
2. Ottava rima.
3. Cento.
4. Villanelle.
5. Sonnet.
6. Elegy.
7. Ode.
8. Sestina.
9. Palinode.
10. Pentina.
11. Lyric.
12. Idyll.
13. Ballad.
14. Eclogue.
15. Rondeau.
16. Pantoum.
17. Triolet.
18. Fable.
19. Fugue. Running wildly. Yes.

This year it seemed that all the young poets were reading Anna M. It was quite sudden, this close attention to one who had never sought it, a woman who had enclosed herself increasingly, who had little interest in being published but continued to write and draw, thousands and thousands of poems written by hand, even more ink drawings, and over eight hundred notebooks. Sometimes she worked on a poem for thirty years [the proper time of writing, as Louis Z. returned to the same poem, 'A', continued, came out of mysteries]. Thin lines of thought were her *raison d'être*. Sean B. wrote about her in 2011, saying that her poems were like walking into a room in the middle of a conversation. He wrote that the work disrupted, no, interrupted, and this was the voice of the poem, its method of communication, under attack, countering attack, in danger of disappearing, no, of being forced to disappear. Anna M. said she was harassed, attacked, threatened with strangulation if she dared speak, that she was silenced. She wrote that some must never be allowed near her poems, her poetry was not for them, and she would speak a language they could not comprehend. It might go like this, for example: [listen/read as though you entered the room where she was speaking and Sean B. and I were listening] grist to the mill Camille Desmoulins free / mistressclasses sc cross coloured glass / scrovlong chiselled pros & cons slouch hat / raised gutted close tense racing singing / lachesis a back was taken for you unwanted. [And now you can leave, this tiny extract ringing in your ears. Sean B. left us and it was too soon.] She changed her name, her names: Anna became Grace and Nancy, 'son' became '*sohn*', and the daughter, the daughter of Morris, the daughter of Clementina, was still the 'son of' in both languages. She was lost at the memory of her parents dancing. She read by the light of the moon. She had become her enemy who she could please. She was imagined to be who she was not for she was not her. She wrote in her *kiosque botanique*.

CCXXIII

In Berne in 1910 Eugen Bleuler spoke of conflicting feelings towards a person or object, feelings held simultaneously in an insoluble concurrence: accounts are kept but cannot be summarised in a consistent record, like the mother who killed her child yet laughed as she cried in despair. Freud took up Bleuler's idea of 'ambivalence' as an opposition between love and hate, between telling and not telling, took it up with enthusiasm, *glücklich, gut, passend, trefflich*, happily chosen, excellent, apt, hitting its mark. Anna F. observed the contradictory consequences of the development of the ego, the intrasystematic contradictions of the id, the oppositions of the drives. Melanie K. formulated her theory of depression on ambivalence, a dialectic of good and bad objects, taken in, spat out, damaged and repaired bodies incorporated. Anna F. was resistant to Melanie K.'s views, but Alix S. felt Anna simply hated her on personal grounds, thinking she was a low woman, and that someone ought to speak to Anna about her general sniffiness. Melanie K. said there should be no mistake, she was a Freudian but not an Anna Freudian. Jacques L. made a new word of oppositions, of two passions of being (the third is ignorance), bringing them into one, a montage-writing, finding 'ambivalence' to be a bastardised name that failed to shake up its setting, one that did not act from within. It is *hainamoration*, hateloving, combining noun and adjective. This is far from being simply a matter of mixed feelings: this is the fundamental split of a subject produced by language. Jacques said he did not think a little bit of hateloving ever killed anyone (*étouffé* he said, suffocated), and not to tell him any stories about Madame F., her system was in an impasse. As for Madame K., she plastered on symbolisations, brutally grafted them, arbitrarily. Jacques raised an eyebrow at her inadequate articulation. There were, he said, two trends in psychoanalysis, associated, in shorthand, with two women. However, he had other fish to fry than to qualify either trends or women.

CCXXIV

Ananda D. wrote in French, but English, Hindi, Creole, wound into the threads of her sentences. Eve said that Saad borrowed words from other people, that they would help him fool them, and yes, he would get out. The real life was elsewhere. He was upset, for he felt that if he used them, they were his, he took them, words did not belong to anyone. Saad listened to his teacher reciting Rimbaud, hearing something that stopped him, held him, made him scrawl the words across walls. He would bring Eve out from her ruins, but her time was not like the others, and violence would be her escape. All she gave was the shadow of her body in the barter for money. She did not want to let Saad take the blame for what she had done; the violence was there, everywhere, and she was like a sculpted rock.

Jacques L. said that knowledge of existence is mediated through the imaginary psychic and social relations that structure a sense of self in the first place. He thought about Anna F.'s work on the ego. He thought *Verneinung*, that is, negation or denial, was fundamental to the misrecognitions that structure the experience of reality and self. He might have put it like this: you are an animal subject to death, to violent instinctual drives; you disavow this dimension so you may function as a 'normal' human being, but the reality of your aggression, sexuality, and mortality does not disappear. No, it does not. In fact, the distressing truths about your nature forms the id, which puts a constant pressure on your consciousness, and actually, it erupts in your dreams, your neuroses, and your psychotic episodes. Oh, what an unhappy animal you are, an animal that dreams, twitching in your sleep, a prey to language, even in repose, and that is where your domestication led you, you poor old imperfect thing, you piteous donkey, you pathetic ass, you dull downtrodden brute, you wretchedly burdened beast. Anna M. wrote that she had been made of no. no certainly. no no, and then nothing, nada, and never, dead from the start, an ass's head. an nn. [I have taken liberties in stringing together her words, in omitting words. I would say to her that I was sorry, to be another mind that by error has been taken in the gentlest of winds, but winds are sometimes gods with dominion over flowers and plants.]

CCXXVI

Jérôme-Adolphe Blanqui noted that the spinning and weaving of Lyon and Nîmes was entirely patriarchal; it employed a great many women and children but without ruining them, allowing them to stay in their beautiful valleys where they cultivated their silkworms and unwound their cocoons. Their work never became a factory industry, though the division of labour took on a special character, remaining independent, not assembled in the same workshop or under a single master. They were winders, throwsters, dyers, sizers, and weavers.

Rosmarie W. wrote that even if a woman sat at a loom, it did not mean she must weave a cosmogony or clothes to cover the emptiness underneath. Later she said she had read how women prisoners who were to be hanged had to wear rubber knickers and a dress sewn about their knees because the uterus and ovaries spill with the shock down the chute. Some women, however, dressed as if they were going to a party, wearing, for example, a large hat with pronounced crimson trimmings or neat white stockings with white slippers. Others walked barefoot to their execution and excused themselves to their executioner, sweetly, with concern, when they stepped on his foot, quite by accident, and *monsieur*, they were sorry, they did not do it on purpose.

Helen was weaving a great double-folded crimson or purple web, working in scenes of the endless bloody struggles being fought for her sake. Iris interrupted her to announce the duel between Menelaus and Paris. Helen stopped her work and the web was never mentioned again. Andromache wove a cloak for Hector; her web was also double-fold, scattered with flowers of different hues. When his death was announced, she dropped her shuttle. She imagined that the cloth she and her servants had been weaving would become the clothes to be worn at his funeral. She was then raped and enslaved by Agamemnon. Circe wove a web that was delicate, exquisite, and dazzling. She was weaving when Odysseus arrived on her island. Calypso was weaving when Hermes told her she must let Odysseus go. Circe and Calypso sang while they wove, but Philomena did not sing as she wove the scene of her rape on her Thracian web, for her tongue had been cut out by the man who raped her; she was sharp-witted, cunning, and would tell the story of her wrongs. Clytemnestra wove a fine web, crimson or purple, for Agamemnon; it enveloped and immobilised him as she stabbed him in revenge for the death of their daughter. Medea had been quite content that Creusa should make friends with her children, but when Jason betrayed her, Medea, the planner, the schemer, did not hesitate to kill his new bride, sending her a poisoned *peplos* that sucked her blood and devoured her limbs, melting them like the resin of a pine tree, burning her to death. [There was also the matter of the death of her brother and of her children, but that is quite enough mythology, as I have said already, echoed by my editor, and my point here, that is, my train of thought, follows weaving and garments, textile and text, sentences and the sewn, frames and bodies, matters that hang by a thread, back and forth, back and forth. *Ah*.]

[However,] Andromache's son by Hector, Astyanax, was thrown from the city walls of Troy. His battered corpse was given to his grandmother, Hecuba. All she could do for him was bury him, though she knew that the dead cared little about burial, that it was the vanity of the living. She was taken as a slave by Odysseus, a man as false in hate as in love, and one account said she cursed him, snarling at him, and the gods turned her into a dog. Another described the madness that fell upon her when she saw the bodies of her children, her son murdered, her daughter sacrificed, the daughter who preferred death to slavery, and she began barking like dog, howling, a she-dog with fiery eyes. She would kill him, yes, she would tear out the eyes of the man who killed her son for gold, and he would cry out in agony, blinded of the light of his eyes, howling like a wild four-footed beast, and she would kill his sons, and that was just and she had cause for delight.

CCXXX

Roland B. used the metaphor of 'unthreading' for describing, material translated into language, *parfiler*, to unthread, to undo, thread by thread, but the equivalent of the word, to unthread a word, said Voltaire to Madame de Pompadour, was not to be found in Cicero's discourses. *Chère madame*, official and chief mistress of a king, Jeanne-Antoinette had her own printing press [imagine that, to be able to print one's own works when no other would publish them, that would teach them, those bastards, the swine who steal one's words]. Madame made engravings after her own image, with the help of Boucher, applying her rouge. Madame engraved onyx, jasper, and other semi-precious stones. Madame did not care about the king's other mistresses; those pretty little girls with no education would not take him from her. She could memorise entire plays and understood the fine art of conversation. She held his heart.

Arlette F. followed the trial of a woman in the eighteenth century, declared as an adulterer by her husband. She noted how the witness statements described a world other than that of the accused, poor innocent Anne-Sophie, scenes that came not from her modest milieu but rather from a painting by Fragonard or a libertine novel by Crébillon, from a class superior to hers, overflowing with luxury, with ribbons and jewels and other signs of wealth. Anne-Sophie's adultery was a libertine fiction. Arlette permitted herself to speculate thus: if the prosecutor, the judge, the clerks, the witnesses had lied in dressing Anne-Sophie in aristocratic outfits, in attributing licentious acts, was it not because this was the world they knew well from attentive observance of those who governed them, fascinated by them while contemptuous of their abuses? That they invented the life of a princess for Anne-Sophie, derived from their reading, from their theatre-going, from a culture in which Marivaux and others had their place? The prosecutor invented the letters between Anne-Sophie and her lover; he wrote a lover's dialogue that echoed the exchange between, for example, a king and his mistress.

CCXXXII

Tromp as writ is the sequence of threading as repeated in treadling. It is the notation, the set of instructions for setting up the loom and for the movement of the weaver's feet: to treadle as written; what is written, once with a quill and ink, is the threading draft. Anni A. wanted to make threads be pictorial again, she said, to find a form themselves to no other end than their own orchestration, not to be sat on, to be walked on, only to be looked at. When she stopped weaving, turning away from the subtle instrument of the loom in order to make prints, she rather bitterly remarked that when it was threads, it was craft, yet when on paper, it was art. She received her longed-for pat on the shoulder, but the loom stood at the entrance to her exhibition, and circumstances still held her to threads. It was an argument whose conclusion was the textile. The loom attended the body of the weaver.

CCXXXIII

Sweetgrass is fragrant, a sacred plant with many uses: a material for basket weaving, a scent, a smudge, purifying thoughts, a medicine. Its scent intensifies with rain, with fire. Braided, the three sections represent mind, body, and soul, or love, kindness, and honesty, the hair of Mother Earth. It is planted by putting roots in the ground, not from seed. Robin K. W. wrote that in braiding sweetgrass, a certain amount of tension is needed, you have to pull a bit, and the best way is to have someone else hold the end so you pull against each other. She said she could hand you a braid, as thick and shining as the one that hung down her grandmother's back, but like that braid, it is not hers to give nor yours to take. Grass, any grass, swept through water, will cleanse it; cattail, soft rush, water mint, caboma and hornwort, water lilies and irises, the sapwood of pine, all filter and clean. Mats of human hair are used to clean up oil spills, separating oil from water. Mixed with cattle dung, hair is a fertiliser or for pest control, repelling rabbits, wild boar, and deer, but only if the deer do not know humans already. Hair ash, if the hair is pure, stops bleeding and heals wounds. *These are facts.*

CCXXXIV

One might dream of taking on a braid, Jacques D. said, without being sure of the textile to come. There was invention, discovery, in the plaiting that covered lack, even if it came from shame, as the old professor noted, as the women, he said, braided their pubic hair. There are other braids and weaves. Hair can be attached to the head with a weave, a band of hair bound by a sewn weft, sewn into thin plaits of the recipient's own hair, or braided, extended from the scalp without a binding weft. There is Remy hair, in which all the strands face the same way, often coming from a single head. There is virgin hair, which is unprocessed, and double drawn, all the same length. There is deep wave Indian hair. There is Brazilian hair and Peruvian body wave hair. There is Mongolian deep curly hair. There is Afro kinky curly hair. There is Vietnamese straight, wavy, curly hair. There are hand-tied wefts and flat silk wefts, nano-linked, micro-linked, tipped, nail-tipped, flipped-on, ponytail. The hair should be very soft and have no smell at all. Women crouched on the ground in hair-processing factories, sorting the hair. Agents toured villages, offering small payments for women to part with their hair. Warders shaved and sold the hair of women prisoners. Women offered up their hair in the temples, praying for a child, a good harvest, a sick person. Husbands in rural villages forced their wives to sell their hair. Girl children swapped their hair for toys. Women auctioned their hair online to the highest bidder, and all this is now, as once they did in the marketplace, where they might have been offered in exchange silk handkerchiefs, a dozen yards of calico, a pair of high-heeled boots. It is a harvest that takes a long time to grow, one that flows most freely from the poorest places.

CCXXXV

The wolf was at the door. What could be done when the wolf arrived, when the wolf was not a kind dog that only looks like a wolf? When the wolf was a figure of speech or a field spirit taking the form of a wolf, a corn demon hiding in the last sheaves at the end of harvest? When the wolf incarnated brutishness, cruelty, voracity, gluttony, cunning, impiety, and hypocrisy? When the wolf lied? When it snuffled at the keyhole? When it wedged its paw in the widening crack in the door? When it whined and howled and scratched its way in? When it bristled hair and breathed fire? When it stole the children and ate them up? When it brought calamity, ruin, difficulties? The wolf was at the door, and it came in winter, in the cold spell when there was no money left for fuel and light. Juliana S. wrote of songs as poems, and that the refrain was when the singer made it clear they understood what was being lost. Her poems were about love and naming and movement: women walked by, migrating geese flew, and in moving, humans and non-humans were together but knew it would not be for long, though that did not stop the wanting to be together, the becoming with. She said that when she got angry, and it seemed to be often, she wanted to call some poets capitalist poets. She said that sometimes it felt like it was over and it was not, that sometimes it felt like it had just begun and it was over. She wrote that she made a list of children's names, alphabetised it, got to O, and the children who were not there yet: O, S four times, Y and Z, she loved those children too. She wrote: that winter the wolf came, and that winter, they were there, close together. How can one put one's head in the mouth of the wolf and take it out again safely? That was in the winter, the time of cold tales.

In 1933 H. D. cried, too hard, she said; she went to a restaurant with paintings of Swiss scenes, mountains, chalets, and also some Victorian snow scenes. In 1913 she visited an Austrian village, like one in the paintings, with her mother. The forest was menacing, and she cried then too, and in 1915 at her first confinement, at the coldness of the nurses, in 1918, at her broken marriage. She cried as she remembered her father's telescope, her grandfather's microscope, and she feared that she would dissolve. It was as if she had a half globe over her head and another at her feet. She called them bell jars, these two convex lenses through which she saw the world and it seemed as if everything but them had broken. She watched snowflakes through a magnified pane of glass.

CCXXXVII

As a child, standing at a window in winter, W. B. felt the flakes of falling snow told him silent stories he never quite grasped. W. B. particularly liked the glass globes containing snowy landscapes, miniature worlds which could be shaken into life in a flurry of snowflakes, a little blizzard that then settles. His friend said W. B. was attracted to everything that had alienated itself from homely aliveness, the petrified, frozen, or obsolete elements of culture, that the snow globes were dead life. Yet these interior scenes of the outside come to life, animated by the intervention of the hand that shakes them. He liked to place the objects he collected into his visitors' hands. W. B. wrote that memory let things appear small, compressed them. He imagined writing an essay that could be squeezed onto a single sheet of paper, that everything might contract. He imagined that the world might be transformed, the material world, *Stoffwelt*, the stuff that is the mute, soft, and flocky element that—like the snow tempest in the small snow globes—clouds over the core of things. Compacting. Covering. Like the irresolute flakes of the first snow.

Sabine was the magician's assistant. The magician was dead. The book opened with the end of the story. That was one of the tricks. But that was not the end of the story, not at all, though Sabine was in despair, alone apart from the magician's rabbit and speaking with ghosts, well, one revenant, the lover of the magician, mourning the magician, her husband, who had a history and a family he had kept from her, and which through his death, she had to encounter. There was a move to Nebraska in the dead of winter to stay with the past of the magician she did not know, to meet it and its violence. There was a dead father. The son killed the father. If the son does not kill the father, the father will kill the son. Here, the snow was an envelope, inescapable, banked in high hills, pooling and vanishing, like walking into something boiling, but bone-crushingly cold. There was violence in the snow, the wind, the icy undistinguished expanses. Ann P. knew how to tell this story, these stories, entwining them with tricks of juxtaposition, sleight of hand, sentiment avoided adroitly, but always telling the same story, its form unchanging, starting with a group of people in a room, say. A magician's assistant has to know the trick; she has to know how it turns out, she has to know it like she knows her own name. She must become an encyclopaedia of magic; she must work the trick and shuffle the cards. It cannot work any other way. The magician needs his lovely assistant. How he needs *her*... The magician had taken her hand; he had lain her down, lifted her, balanced her on the point of a chair, brought her back down, and magic was like love, she thought. She was a floating woman.

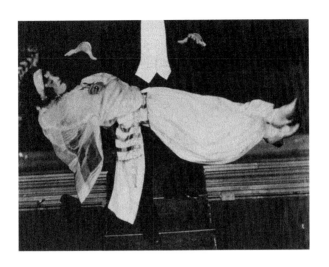

CCXXXIX

In Massenet's opera *Cendrillon*, a prologue invited the audience to escape from dark realities, to believe in the fabulous tableaux. The invitation was repeated at the end. This was only one version, of course, but the story was familiar: Lucette, Cendrillon, was one of three daughters, but the other two were not her sisters. Lucette, Cendrillon, could not go to the ball. Her stepmother forbade it, and her father was too weak to protest. Thank goodness for fairy godmothers, who produced beautiful dresses and magical slippers of glass, so the poor girls who were sleeping in exhaustion by the fire, having completed their household tasks, could go to the ball after all, unrecognised, but they had always to leave by midnight, and then they always left one slipper behind, and the princes, the handsome melancholic princes—in this case, played by a *soprano de sentiment*—had to look for them, and in this case, the girl recalled her mother's death and fled into the night to die on her own. And then the princes found the girls who ran away and they put the slippers on them, and obviously, the slippers fit. In other cases, the stepsisters tried to force their feet into the little glass slippers, which might also have been little slippers made of fur, but they did not succeed, and the slippers slipped as smooth as anything onto the feet of the poor girls who had to work as kitchen maids, fitting their little feet as if the slippers were made of wax, not of glass or fur. These girls then married the princes and they lived in the palaces, and sometimes they invited their stepsisters to live there and married them off to courtiers. That was the general account, though the Grimm brothers embellished it: the slipper was golden, and the stepsisters, who had beautiful feet, cut off a toe in one case, a heel in the other, the knife given by their mother, in order to squeeze their feet, their no-longer beautiful bleeding feet, into the slipper, and in both cases, the slipper filled with blood, which gave the game away, and the prince found the right bride, the girl of his dreams.

The mouse queen took her revenge for the death of her mouse children in Drosselmeyer's traps on the princess Pirlipat. Surrounding the princess with cats did not work, for the nursemaids who were supposed to keep the cats awake by stroking them fell asleep. The mouse queen turned the child into a nutcracker, giving her an enormous head, a wide grinning mouth, and a beard. The astrologers said the only way to cure her was to find a magic nut that must be given to her by a man who had never worn boots, who must not open his eyes when he put the kernel into her eager little open mouth nor stumble after he placed it there, popping it in while taking seven steps back. The nut was at last found in the possession of a puppet-maker. The bootless puppet-maker's son cracked the nut easily and Pirlipat was once again beautiful, but he stumbled, the clumsy lad, stepping on the mouse queen, and so he was cursed himself and become the nutcracker. Oh, how ugly he was, too ugly for the ungrateful princess to marry him, and so he was banished. [I will cut a long story short.] Mouse king whispered to Marie in the night. Mouse king threatened to bite the nutcracker to pieces unless she gave him sweets and dolls. Girl gave him what he asked for in the night, but he wanted more and more. [They always do.] Nutcracker said if he had a sword he would kill the mouse king. [Again, I will make it short.] Mouse king dead, magic kingdom, girl fell asleep in the palace of the ugly nutcracker, girl came home, told mother, mother did not believe her even when shown the evidence, girl forbidden to speak of her dreams, *et cetera*. [Same old, same old.] Drosselmeyer was repairing one of her father's clocks, Marie swore she would love the nutcracker whatever he looked like, and then bang! she fell off her chair and fainted.

CCXLI

That was not quite the end of it. The nephew of Drosselmeyer arrived, announced by Marie's mother. Of course he was the nutcracker, the clumsy recipient of the mouse queen's curse. He asked Marie to marry him and returned for her a year and a day later, according to one of the usual arbitrary laws of fairy tales, to take her to the magic kingdom of the dolls, where she became queen, according to the usual pattern of wish-fulfilment in fairy tales. In the ballet, the story was different: the death of the mouse king broke the spell, Marie or rather, Clara, and the prince had delicious cakes on a glittering throne, there were dances: Spanish, Arabian, Russian, Chinese, the Mirliton Dance, the Waltz of Flowers. The Sugar Plum Fairy and her escort danced a *pas de deux*, and Clara and the prince departed in a sleigh pulled by flying reindeer. There was an army of mice, and while some girls might prefer a tulle skirt and to dance with the snowflakes, others might be delighted by an over-sized furry head and a long whip-like tail, as Ann P. wrote, and the child May, the daughter of Ann P.'s narrator, stayed in character during rehearsals, scurrying, nibbling, irritatingly mouse-like. When the curtain rose on the ballet, her father felt it might have been the house of his childhood, the house under dispute, the house he and his sister had lost, an architectural mirage. On the stage, he could have recreated his past by a simple rearrangement of the furniture. However, he knew that it was not really the house they had lost but their mother and their father. Over the years he and sister drove to the house, watching it from outside. When eventually they returned, the interior of the house looked exactly as it had done when they walked out thirty years before. It had been maintained with great tenderness.

CCXLII

Heimlich describes what belongs to the house; it is not strange, not unfamiliar, not unfriendly nor untame. It belongs to the house or to the family, comfortable in a friendly way, agreeably restful, secure, where one goes to sleep so soft and warm, so happy, so cosy, so intimate. But it carries its opposite among its shades of meaning and what is homely becomes unhomely, full of terrors, something concealed and kept out of sight, and vague forms glide about in the night. One might call it the return of the repressed, a disquieting strangeness, arising from the child's fear of the dark, the fear of the Sand-Man, but not the Sand-Man who sprinkles sand into the children's eyes to make them sleep and dream, blowing softly on their necks and does not hurt them, for he is very fond of children and wants them only to be quiet so he can tell them lovely stories, but the other Sand-Man, the one who comes when children will not go to bed and throws sand in their eyes so they jump out of their heads all bleeding, carrying them off in a sack to the moon where he feeds the eyes to his own children, who are like horrible little birds in their nest, and the Sand-Man's nasty children have sharp beaks which they use to peck the eyes of naughty children.

Some characters: Nathaniel, a student, happy but with terrifying memories, Coppelius, a lawyer, a frightening and repulsive person, Nathanial's father, now dead, a nursemaid, Coppola, an itinerant optician, Spalazani, a professor, Olympia, the beautiful daughter of the professor, strangely silent and motionless for she is a clockwork automaton, Clara, the student's betrothed.

Some scenes: two men working at a brazier with glowing flames, a little eavesdropper who heard a man calling out and screamed aloud, a father who saves his son from blindness, weather-glasses on sale in the street and eyes also offered, men quarrelling over a wooden doll, a curious object moving through the streets, seen from a high tower through a spy-glass, attacks of madness, a leap over a parapet resulting in a shattered skull.

Some themes: intellectual uncertainty, the fear of damaging or losing one's eyes, the punishment of castration, the relation between eye and male organ, the disturbance of love, dreaded fathers, childhood life, living dolls, the double, telepathy, primary narcissism, pathological mental processes, regression, repetition (under certain conditions), compulsion, repression, the return of the dead, the reanimation of the dead, the phantasy of inter-uterine existence, social parody.

Conclusion: The anxiety, not of loss, but of gaining too much, through too close a presence; as Jacques L. might put it, the lack of the support of the lack, whether blinded or orphaned.

CCXLIV

A child, Anne, in Anna's and Dorothy's war-time nursery wanted big bombs and lots of guns. She wanted to make a big hole in the wall and the house would be all open and she would bleed and everyone would bleed.

CCXLV

Aimée's mother had another child, Aimée's older sister, who fell into an open furnace and died from her burns. Aimée dreamt of open coffins. Her daughter was stillborn, choked by the cord. When her son was born, she feared others would harm him. She would not leave the house, she was completely mute. She was torn between care for her son and the desire to live her life. Her novel, which no-one would publish, was entitled *Le Détracteur*; Aimée was the name of its heroine who wanted to be thought as lovely as a stone in the water. She wanted to write, to become a writer and be published, but instead she was written: the poets killed her in effigy and the bandits killed; they cut in pieces and the bandits cut in pieces, they made secrets and the people made secrets. Lacan did not even return her manuscripts to her, despite her repeated requests for them. In hospital, she stopped writing, devoting herself to embroidering instead. However, later, her son said that his mother became God's chosen one, moved by her qualities in overcoming so many trials. She was writing the story of the women in the Bible in alexandrines. She read him one stanza, splendidly. Her son placed an emphasis on the maternal voice as a sound envelope, a fine, ephemeral membrane.

CCXLVI

Anne T. wrote a story about a woman who walked away from her family on a beach and just kept on going until she got to a new town to make a new life. She left one cat behind, Vernon, and on the point of making a new life, she acquired another, a kitten, George, when she was determined that she would no longer care for anything. His fur was startlingly soft. It reminded her of milkweed. When she lay on her bed in her lodgings, she felt the denting of the mattress. The kitten passed behind her, brushed the back of her body as if by chance but it was not. She felt they were performing a dance, courtly, dignified, elaborate. It was a delicate account of negotiated relationships. This was one way, a clear way, to tell a story of departure, of becoming.

CCXLVII

From Rome on 16 September 1923, halfway through his analysis of Anna, Freud sent the postcard on which he wrote that Anna was as gay as a chaffinch. On their return from their 'Roman adventures', Anna re-read their notes—all that they experienced there came to life again. She sought to record the memory, to remember better. She noted down the journey from Florence to Rome, on 1 September, hot and uncomfortable, too many noisy Americans from Cincinnati, who took her father and her for Italians, wives who demand information about Roman pearls, hills that reminded her of the background of numerous images of the Madonna. From the train, she did not see many people, but there were many small olive trees, among them the garlands of vines. Thirty minutes before arrival her papa pointed out the dome of St Peter's, and at midday they arrived in Rome and were taken to their hotel, the Hotel Eden, by the hotel's omnibus. It was hard to see anything from the bus, but her papa showed her the baths of Diocletien near the train terminus. They were given two comfortable rooms, with a huge bathroom, numbers 119 and 120, the windows giving onto the Via de Porta Pinciano. At first they feared the south-west aspect would make their rooms too hot, and wondered if they should change them, but their fears were groundless. Except to protect the rooms from the sun, they never had to draw the curtains, for no-one could over-look them. In front of the window of her papa's room was a line of particularly pointed cyprus trees, solemnly nodding their heads in the light current of air—as they did in 1913, said her papa. They rearranged the furniture, turning a marble-topped washstand into a games table. Her papa's desk had to be protected from the wind.

An excursion to the cinema one evening was noted. Perhaps, it is thought by some, Freud remained at the Hotel Eden, while Anna went out to the flick with the daughter of the shareholder of the hotel, for there was a letter written on the same day to the family at home that Anna was going out with that young woman. If so, perhaps the father waited up for the daughter's return, catching up on his correspondence in his hotel suite. In 1923 in Rome, the Italian films that they might have seen included *A morte! Signor ladro*, 'To death! Mr Thief', though it was not released until December, or *La dama de Chez Maxim's*, after a farce by Feydeau, or *Ali spezzate*, 'Broken Wings'. They might have seen *The Ten Commandmants*, of course, for Cecil B. DeMille's film was released that year, which told the story of Moses leading the Jews from Egypt to the Promised Land, or *The Eternal City*, a film now lost, directed by George Fitzmaurice, in which there is footage of King Victor Emmanuel III and Benito Mussolini reviewing Italian troops, or *Salomé*, directed by Charles Bryant, in which Salomé, the daughter of Herodias, seduces her step-father Herod, governor of Judea, with a salacious dance.

Lucie F., Ernst's wife, wrote a letter to Felix Augenfeld on 2 October 1939, following Freud's death on 23 September. She said that the last month had been long and infinitely painful. Her father-in-law's agony started on 3 September, and the injection given by his doctor simply prolonged it, consciously, under their eyes. Until the last moment, when he was not sleeping or in the throes of pain, he was himself, gentle, kind, patient, desiring to live. Anna, she wrote, had not slept for weeks, but despite this, her father never saw her without a cheerful expression. Anna was always in his room; for four weeks, he was in bed, the doors were opened to the garden, and there was always a peaceful atmosphere, gay, almost cosy. (Lucie did not mention the terrible smell from his cancer, so awful it caused his beloved dog to run from him, and at this, only this, he faltered.) Perhaps the happiness read on Anna's face was the explanation for what Lucie was unable to understand, the fact that without mentioning it once, Freud accepted so entirely Anna's selflessness, which was destroying her. Lucie questioned Anna, who confirmed her suspicion: never, absolutely never, had he addressed a single word of thanks to her. Lucie wondered if perhaps, even in the light of this situation, he had always to be the one who gave.

Anna cried for the first time on the Friday morning when the doctor told her that her father would not regain consciousness. He had asked his doctor for morphine for it was nothing but torture and to suffer made no sense any more. He asked his doctor to tell Anna. They all watched over him that night. Anna and Lucie did not sleep. He slept for forty hours, breathing calmly. His heart stopped a little before midnight. Anna's aunt died two years later; Anna's mother died twelve years later, and Anna wrote then about losing and being lost. She remarked that a child clung to its toy as though the toy, like the child, felt hurt, discarded. Dorothy died in 1979 and Anna wore her sweaters for comfort, stroking them in a way as she had never been seen to touch Dorothy. Anna said that people forget to consider that a child or a sick adult must suffer from the fact that they need help. Her father called her Anna Antigone, his Antigone, his Anna, passionate child of passionate sire, her father's guide. He did not call her Cordelia, and he was never her mad old father, blind and raging. She was not death, the third of the Fates, and he did not have to renounce love, though he did have to make friends with the necessity of dying. Freud was seen to weep for the first time when Anna returned home from the Gestapo's roundup in 1938. Anna said that in mourning, the dreamer (it was her dream) felt caught by conflicting emotions: the joy of reunion and the remorse and guilt at having stayed away, neglecting the dead one. Dreams, like hers, were a way of overcoming mourning, of remaining loyal to the dead and turning to new ties with the living (of burying the father while incorporating him).

The Freud children enjoyed ice-skating. In Vienna, in the winter months when the temperature seldom rose above freezing-point, they used to skate on the open-air rink in the Augarten in the Leopoldstadt. They used to sail in wide circles on the ice, joining hands. Mathilde, the eldest, never lacked for admirers at the rink. Once there was an unpleasant incident [of which I shall say nothing]. Ernest Jones had a keen interest in ice-skating, comparing psychoanalysis with the sport. He said that his book *The Elements of Figure Skating* was motivated by his interest in the psychological problems of the novice skater. The book was illustrated with drawings of the elegant marks skaters left on the ice, from which the name of the sport derives. The marks are examined: the residue of jumps, toe, loop, salchow, flip, lutz, butterfly, and axel, and spins, forward, backward, scratch, biellmann, upright, sit, camel (including the illusion). The blades of the skates inscribe the surface of the ice, and more blades cut into the inscriptions. Why! It is just like the mystic writing pad, ice replacing the slab of brown resin or wax over which is the translucent sheet of waxed paper covered with a celluloid sheet, to prevent the stylus tearing the waxed paper. The permanent trace of what was written is retained on the slab of wax or resin, legible in suitable lights. Memory traces. Unlimited recording and a lasting record. Family romances. The surface must be renewed or the inscription must be destroyed.

A. was alone now, in a salon or a passageway, her costume quite different from anything she had worn before, a kind of travelling suit, elegant, severe, perhaps dark. She sat on the edge of a couch, occasionally looking at a baroque clock, an enormous object decorated with bronze figures. She looked for something in her bag; she found a letter that she began to read then tore it into sixteen pieces, dropping the pieces on the long, low table in front of the couch. She started to arrange them in the form of a game, but before she had finished, stirred them up with a sudden gesture. She gathered up the bits, tore them again, finally abandoning them in an ashtray. X appeared and she looked at him, her face blank. She remained seated; he stepped towards her. They said nothing to each other. They did not look hesitant, but resolute, though as if they were at the end of their strength. The clock struck midnight and at the second stroke she picked up her bag and walked away, stiff, expressionless. He followed her. It was as if she were a prisoner and he her guard. The strokes of the clock continued.

Agave thought her son was a lion, a wild beast to be captured. In Anne C.'s translation: she picked up his head, *the terrible head*, impaling it on her thyrsos, a staff of wild fennel covered with ivy leaves and berries, and carried it down the mountain to Thebes, leaving her sisters, exalting in her dark and bloody prize. She caught him with her bare hands; the hunt, the spectacle, was magnificent. She asked for Kadmos, her father, and for Pentheus, her son, for she wished to show them her trophy. She boasted that she had left her loom and weaving to go after bigger game. O sorrow, cried Kadmos. He cried, O grief without measure, O pity. He asked his daughter to look up at the sky; he asked her what child she bore to Echion; he asked her whose head she held in her hands, to look straight; he asked her to understand and there was unimaginable pain. Truth was an unbearable thing. O the dear body of the son, pieced together by the grandfather. There was only exile then, the departure from home and honour, only exile and despair. Kadmos would make his way as a stranger in a strange land, to live as a snake, without release from his misery; there would be no sailing down the river of death to peaceful oblivion. Agave asked where she should go, as no longer did she have a home. She bid farewell to her house and to her city, she asked to be led away to her sisters to the place of their pitiful exile. She asked that she might never remember a moment of all that had occurred. Anna F. wrote that lost souls, those condemned to wander, moan and sigh and beseech the living to help them find release, but that may only be achieved when they have detached their hopes, their demands, their expectations from the image of the dead.

L. died in June. Once she wrote that the object of desire had no proper name, but it spoke passionately, framing one's life. She wrote that it bobbed and wove, and one must be dented by it, incidentally, weaving, recovering, and maybe reaching out again for it from within the relation that was at once possessing and dispossessing, forcing one to scavenge for survival while remembering that there was a better beyond to it. The impact of the object, and the impulse that involved the patterning of attachment, were the materials of sexuality and of the optimism (at least for affective relief) that must accompany taking up a position in it. An object gave optimism, then it rained on your parade. Although that was never the end of the story, she wrote, and she was right.

Freud wrote to his daughter, signing his letters:

> With all my love
> Farewell with all my heart
> Greeting with all my love
> Father
> Papa
> Your Father
> Your Papa
> With all my heart
> Many greetings with all my heart
> Warmly
> Cordially
> Greeting from the bottom of my heart
> With all my heart, Pa
> Tender greetings to Wolf and family
> Love, Pa
> From Papa
> With the best wishes of Papa

She was his dear and unique Anna, his dear Anna, his only Anna, his dear child.

CCLVI

[How to stop writing? I had to stop and the only measure I had was the rule I imposed upon myself before I started. The end must be an unravelling, when threads are combed or carded, spread into webs or lines, and things had to be made clearer, even if only to myself. Danielle R-G. once wrote that my work was like a ball of string and when one tried to tease out a strand, others followed, came tumbling out and not one would not be returned neatly. Who was there to read me, in any case, not more than three hundred, and like S., I would prefer to live in the woods and give my visitors a good wine and lovely salad from my garden and a morsel of fine camembert and eke out my slender livelihood while listening to the birds and jostling my arguments. I gave myself a year. I set myself the limit of a page. The words would come as they would. I determined that I would not change anything, for once spoken (written), words could not be taken back, even though the words were not mine as I wrote (spoke) them. I was resolute in refusing to make connections or identify themes, even as they emerged. An analysis begins with the analysand speaking without speaking about herself; it ends when the analysand speaks about herself and so it must be over. It is a matter of going round in a circle, and in an analysis, twice round, but of course, this was not an analysis. I knew I could continue but it was the end of August then and it is the end of August now. There was a logical end-point. A song, perhaps, from a child's memory: the stepmother killed her, the father ate her, the sister gathered all her bones and tied them up in a silk scarf and buried her under a juniper tree, and she sang *tweet tweet* what a beautiful bird she was. The year passed. And years passed.]

So it could end with a song. It might be like this one, Anabelle H. singing as Sam Moore and he singing as she sang, and in that case, it would go Mountain, hill my best view, and the wolf would sound the la. This Sam was her sower, the sower of poppy seeds, in gardens, on balconies, in palaces (that were now museums). *Papaver somniferum.* Seeds and milk and honey to calm a crying sleepless child. Seeds and sugar and cinnamon with ground almonds or walnuts for *Mohnstriezel* or *Mohnkuchen*, delicate and gentle, *schmackhafte*, delicious. Or it might be the song of Daniel, the one written by Ali S. in autumn, and this one went Snow is falling in the summer / Leaves are falling in the spring / Gone are the reasons / Gone are the seasons / Time has gone and taken everything. There, the purpose was noted: to tell of bodies transformed into shapes of a different kind, following what was ignored, lost, rediscovered years later, and that this pattern would continue to repeat *ad infinitum*. Women would continue to turn into trees, giving up their bodies for garlands, their hearts beating still. That song went that Sweetly rose the sap of earth throughout her and virginal light stretched out in leaves and branches, and happy birds dwelt in her, and the tree was in moonlight as her voice sounded wordlessly from the branches. And yes, one could die from a broken heart. Or this song, yes, this one for the ending, that went It had been a long long time, and the days grew short, and the autumn weather turned the leaves to flame, and no one had time for the waiting game, for the days dwindled to a precious few, and these few precious days... Or a swan song: the last gesture or performance, ready for the final curtain, and then *encore un effort* if one were to leave in style, nicely turned out in hat and gloves and jewellery and red lipstick, in a smart coat for the coming cold season, without hissing or grunting but with fists clenched. Let it stand.

ABÉCÉDAIRE
HOW THIS BOOK WAS WRITTEN

In 2020 I was sixty-five-years old. I could not imagine how this happened. I wondered if the years simply slipped by, without me taking account of them. Yet I knew this is not true. In the recurring bouts of insomnia from which I suffer, I lay awake, calculating how many years remained to me, an estimate based on longing and family history (my mother is in her mid-ninties, while my father died in his early eighties, quite mad by then), and at the worst times of my anxiety, a longing arises that it might be over and thus, I would not have to face the day. I made a promise to myself about writing, about writing something I had no idea how to write, but which nonetheless I undertook. I established the strict internalised constraints without which I am unable to function. I ended it a year later, almost exactly.

I wrote (more or less, for promises are always hard to keep, even those made to oneself, perhaps especially those made to oneself) for five days a week for a year. I wrote no more than a page or rather, I wrote only for the length of the analytic hour, fifty minutes (though I also practiced the variable session at times). I wrote in as/in free association, on/in the page, in the production of new material from extant material, and with what preceded, from memory, but not entirely. I followed Freud's model of train travel for his theory of free association, acting 'as though, for instance, [you were] a traveller sitting next to the window of a railway carriage and describing to someone inside the carriage the changing views which [you] see outside'. I stripped back what I wrote as I wrote it, so it was short, exact, and flat in tone. (I believe the term used now is 'modern neutral', as I discovered in the course of writing/reading, although I had written like this for over twenty-five years). I practised each time a secondary revision of what had been written, reading backwards, then reading forwards.

This echoed the structure of the dream work, in which revision provides some order and intelligibility to the dream by supplementing its content with narrative coherence; as Freud writes, it 'fills up the gaps in the dream-structure with shreds and patches'. The work was intended to develop according to the addition of new material after unconscious patterns. In consequence, the content of the final work could not be fully predicted. The book was subjected to a final revision at the end of its construction, something more than (or different from) editing, though not unlike it. Some entries had to be shortened, while others were divided to become two entries. I assumed a line of thought that revealed the hidden logic that connected seemingly disconnected ideas, without attempting to enact this—indeed, this was strenuously resisted. There was to be no tethering.

As for my characters, many of their names begin with A. These are their first names; there are few surnames here, save those of the secondary male characters (sometimes). I add a surname initial. It is inconsistent. Some of these women exist or existed, others are from fiction, or write fiction. Some are friends or acquaintances. Many are absent but that does not mean they do not inhabit me. All are comrades. Gladly, I would drink with any of them in a bar, though they might try to avoid me as I thrust my too-eager friendship upon them. None are credited but a keen reader could recognise many of them, even themselves. I ran my hand along the shelves of my library or unearthed years of notebooks to extract them. None of them are me. The words are not my own; the words haunt me and inhabit me.

I invented nothing. I am the aleph.

ACKNOWLEDGEMENTS

Oh, whom to thank? Gratitude to writers and artists and my family and my friends and my students, past and present, overflows from me. Yet, to tell the truth, I did not really speak about this book with anyone while I was writing it nor did anyone ask me anything much about it: so thanks to Florentine Kehm and Sarah Wood, who did, encouraging me to continue. I thank especially the four diligent readers who read and commented on the final manuscript, kindly, thoughtfully, critically, acutely: Felicity Allen, Alison J. Carr, Jo Aurelio Giardini, and Naomi Waltham-Smith. I am also grateful to Elizabeth Legge, for her steady enthusiasm, who reminded me that I present myself 'along the lines of the spinster companion of fiction, modest and resourceful' at the right moment. Susan Finlay is responsible for the book's existence, calling it into being from a passing remark I made about something I was working on, and hooray, huzzah, to her, for her challenge, persistence, and support. Thanks, of course, to MOIST: Paul Finlay, Sarah Smith, and Maggie Panikkar. And immense gratitude to Clair Le Couteur for their work on the cover, wild thanks (and your debt is paid, in spades). Lastly, eternally, and first, *toujours, toujours, toujours,* thanks to those who are here.

ABOUT THE AUTHOR

Sharon Kivland is an artist and writer (she has been called a poet, much to her surprise). She is also an editor and publisher under the imprint MA BIBLIOTHÈQUE. Her books and pamphlets include the series *Freud on Holiday*; *Unable to achieve broad recognition in my lifetime, I laboured in obscurity until my death last year*; and *A Lover's Discourse / Un discours amoureux*, which was shortlisted for the Bob Calle Prix de livre d'artiste in 2017. She lives in London and rural France.

ABÉCÉDAIRE is the second book in MOIST's second season. The other titles in 'Strange and Ha Ha' are:

Best Practices by Habib William Kherbek
The Jacques Lacan Foundation by Susan Finlay